BROKEN BITS

Kel O'Connor

Enjoy!

Kel O'Connor

Cover Design by: Romanced By the Cover

ISBN-10: 0-692-77208-1
ISBN-13: 978-0-692-77208-9

For JK

Chapter One

THIS TRIP HAD to be in her Top Ten List of Bad Ideas, Kit realized as she gazed up at the starry sky. Well, she relented; the idea itself had been solid. It was just that it had not provided the solution she had hoped for.

A week alone in the woods, hiking and camping, was supposed to give her insight into what to do with her upended life. She had hoped to reclaim the part of herself that she had misplaced this last year. The part that made good choices with sound judgments. That innate trust in herself had taken a beating this last year. She had been woefully wrong about someone.

Friends understood that she needed this trip to reclaim herself. She needed to prove to herself that her instincts were still functional. That believing in one wrong person did not mean her gut was faulty.

Despite her skills, people had cautioned against this jaunt. However, Kit had been adamant. In order to think, she needed to be alone. It wasn't as if she didn't have backcountry experience. She'd led several camping expeditions on this very trail. Since it was off-season, she had assumed she might pass a handful of hikers, but so far, she had been alone. Which was what she had thought she had needed.

She'd spent the last few months in denial and avoidance, piling on activities and visits to ensure that she was rarely alone to worry. This trip had been a way to force herself to look at reality. She had to change careers, but to what? Moving to another state might help, but that involved making a choice. Where to go?

Now that she was over halfway into the outing, she still had no answers. She needed to face the fact that she was no closer to a decision than before. Perhaps she should just go home, open an atlas and blindly pick a town. She looked from the sky down to the contents of her thermal cup. Too bad she couldn't read tea leaves. Kit sighed and rubbed her forehead. She'd had enough time to see that this trip was not going to give her the insight she needed.

She started the day by looking for anything to break the monotony. She was bored, and, unfortunately, the animals she crossed paths with did not respond to her greetings. Back when her destination had been selected, the idea of being alone to think was appealing. However, right now, she would give anything to have someone to talk to.

Kit snarled up at the clear sky filled with twinkling stars, "C'mon universe! Give me a clue!"

Then she snorted at her own folly. It wasn't as if the universe had been kind to her during the last year. Why start now?

She sighed and dumped the dregs left from her after-dinner drink. She had put out the campfire, so she cleaned the cup by the glow from her lantern. She was dawdling, and she knew it. The fact that she was putting off a decision itched like a wool sweater. But this was the new, cautious Kit. She would just adjust to the irritation.

Before entering the tent, she spoke one last time to the brilliant sky. "Send me a sign by daybreak. Otherwise, I'm outta here."

The next morning, Kit admitted to being disappointed. There had been no sign that she was on the right track. No sign that she was finally making good choices. She had awoken to just another cool, foggy dawn. It was time to admit defeat and head back to civilization.

Ugh! She threw her pack across the site, scattering its contents. She finished her power bar and began taking apart her tent. The bright blue and yellow material burned her eyes. She should have chosen black or gray. Those were appropriate colors for a failed trip. She blinked back tears and bared her teeth in frustration. Yes, it was definitely time to get on with a new life. The idea left her feeling hollow instead of energized. She wanted her old life back, damnit.

Kit heard the helicopter long before she spotted it. The whirl of the blades was thunderous. As it came closer, she watched the branches overhead twist violently, loose leaves fluttering down to land around her boots. She tried to identify the bird, but the tree canopy around the campsite was too high for her to see it.

What the hell was it doing, flying so low over the isolated forest? It could be a rescue team, searching for a stranded hiker. She had trekked through the eastern half of the forest for the past week and hadn't seen a single flare or even a remote sign that someone else was in the area. Only an idiot who deserved to get lost would venture this far out without emergency flares.

Kit pulled a well-worn topography map out of the side pocket of her pack and studied it. There should be a clearing up on the left – that had to be where the helicopter would touch down. If it was a rescue operation, she was trained and could help. Adrenaline flowed through her veins and she laughed. Finally, a distraction!

Stowing the map in a pocket, she scrambled to find her first aid kit.

"Stupid!" she mumbled under her breath. "You are an idiot for throwing your shit around!"

Finally, she spied it lying beside her discarded sweatshirt. Despite the cool temperature, she'd gotten overheated as she'd began to break camp. She tossed the first aid kit and whatever supplies that were nearby into her backpack and threw it on.

She strode forward, hopping over a slender tree that had fallen across the path. Her hiking boots left marks where yesterday's rain had puddled in the dirt. Once on the nearby trail, she orientated herself and set off. A chuckle escaped her as she trotted down the trail as fast as she could manage without having the pack throw off her balance.

Luckily, the trail was smooth here, with few rocks or tree roots. The closer she came to the clearing, the louder the helicopter noise became. Peering around a thick tree trunk, Kit lowered her head so that the bill of her cap blocked most of the dirt blowing past her. From here, she had a good view of a meadow filled with plump bushes that were beginning to bud. The morning fog collected around the edges, leaving the field easy to see. There was no stranded hiker. No human was waiting for her help among the tall grass. Damn it.

The sound of the rotors was almost deafening this close. More debris flew by as she watched the helicopter descending. Something wasn't right. The helicopter...there were no rescue agency markings on the outside. The expensive looking machine was all black and shiny like the forewings of a beetle. The sun reflected off the windows so she could not see how many people were inside. Goosebumps rose on her arms as the theme to *The Twilight Zone* played in her head.

"Oh shit!" She ducked behind a tree in order to avoid being slapped by a stray branch that whizzed past.

Whether it was her over-active imagination or not, she wanted to remain hidden now. Pain stung her palm and she loosened her grip on the knotty tree trunk. She peeked back around to see the helicopter hovering about twenty feet off the ground. Thankfully, it was also now facing away from her. Her eyes narrowed as she noticed that even the tail lacked any identifying numbers.

Not a good sign, Kit thought, and then watched in horror as a body tumbled out of the opened door. It landed in the meadow with a thump, and the helicopter flew away.

Kit froze as the noise faded away with it. *What the hell? Was that a dead body?* If not, he was certainly injured after that fall. She moved out from behind the tree, keeping an eye on the spot where the body had fallen. The tall grasses swayed in the light breeze but were undisturbed by any other movement.

Even though her heart was about to burst out of her chest, she knew she had to at least find out if he was still alive. True, the person could be dangerous, but there was no way she could just leave.

She slipped off the backpack and pulled a small canister of pepper spray out of the side pocket. There was also a coil of tent rope there. Pulling it out, she thought, *better to be prepared.*

Quietly, she picked her way through the thick grass and briars toward the lump of black clothing. There was still no movement. Luckily, the body had landed where there were no bushes or rocks, just dense grass that was almost emerald in color. Their wild smell tickled the inside of Kit's nose as she sucked in air, trying not to hyperventilate.

Please don't be dead, Kit chanted in her head. Although, if he were a "bad guy," it might be better if he were dead. While her background working with children meant that Kit was well-trained in first aid and CPR, she was not equipped for anything worse. Like a coma or internal bleeding. Since the only way to call for help was to shoot off a flare that would surely alert whoever had been in that helicopter, she did not think that idea was wise.

As she got closer, Kit saw that the person was indeed a man. He was lying on his back, his head facing away from her. He wore black cargo pants, black boots, and a black jacket. His hair was short, straight and also dark. She didn't see any traces of gray in his hair and guessed he was probably in his late-twenties, early-thirties – close to her own age.

It's silly and superstitious, but black is the color of bad deeds, Kit thought as a shiver traced her spine. Why couldn't he at least be wearing something white? Or a "Hello My Name is Good Guy" label on his jacket? Trying to make as little noise as possible, she edged around his inert body until she could see his face.

The bottom half of his face was covered in short beard stubble, coated in areas with drying blood. Even white teeth peeked through where his swollen lips parted. Upon a closer look, she saw that two of his bottom teeth were crowded, crooked. That small imperfection made her feel more at ease. There was dried blood on his chin, and he was sporting a black eye. That and his busted lip must have happened earlier, judging by the color and swelling.

The guy had taken a beating, but he was still breathing. She could see the rise and fall of his chest under a gray t-shirt. Her own breath *whooshed* out in relief.

She inched closer, still holding out the pepper spray, her finger steady on the trigger. She nudged his shoulder with the toe of her hiking boot. She took a deep breath, ready to run if he should suddenly grab her.

"Hey!" Kit tried to keep her voice firm and sharp. "Are you okay? Wake up!"

The man groaned in response and turned his head to face the bright blue sky. Kit made an involuntary panicked noise when she saw that the other side of his face was covered in fresh blood.

Cursing freely under her breath, she quickly put

down her defense spray and grabbed the rope she had brought. Tying his hands together with the rope, she saw that his knuckles were bruised, the skin abraded on his right hand. She had to wonder who looked worse – the fallen man or the person he'd fought. As soon as she had him secure, she ran back to fetch the first aid kit out of her pack.

Fuck! Where was it? She fumbled through the main compartment where she had thrown the supplies. When she finally found the small nylon case, she dropped it twice before tucking it under her arm. Hurrying back to the injured man, she managed to get the case open and find the pack of sterile gauze.

"This is what you get for being fucking bored," Kit chastised herself as she tried to find the source of the blood.

Luckily, it did not take long. The small gash was just outside his hairline. She applied pressure with one hand and used more gauze to wipe the blood off his face with the other.

"Wake up," she pleaded, hoping to see his lashes flicker in response, but the man remained still.

His clothing was non-descript and well-made. Not shiny or cheap. The combat-style boots on his feet were worn. She could see the creases in the leather around his ankles. Was he a cop? Undercover agent? Mercenary? Did such people really exist outside of books and movies?

"Wake up!" Kit patted his arm in frustration as she tried to control her runaway imagination.

She needed to stop reading so many mysteries and thrillers. While her reality seemed surreal now, she had not imagined the helicopter. As far as she knew, it could be headed back for them right now. Discarding the gauze she had been using to wipe his face, she laid her hand on his chest and shook him. Hard muscles moved under her hand as he coughed.

The man groaned, and this time she noticed his eyelashes flicker. She held her breath as his eyes slowly opened. They squinted up into the bright morning sky before shifting to her.

Wow, Kit thought as she reached for the pepper spray with her free hand. *Gorgeous eyes.* His eyes were a few shades darker than the sky and framed with dark lashes. Even though one eye was bruised and puffy, they were still striking. As they met hers, she was held in place by his gaze as he studied her in confusion.

EXCRUCIATING PAIN IN his body brought Mick slowly back to consciousness. His senses quickly told him he was outside. He smelled clean air and dirt. He heard leaves fluttering and the far-off cry of a bird. Bright light pulsed behind his eyelids, signaling that it was daytime.

Good Lord, where was he? The last thing he recalled was fighting with Peck's goons. That had been at night in downtown Chicago. He must be far from there, since there were no sounds of humans at all. *Christ!* How long had he been out? How injured was he?

Every part of his body throbbed, especially his head. Fortunately, nothing stood out, so he was hopeful that there were no broken bones or internal injuries. He should get up. Mick knew this but still hesitated. His assignment had turned into a cock-up when he'd been discovered. Now it appeared it had taken an even worse turn.

Gritting his teeth against the knowledge that the sun would make his headache worse, he slowly opened his eyes.

What he hadn't sensed was the woman hovering over him. She looked terrified, so she was not an immediate threat. His brain called forth a memory of a hidden café in Paris where he'd eaten the most delicious dessert of his life. It was *soufflé au chocolat* and it had been the same color as this woman's eyes. Exquisite.

He blinked, trying to bring her into focus. That action caused one eye to throb and he recalled the last mighty blow that had knocked him out. Bloody bodyguard.

"Are you okay?"

The mystery woman's voice quivered. Nerves, he surmised. She tilted her head, causing the bill of her cap to block the sunshine from his eyes. Without the bright glare, he could inspect her more thoroughly. Other than wisps of brown near her ears, her hair was completely covered by a worn, navy baseball cap. She wore no makeup, so Mick could easily see the faint freckles scattered across her face. Other than her lovely eyes, her face was cute, ordinary. He put her age near to his own. Judging by the faded t-shirt she wore, he wondered if she were a jogger who happened upon him.

Speaking of that…where the bloody hell was he? The sky above him was a bright, cloudless blue. No buildings in sight, just trees. His stomach sank. This was not Chicago.

"Wh…"

He started to ask the woman where he was as he raised a hand to his aching head. However, the first word trailed off as he saw that his hands were bound together with a thin nylon rope.

His gaze flew back to her, and something in his face made her scoot back and raise the trembling hand that held a canister of pepper spray. Mick relaxed a bit. She was not a viable threat. Nevertheless, he needed her to untie him so that he could get the hell back to DC.

He spoke, trying to keep his tone soft. "Where am I?"

"Smoky Mountains…wilderness area," she answered, not lowering her arm.

"Where?"

"Uhm…North Carolina."

His brows rose in shock, "How the bloody hell did I get here?"

His loud voice caused him to wince in pain, likely because of whatever head injury he'd sustained. Damn, but it hurt.

"Actually, you were dumped here," she explained, "If you'll just stay still, I can finish treating the gash above your eye. Just…be still."

Mick lowered his hands, eyeing her sharply as she put down the pepper spray and moved closer to root through a first aid kit. North Carolina? That seemed impossible.

Making himself lie still, he winced again as she pressed an antiseptic cloth on a spot near his hairline. As soon as she was satisfied the area was clean, she went about applying bandages.

"It's not a deep gash," she said as she worked. "Head wounds just bleed a lot. You could use a couple of stitches, but maybe the butterfly bandage will cut down on the scarring."

"Thank you," Mick said.

"You sound British." Her brown eyes flicked down to his face in suspicion. "Are you? What the hell is going on? What's your name? Do you feel sick? Having double vision?"

He did not think he'd suffered a concussion, but her incessant questions were making his head spin. He remained silent as she placed a non-stick-pad over the wound and sealed it with tape. The woman returned the supplies to their zippered pouch and sat back on her heels, waiting for his answers. Mick wanted to smirk. He'd outlasted professional interrogators before. This woman was no match for him. He continued to look at her until she started to squirm and fidget with the pepper canister.

"Now may I have my hands free?"

He tried to keep the arrogance from his voice even though he was becoming frustrated. He needed to be free and get back to DC. He had little time to placate a civilian.

She swallowed nervously. "Look...we are in the middle of nowhere. You are a large strange man who was shoved out of a helicopter —"

"I was thrown from a helicopter?"

Mick shifted on the ground, amazed that he could feel no great pains. No broken bones. Amazing. Peck's son dumped him out of a helicopter? Mick wanted to smile at the ingenuity of the idea. He looked around as best he could without raising his head. They appeared to be in a field. This was bad. They needed to get out of the open. But he didn't want to alarm his frightened rescuer.

"Yeah." Her voice firmed up. "You look like a tough guy. This could turn out very bad for me."

He didn't smile, sneer, or even look offended. He kept his face passive and forced his body to relax. She felt threatened. Of course. She had no clue that he would never harm a woman.

"No," he answered, his voice less harsh than before. "I am not going to hurt you. You have my word. Please untie me."

The woman chewed on her thumbnail, still looking at him with narrowed eyes. Moments passed, and then her chin jutted out. They were sitting ducks out here in the meadow. Mick strained to hear any faint engine noises. All he heard were tweeting birds and rustling leaves. Good. They had time to hide.

"Tell me your name," she ordered.

Mick wanted to smile, but realized that would be a bad move. Her hands had stopped trembling, and her lips were set in a straight line. *Bravo, brave girl.*

"My name is Mick. And I would prefer to answer any other questions away from this exposed area."

Her luscious eyes widened. "They're coming back?"

He grimaced. "I have no idea. Best to be safe."

He didn't move, just watched as she came to a swift decision. The woman popped the knot with a quick tug and scooted back, holding onto the pepper spray for dear life.

He eased into a sitting position, swearing at all the aches and pains the fall had caused. *Christ*, his entire body ached! He flexed each arm and leg and then bowed his back, testing each muscle group and waiting for the sharp pain of a broken bone to hit. A heavy sigh escaped when he found nothing agonizing, except his head. Gingerly, he touched the bandage she had placed on his forehead.

"What is your name?" He glanced over to her.

"Katherine, but I go by Kit." She continued to eye him warily. "Do you have any broken bones?"

"No." He pulled his jacket away and looked for blood.

"*Who are you* and why did people just fucking dump you out here to die?"

"Questions later, remember?" He let out a groan as he slowly rose to his feet.

Still holding onto her pepper spray, Kit grabbed the first aid pack and motioned for him to precede her to the tree line.

After a few more minutes of annoying silence, broken only by the twigs snapping underneath their feet, she asked again, "What the fuck is going on?"

They reached the shelter of the trees that overlooked a dirt path and Mick sat down heavily on a nearby fallen tree trunk. He must look like hell, but that wasn't buying sympathy points with Kit. His refusal to confess had her frowning and shooting daggers at him with her eyes.

"I am not moving until you talk!"

Mick's lips almost formed a slight smile that hurt,

and he touched his battered gums with his tongue. Good – no loose teeth, just a busted lip.

"I need to get out of here and find a phone," he announced, and was rewarded with a snort.

"Good luck. Civilization is two and a half day's walk away. That includes cell service. And I refuse to set off a rescue flare as long as there is a chance the helicopter men could come back."

Fuck! Now his predicament made more sense. If the intel he had did not make it back to DC by Friday, it would be useless. Moreover, his mission would be a failure. Mick closed his eyes and whispered many other foul words under his breath. Strangely, that seemed to put Kit more at ease. She pocketed the spray, leaned against a nearby tree, and let him fret.

He checked the black watch strapped to his wrist. It was Wednesday, so he had been out only a few hours. The thumb drive was still safely disguised as part of the metal watchband. Could he hike for almost three days straight? What about food, water?

"Look, you are obviously on some expedition or whatnot." He gestured to her clothing and hiking boots. "But can you help me get out of here? Quickly?"

Despite his impatience, he let her work through her options. He saw no supplies other than a discarded backpack, but they must be nearby. She was smaller than he was, so he could easily overpower her, make her lead him out. But it would be easier and less distasteful if she were willing.

She had returned to chewing on a thumbnail as she looked him over. Mick held his breath. He truly did not want to force her, but if needs must…

"I was on my way back out. I have enough food left for two people. I always over pack. Fear of starving," she explained.

"I would be eternally grateful." Mick tried to put her at ease with a smile, but with the busted lip, he doubted it looked genuine.

Nevertheless, he was thankful for her capitulation. Even though it was terribly risky for her, a woman alone in the forest. There must be a story there, but he had no time for puzzles. They needed to get going.

"Soooo…" Kit drew the word out to get his attention. "Are you a cop? A drug dealer? A mercenary? A spy? A delusional rich dude? An actor with amnesia?"

Any other day, Mick would be impressed with her imagination. Today, he needed to stay focused on getting his intel back to DAG.

"I am someone who will do you no harm and will repay you for your time and expense."

Kit waved the offer away. "No need for that. Let's get you some painkillers and water. I need to finish packing up my campsite. I want to get as far away from here as possible, just in case that helicopter comes back."

They set off, Kit slowing her pace to allow Mick time to walk out his soreness. His body felt stiff, awkward. There were sure to be dozens of new bruises to add to the scars he already carried.

Thrown out of a helicopter and walking away with minor injuries! He could not wait to tell Archie. His teammate would be jealous. It wasn't polite to gloat, but this might be his only chance to one-up his co-worker.

First, he had to ensure his legs stopped wobbling. If the woman in front of him could make the trek in less than three days, so could he. Mick gritted his teeth and kept walking.

What an odd creature, he thought as he studied her from behind. What sort of woman ventured this far out by herself? She acted comfortable and capable, even miles away from civilization. The Universe was looking out for him for once. She certainly looked the part of an experienced hiker. Her brown boots looked impenetrable and she wore a large black watch that hung loose around her left wrist. It wasn't her normal watch, he idly noted. There was a thick band of un-tanned skin further up her arm. Her current timepiece must be full of technical features that would be useful camping. Loose cargo shorts and a baggy t-shirt hid any curves that she might have. Well, it wasn't as if he were here to secure a date. Nevertheless, there was no harm in letting his mind wander.

With her shapeless clothing, her lower legs were also the only body part he could really see. Mick found he was quite taken with them. He loved women with strong, shapely legs. That was his weakness, not big tits or a round arse. Focusing on them as they walked helped him ignore his aches and pains. *There's no harm in it*, he told himself as he watched, fascinated as the muscles contracted and loosened. Was her skin as soft as it looked?

His musings were cut short as the woman veered off the path to the right and led him to what must be her campsite. Her tent was half-collapsed, and bags and supplies were scattered about. On instinct, he looked around for the culprit, his hand automatically reaching for a gun at his hip that wasn't there. She must have noticed his alarm, for she laughed nervously.

"Yeah…uhm. I am not normally so messy. I was in the middle of packing when I heard the helicopter."

"And you just ran to the rescue? Are you daft?" he asked, incredulous at her disregard for her own safety.

While her coloring was not pale, he could still see the flush that stained her cheeks. Her eyes narrowed at him again. Damn. He much preferred her friendly face.

"I thought it was the park service, coming for an injured hiker. I have first aid training and thought I could help."

She gestured toward his bandaged forehead. "And good thing I did, Mr. Smartass."

He dipped his head, conceding her point. For all his skills, surviving in a foreign forest was not one of them.

"I am grateful," he said, and placed a hand over his heart, hoping to look contrite. "And very lucky you were nearby today."

Kit huffed out a breath and relaxed. She proceeded to rummage around in a purple nylon sack lying on the ground. After a few moments of searching, her hand emerged holding a pill bottle. Grabbing an aluminum water bottle and a packet of peanuts, she motioned for him to sit on the dusty ground.

"Over the counter migraine medicine," she explained as she handed them off. "There are regular painkillers in the first aid pouch, but you might want to start with these. Try to eat at least a handful of nuts so the medicine doesn't upset your stomach."

Mick silently agreed. The pills should be full of caffeine, something he sorely needed now. His thinking still felt muddled. Kit turned down his offer of help, so he sat and watched her pack her belongings in record time. She had the large pack strapped onto her back before he could even rise to his feet.

Lastly, she picked up two slender red metal poles at her feet, handing one to Mick. It was similar to a ski pole, but lighter and slimmer. Since it was early spring, he looked at her in confusion.

"It helps with balance," she explained. "Some parts of the trail are rocky and it's hard to keep your footing. There will also be times when one wrong move could send you down an embankment to your death. So we will walk carefully, mystery man in black."

She set off, leaving Mick again wondering what she was doing in such a dangerous area all alone.

Chapter Two

A S THEY LEFT, Kit slowed her pace to allow Mick time to loosen his muscles. Despite the strangeness of the day, she felt lighter. She had made the right choice to help Mick. It felt like she was actually in control of her own life again. Even if it turned out badly, *she* had made the choices. While the trail was not wide enough for them to walk side-by-side, it did allow her to keep him in focus out of the corner of her eye. She divided her gaze between the damp forest trail and her new cohort. After all, he was still a stranger in black, and she was not a pushover for an attractive man.

Keep telling yourself that. Goosebumps raced down her arms whenever their gazes met. How silly was that? Was it the fact that he was walking away from an event that could have killed him? Or that he had not complained, not even one groan? Stoicism was just as appealing to her as his looks and accent were.

She bit her lip to keep silent. Questions buzzed around her mind. Without actual answers, her imagination was creating all sorts of absurd scenarios. Why couldn't he just explain? His silence made her want to talk all the more, but it was just her nature. Her friends had nicknamed her "Chatty Kathy," and she knew it was spot on. That was the only thing about this trip that had grated on her. Animals and trees could not hold a conversation.

Let the painkillers work first, she thought. He might not appreciate her adding to his headache with chatter. There would be plenty of time for questions later.

It was turning out to be a spectacular day. The tree canopy above the trail had thinned to where she could feel the sunlight. She caught a glimpse of a wild turkey in the distance, but it ran away before she could point it out to Mick. All in all, the day was turning out to be better than most she'd had the past year.

"Whoa, stop!" Kit commanded, holding up her left hand.

They had been walking at a brisk pace, so Mick stumbled in an effort not to crash into her. They had just come around a bend, moving from shade to sunlight. She was thankful to note that Mick froze upon her command. After a moment, though, he began scanning their surroundings, his head cocked for any noise. Interesting.

"Kit?" His voice was hushed.

The trail was narrow, penned in on one side by thick bushes and on the other by the rocky mountain slope. Kit shifted to the right so that he could see what was in front of them.

A rather small snake was slowly gliding across the path, heading toward a thicket of bushes with bright green leaves. Kit wanted to laugh when Mick eyed the small animal skeptically. It was less than two feet long, thin with gray and brown markings. Hardly fearsome if you did not know what it was.

"Would you like for me to remove it?" he asked, his voice hushed.

"No!" She looked at him in horror.

"Are we waiting for it to move off the path?" he asked.

He did not try to wipe the condescension from his tone, so she rolled her eyes and sighed.

"Look Mystery Man, that is a rattlesnake. It's venomous. Yes, it is better to wait than try to walk around it. They strike when they feel threatened."

Mick studied the snake. "Are you certain? I do not see rattles on his tail."

Kit huffed and ground her teeth together before speaking.

"He's young, which makes his bite twice as deadly. The rattles come from molting, like humans get wrinkles as we mature. Sometimes the rattles fall off, so I may be wrong about his age."

She threw him a look full of disdain. "I promise to show you proof when we get back to civilization. Until then, you just have to trust me."

"Of course," he whispered, and leaned against the rocky wall to rest.

Kit looked at him in surprise, but relaxed when she saw he was sincere. She had expected an argument. Or at least a macho display. But he seemed satisfied to follow her lead. She shifted her feet, glancing from him to the snake and back again.

"Luckily, snake families don't stay together long after birth. A normal rattlesnake litter can be from eleven to thirty babies. Wouldn't that be fun to stumble upon?"

She continued to ramble, schooling him on all things related to the snake that was almost out of sight. She saw his stifled grin, but kept going. Now that she'd started talking, it was hard to stop.

Kit paused and took out two water bottles from the sides of her pack. By the time they had slaked their thirst, the snake had vanished. Kit hurried past where it had been and Mick followed her lead, both anxiously watching for any sign of the animal to strike.

"I didn't mean to scare you." Kit's words floated back to him. "Out here, it's just better to be safe."

"Indeed," was his only reply.

They hiked on, Kit managing to keep quiet until her growling stomach reminded her of the time. She'd been so intent on keeping an eye on Mick and keeping her mouth shut that time had flown by. There was a nice rock outcropping at the top of the next hill where they could eat.

She watched as he sat down and began stretching his long limbs. *Smart guy*, she acknowledged, and knew she would be loosening her muscles after she ate. However, her sunny mood faded when he removed his jacket.

She unpacked the food and water, trying not to stare at the tattoo that was now visible on his arm, below his short sleeve t-shirt, right under the crook of his left elbow. The skin there looked soft, touchable, but that fact barely registered with Kit. The small tattoo was rendered in dull, dark ink. His forearm had four black dots forming a square that held a single dot in the center.

Even though the sun was out, it was cool down in the forest. A light breeze swept through occasionally, adding the swish of tinkling leaves to the sounds of birds that filled the air. Kit was sweaty from the hike but now felt clammy. Had she made a huge mistake? Shit, she knew what those dots on his arm symbolized. Were her instincts really that fucked up?

Just act normal, she told herself, and tried not to laugh. There was nothing normal about this day. Especially not now.

She handed him a bag of crackers, a small can of tuna, and a packet of granola. She sat her own lunch nearby and switched out the empty water bottles for full ones. Even with her back turned, she could tell he was watching her. That twitchy itch between her shoulder blades. On the trail, it hadn't alarmed her. She had just felt *noticed.* Now...now she felt exposed.

Her thoughts went to the emergency flares in her bag, and she flushed. It felt deceitful to be thinking of a way to escape him. Moreover, there was no way to know who would come to her rescue – park rangers or the black helicopter. If he triggered her alarm buttons, she could veer into the forest and lose him. As long as she had her map and compass, she could find her way back to the trail. That was the worst-case scenario plan that she did not want to do. She was stuck, and this time she flushed with anger. Damn him for putting her in this predicament.

They ate in silence, and Kit tried to relax, taking

deep breaths in between bites of food. The salt from the cracker was like heaven on her tongue. On the trail, any food was a delicacy, and right now she was starving. She tried to keep her eyes on the dirt around her boots, but could not help sneaking glances at her quiet companion. She needed answers before they went any further. Was she truly safe with him?

The crazy thing was that she still did not feel he was a danger to her. He had been helpful so far and had not questioned her knowledge about the snake, or the route. Realistically, it was safer if they stuck together. It goaded her that there were no other options.

Kit ground her teeth until her jaw ached. She needed to be cool and get him talking. Find a way to get some real answers out of him. Remind him who had the map and the supplies to get them out in one piece.

She was so intent on her thoughts that a sudden sound from Mick made her jerk. He had not said a word, just made a strange chattering sound. At first, Kit thought that his head wound had caused neurological damage. Then she saw the small animal.

Two yards away, a gray squirrel sat swishing his fluffy tail, his eyes captivated by the sliver of cracker Mick was holding out to him. He repeated the noise and Kit realized he was talking to the animal. Or trying to. The large man didn't move as the squirrel crept closer, ready to run at the first sign of danger.

Many of Kit's apprehensions vanished as she watched him carefully throw the cracker bit so that it would land at the animal's feet. The squirrel snatched it up and raced away, but not before chittering back at the man in black.

Kit broke the spell by laughing in delight. Her hiking companion was an animal lover. That made the situation much better in her mind. Animal abusers were frequently serial killers, not the other way around.

Mick looked at her and flushed. "So sorry. I should not be wasting your food."

"Feeding crumbs to animals is not a waste," she admonished. "I didn't realize you spoke squirrel."

He looked back at her, and the air grew heavy and hot. Kit's twitchy itch was back but had settled low in her abdomen. Not knowing how to act, she jumped up and began to gather their trash.

"There's a stream nearby." Kit gestured to the knot of trees off to the right. "We'll need to fill up the water bottles. I have a filter pump so don't worry about contamination."

Mick nodded and smiled as best he could with the busted lip. "Thank you again for being so generous."

Kit smiled tightly and tried not to stare at the symbolic spots on his arm. She obviously was not successful because Mick noticed. He looked down at the tattoo and then back up to her. His eyes were so blue, her breath caught.

"Youthful indiscretion," he explained with a negligent shrug.

With that lie, all of her former goodwill vanished and she was back to feeling peeved. Seriously? She'd been under the impression that he held her in good esteem, but he obviously took her for an idiot. She had sworn that no one would ever make that mistake again. She was through looking the other way and being labeled obtuse.

The deep breath she took was not to calm down; it was to ready herself for a fight.

"No." Kit's eyes sparkled with anger, and she spoke before she thought. "I am not stupid. That's a prison tattoo."

Shit. She clamped a hand over her runaway mouth. It was too late to take it back. Mick's eyebrows went up along with her heart rate. What had she done? She needed to get her blabbering under control, but that was a life-long job still in progress, and she was furious. She could not take back her accusation, so she kept going, faking bravado that she only half felt.

"Look. Don't lie to me." She looked at the man across from her. "I need to know why you have that tattoo."

He cocked his head, searching her eyes. She hoped she looked as serious as she felt. She did not want to leave him to die in these woods. Fact was, she needed more information from her tight-lipped companion. She could sit here all day if she had to. He wanted to get back to civilization so badly; he could cough up the truth.

"And where does this vast knowledge come from?" Mick finally spoke, his voice and expression bland.

Kit snorted. What would it hurt to divulge some of her past? Perhaps it would make him wary.

"I come from a long line of bootleggers, pot farmers, poachers, you name it. My family picked up a gallery of body art over all of their various incarcerations. So now I know that the dots forming the square are the prison and the dot inside is the inmate." Kit gestured to the ink on his arm below the crook of his elbow.

Kit finished with a wave of her hand. "I am not only the first to graduate college, but I am now the only one without an arrest record."

Mick smiled thinly and continued eating. Kit gritted her teeth. She needed answers.

"You are not making me feel very comfortable here. My ass is not moving until you talk."

Mick's mouth twitched. She wondered if it was in anger or amusement. She prayed it was the latter, but right now, she was so pissed, it didn't matter. Thankfully, her speech sounded quite badass to her ears. Lord, she needed to learn to control her mouth. Nevertheless, she wasn't budging until he was truthful.

"Kit," he looked her straight in the eye, "I will not harm you. As long as I am with you, I will not let anyone else harm you. I have never hurt a woman. Yes, I have a prison tattoo on my arm. It's a private matter, but I can assure you I was not incarcerated for rape, murder, or anything else along those lines."

His deep voice sounded so sincere. She was glad she had seen the tattoo. It was proof she needed to stay on guard around him. Like her relatives, his crime could have been minor. While she had little contact with those relatives, she did not feel unprotected around them. The tattoo was a way of making them look frightening to strangers. Like animals who fluff themselves up when threatened.

OK, so perhaps her instincts were still effective. She exhaled such a deep breath it made her dizzy. She chose to believe the earnestness she saw in his face. It was foolhardy, but she was trying to trust her gut again. She only hoped her gut was not too influenced by this bizarre situation and all the turmoil from the past year. She glared at him with the last of her anger.

"OK," she finally agreed. "I'll go get more water. There are more painkillers in the side pocket of the pack. Take another dose."

Gathering the supplies, she hurried off toward the faint sound of running water. The best aspect of the trail system she had chosen was that water was never more than half a mile away. This would be crucial now that she needed to double the hydration supply. She would have to factor in more frequent water collection breaks.

She was going to trust him…for now. It had nothing to do with how he looked. If not banged up, his face would be stunning. It didn't matter that his ears stuck out from his short hair or that his nose was large. He was arresting, with his accent and muscles. Put the voice, the body, and the face together, and it could prove distracting. She needed to make sure that attraction didn't cloud her judgment.

"You are a damn idiot, Katherine Hale Foster!" she chastised herself as soon as she was out of earshot. "You've worked around kids too long. You are too trusting. Did the last year teach you nothing?"

She continued to rail at herself while she made the stream water fit to drink. Not that it made much difference. She would continue trying to weasel information out of her secretive hiking partner, as well as keep an eye peeled for any suspicious behavior. But she would also share her supplies and get him back to town.

"At least I now have someone to talk to," she mused.

"Or rather, talk *at*."

She ran the clear stream water through the filter decanter before filling up all four of her aluminum sport bottles. The brook was shallow here, making it easy for her to avoid scooping up any fish or debris.

Kit had just gathered up all her supplies when she heard the first snarl. She froze, her eyes seeking the source of the noise. The bushes to her left rustled, and an animal crept out. It kept low to the ground, inching forward in her direction.

It was perhaps a fox or a small coyote. Kit could not be sure. It wasn't very big, and its reddish-brown coat was matted and filthy. When she got to its face, it felt like everything inside her melted and ran down through her legs. Bloodshot eyes stared back. Foam dripped from its muzzle as it growled and began to slink closer.

"Shit, shit, shit," she mouthed, and tried to form a plan.

Her arms were full, so she couldn't reach her pepper spray. The same spray she realized she had left in her jacket pocket back where she had left Mick. *Fuck!* She looked around, hoping for a small, sturdy tree. None of the nearby ones were climbable by someone her height. She doubted she could outrun it. The stream was too shallow to hope it would drown if it followed her in. Her only hope was the knife holstered on her belt.

Out of time to formulate a plan, she screamed and began chucking the full water bottles at the animal, hoping it would give her enough time to unsheathe the knife. Panting in panic, she had no idea if she could even hold onto the knife, much less use it, before the animal attacked. She had been in some hairy situations in the woods before, but not like this. If she were bitten, she would have to set off the flare in order to get to a hospital in time. And that could alert the spooky helicopter.

A couple of the full bottles made contact, and the snarls were interrupted by a yelp. But that did not deter the beast. Either its sickness or the smell of the tuna oil she had spilled on her boot kept it coming forward. The animal was closing in as she pulled the knife out. Amazed that it didn't fall out of her hand, she tightened her grip and crouched lower. Kit heard high-pitched moaning and knew it was coming from her own throat.

Suddenly, a good-sized rock flew past her and made contact with the animal's flank. As she watched it wobble in a daze, Mick strode past her and kicked the stunned animal with his boot. It went down with another yelp. Kit observed in stunned silence as he approached her, lifted the knife from her unresisting hand, and then stabbed the downed animal.

What was more frightening, the rabid animal or the look on Mick's face? She wasn't sure, but his cold, detached expression made her shiver. Kit's legs gave out and she went down to her knees on the mossy creek bank. All she could do was stare at the unmoving pile of nappy fur. From the corner of her eye, she watched Mick rinse the knife off in the still water and swipe it dry on his pants. Handling it like a pro, he returned it to the sheath on her belt.

"Are you all right?" Mick knelt beside her, speaking in a quiet voice.

Kit nodded, still not wanting to look at him.

She felt his warm hand squeeze her shoulder before he rose to collect the water supplies. He came back and hauled her to her feet with one hand. Mick nodded for her to precede him and they walked in silence back to the trail.

By the time they made the short trek back to the path, Kit was light-headed. Loud buzzing filled her ears, but she did not see any evidence of bees flying around her head. The forest looked foggy, out of focus. Her breath came in short gasps because she could not seem to get enough air into her lungs. Dark spots danced in front of her eyes. The next step she took caused her to list sideways, as if she were on board a boat on the open sea.

"Hold on." Mick spoke slowly as he helped her back onto her lunch seat on a rock. "You're in shock."

He dropped to his haunches in front of her so they were face to face. His big hands squeezed her smaller ones. *That's nice*, Kit thought absently, feeling how warm they were. Her own hands were ice cold. *Shit*, she could have died. Despite being at home in the woods, she had never been this close to a catastrophe.

"Just breathe with me now, Kit," he commanded, and took long inhales and exhales. "That's it, brave girl," he murmured as she began to follow along.

Kit focused on his face, trying to block out what had just happened until she was able to deal with it. *Just focus on Mick*, she told herself. She desperately did not want to throw up, even though her insides were churning. His eyes were too blue, so she concentrated on the small split on his lower lip. It sported a healthy scab, and she hoped the inside tear wasn't causing him too much discomfort.

Yes, she thought again, *it was good he had the big nose and elfin ears.* They kept him from being a knockout. With his pale, English skin, dark hair, and those electric eyes, he looked like something out of a movie, but she could not place the exact film. Even with the battered face. The swelling in his bottom lip was beginning to go down, she noted as he continued speaking in a low tone. It was too bad she couldn't discern the words over the bees roaring in her ears. With his accent, she was sure he sounded lovely.

He had saved her life. He could have taken the pack and left her to the mercy of that animal. Perhaps he was Team Good Guy after all.

As her heartbeat returned to normal and the nausea subsided, she noticed he was rubbing his thumbs along the insides of her wrists. As soothing as it was, it was too familiar coming from someone she had just met. But before she could do anything about it, he dropped her hands.

"Well then," he sat back on his heels and his eyes sharpened. "What in the bloody hell are you doing out here all alone with no weapon?"

Kit bristled at the accusatory tone. "I'll have you know I've gone wild camping dozens of times! I have pepper spray and a knife! Those are all I have ever needed!"

"Oh?" His eyebrow quirked up skeptically.

Ugh! She hated people who could do that! Such a smug, superior ability she had not been able to teach herself. She had spent hours as a child trying after seeing it in a comic book.

"Yes." Kit ground out from behind clenched teeth. "Normally, you only have to worry about bears and snakes and elk. They tend to stay away from humans."

Still frowning, Mick stood up and dusted the knees of his cargo pants. He took a few steps back and repeated, "So what are you doing out here all alone?"

She would have been fine if his tone had not changed to one of concern. All of her bluster fled, and she sagged. When she hugged her knees to her chest, he sat back down. It all came back to this. Kit snuck glances at him before her worries came tumbling out of her mouth.

"Have you ever ruined your life with one mistake? Literally, one thing that destroyed almost everything and you had to start from scratch?"

"Ha!" Mick's short laugh was so sudden, even he was surprised.

Kit ducked her head as a blush stained her cheeks. So much for sharing personal feelings. *Fuck.* She wished for a cave to hide in.

"Kit."

When she would not look at him, he placed his hand on her arm. Wishing he would just disappear, she held out until it was obvious he was not going to move until she listened. She finally cut her eyes to him and saw sincerity with no judgment. Why had he laughed at her?

"I am so sorry. Your question was so spot on. It was as if you read my mind. I have, and I am proof there are second chances. I know the aftermath feels suffocating. But it is possible to overcome."

Kit studied his face and he let her, not moving until

she could find no artifice. If he was lying, he was dreadfully good at it. The slight smile on his face was fascinating. His upper lip made a perfect bow. Her dizziness returned, but this time because of Mick, not shock. *Not good.*

She blinked her eyes and cleared her throat. She needed to get back to flippant-Kit right away. It would be horrifying if he guessed she was attracted to him. Biting the inside of her mouth, she managed to stand up without wobbling. So far, so good. He was still eyeing her so she turned the focus back to him.

"So what is your deep, dark secret, Mick?"

Mick sighed and shook his head. "I cannot say. As much as I want to know your story, I cannot divulge mine."

"So what can you tell me?" She took a drink of water and side-eyed him again.

"Hmmmm." he took a drink of water as he thought. "I believe I can answer any questions that pertain to my life before the age of 22."

He had to smile as she rolled her eyes. "Well, that is better than nothing I guess."

"So we have a bargain?" Mick stood. "You will finally reveal why you are on this outing?"

"You first." Kit reloaded the water bottles in her pack. "What is your college degree in?"

"You assume I attended university?" At her glare, he stopped teasing. "Maths."

Her boisterous laugh startled birds in a nearby tree. They flew away, squawking their indignation at being disturbed. She tried to pick up her pack, but her wobbly arms would not cooperate.

When he saw her struggling, Mick insisted upon dividing up the load. He bundled his part up in his jacket and then tied it around his shoulders. Kit checked to make sure his dressing was still in good shape and they were off. As much as she hated her sordid personal story, she was actually looking forward to telling it this time. Anything to get her head back on straight and to hear his answers.

Chapter Three

THEY WALKED SINGLE-FILE on the narrow path, sidestepping large rocks and ducking under branches. This time, Mick insisted upon being in the lead. Kit didn't argue. When she had been in the lead, she could feel his gaze on her back. It had made her jittery, clumsy. That was the last thing she needed now. Her story was bad enough, and she didn't want to see his face as she told it.

"Every job I have ever held has been with a charity my family established," she began. "It focused on abused children. My father and uncle were born while their mother was a member of this insane, religious cult."

Wait…was she really going to tell this man in black all about her and her fucked-up family? Why not? There was nothing left to use against her, even if he wanted to. Talking was one thing that made her feel normal. It wasn't as if he could run for the hills if he thought she was crazy. He was stuck with her, and he had been the one to ask why she was here. Maybe this telling wouldn't hurt so much. Maybe one day she would be able to share this story without bleeding.

She drew a deep breath in hopes of easing the ache in her chest. "Their grandparents finally won custody, but it took so much time and therapy for them to acclimate to what we consider normal life."

"Luckily, my great-grandparents had the money to pay for all of it. Then the story was picked up by newspapers and soon other 'escapees' came asking for their advice. They decided to start the non-profit and it grew from there." Kit hoped her tone sounded matter-of-fact and not pained.

She blinked away the moisture in her eyes. "Did you play sports growing up?"

He surprised her by answering, not evading. "What you term soccer and some rugby. I was a respectable athlete. Not the best, but good enough to make the team."

He fell silent once more, so Kit forged ahead. Surely, she could come up with questions to cleverly discern some of his secrets.

"The past few years I have been the Outdoor Director of the summer camp." Her voice brightened with affection. "I worked my way up. We hosted different age groups each week. The kids had normal camp activities like swimming and crafts, but we mixed in group and individual therapy sessions."

Mick remained silent, but she could tell he was listening. She had an idea that he was talented at that – listening and dissecting what the person was really saying. Many quiet people had that gift. It was a skill she'd had yet to learn because it required keeping her mouth shut.

"You loved it." Mick finally spoke.

Yes! Kit chalked up a win for herself. He *was* good at listening.

"Yeah… in the fall we hosted family camps. The rest of the year, I was sent out to speak at different fund-raisers, and I also drafted grant proposals. When I had free time, I led weekend camping trips. That's how I know how to handle myself out here," she added, her tone snarky.

"Something happened," Mick prompted after she had been silent too long.

Kit snorted in disgust, a lump in her throat. "My mother and cousin were caught embezzling. Seems they had been taking money for over a year and finally got too greedy. Did I mention my cousin was also my friend?"

"Ouch." She could hear the frown in Mick's voice. "How did the rest of your family react?"

"My uncle died awhile back." Kit's voice softened. "My dad has been in a nursing home for three years. Early Alzheimer's. He doesn't recognize me. My cousin's family knew about the thefts. Seems like I was the only family idiot."

"I am so sorry, Kit," Mick said quietly. "Believing in your family does not make you an idiot."

Kit grunted in disbelief. The pain in her heart still felt like she had been stabbed, and the knife was left to remind her. No matter what anyone said, she still felt like that word – IDIOT – was tattooed on her forehead for the world to see.

"I didn't even ask if it were true." Her voice was

thick with self-disgust. "I never thought they could do such a thing. And when they confessed…I looked guilty for defending them."

Kit reached out and ripped off a branch from a near-by bush. She started snapping it into small pieces. She was so intent upon her makeshift anger therapy that Mick's questioned startled her.

"What happened to the camp, the charity?"

"The courts had to sell everything – all the assets – to pay the creditors. My mother and cousin are going to jail. And even though I was found innocent and ignorant, I'll never be able to work in the industry again. Tainted name, you understand."

"That is deeply unfair." Mick glanced back so that she could see his sincerity.

Kit waved it off, still angry and embarrassed. "Since I lived on-site at the camp, I lost my home. I would have been out on the streets if not for my friends and a small trust my great-grandparents set up when I was born."

"So here I am!" Trying to sound upbeat, Kit knew it came across as shrill and panicked. "And here I thought a week in the woods could help me determine what's next."

"Any luck with that?"

"Not one fucking clue." Kit made herself laugh. "But you falling out of the sky made it more interesting. I do have to warn you though: If you are a serial killer and make me your next victim, the papers will focus more on my scandalous family than on you. Just FYI if you're one of those nuts who kill for fame."

Mick looked back with an exasperated glance, but

kept silent. When he turned back around, Kit stuck her tongue out at his back. Another blown opportunity to tell her his story. She'd let it pass for now. His understanding made her feel better. Less of an idiot.

"Did you get along with your parents growing up?" Kit discarded the remnants of the branch.

She could see his shoulders tense, despite the bulky jacket-pack. *Bingo*, she thought, but then reminded herself almost everyone has parental issues. She was one to judge!

"I was an only child. A late in life surprise. They were fine parents. I never felt un-loved."

Well, so much for her cunning questions. Kit sighed. He now knew her life story and she was still left with questions. So she racked her brain for an innocuous topic to bring up next.

"Uhm…what's your favorite card game? I am awful at poker, if you'd like to play and win some rocks off me later tonight," she teased.

"I am rubbish at it," he admitted. "But I believe I remember the rules to gin rummy."

Even though they were from such different worlds, Kit found they had some things in common. They had both grown up in the country, they enjoyed classical music, and neither understood modern art. She soon had him describing countries and places overseas that she had yet to see.

They walked in silence for a short time. The afternoon was warmer and the breeze had backed off. The forest was still filled with sounds of birds and small animals. Kit wished that the peacefulness had made more of an impact on her. She was still tied in knots of anxiety. The job she loved and was skilled at was no longer an option. And she was so very weary of worrying about it.

There was also a problem with Mr. British Man in Black walking in front of her. Now that he was using his jacket as a makeshift pack, everything below his mid-back was in full view. Jeez, for such a tall, lanky guy, he had a fine ass that was accented by the no-back-pocket design of his pants. His thighs looked pretty good, too. Kit found it hard to speak while staring at the way his ass moved as he walked. It was almost hypnotic.

Realizing what was going through her mind caused Kit to stumble. What the hell? Since when did she ogle backsides of strange men? While she loved a nice-looking butt, it wasn't something she usually focused on. Must be the shock from earlier.

"Soooo," Kit drew the word out again. "Are you a mob hit man? An undercover superhero? James Bond's second cousin?"

Mick did not rise to her bait, merely shaking his head at each guess. Now Kit wished she could see his face. Perhaps he had given away a clue.

"That's okay." She warned, "I have two days to wear you down and figure you out."

Mick's groan actually made her chuckle out loud. It felt good after months of lawyers, hearings, shame, and fury. She couldn't remember the last time she had really laughed.

When they stopped for another rest break, Kit managed to remain quiet for most of it. Rude to talk while eating. She also thought Mick's ears needed a break.

Kit was impressed when she glanced at her watch. With Mick being injured, she had expected him to slow her down. Despite what must be a horrific headache and all sorts of body aches, he had made great time even while carrying part of her load. Pretty remarkable guy, she had to admit. Most men she knew would have bitched and whined while lagging behind or insisted upon leading the way despite being lost. Clearly, she knew too many losers.

"I think I have you narrowed down to drug dealer or super spy," she announced once they had set off again.

"Oh?" Mick actually had a half-smile on his face.

The trail had widened so they could walk side by side. Encouraged by that slight smile, Kit decided to go as outrageous as possible. Perhaps she could get an actual smile.

"Yes. But I am going to say super spy because you have a British accent and I like James Bond movies."

"Your reasoning is not very scientific," Mick pointed out, looking amused.

"True," Kit agreed with a wide grin, "but spies do exist. Although the real thing must be more mundane than the fiction.

"For instance," she continued, "do spies buy their own groceries? Pick up their dry cleaning? Or does the government do that for them?"

"I doubt it is done for them," Mick replied dryly. "Governments are not the most lavish of employers."

Kit locked her knees to keep from swooning. So now she knew that an accent and fancy words made her loopy. *Behave*, she scolded herself; he could still be dangerous even if he had saved her life.

As irrational as it was, she believed he was not going to hurt her. And it wasn't like he was going to jump her. Normally, she considered herself attractive. But right now she was dressed in baggy cargo shorts and a loose t-shirt with no makeup and hair that had been smashed under a ball cap for days. Someone like him would never be so desperate.

"What I would like to know then," she asked, "is if you are a spy and you do all these normal activities, how do you keep from losing your cool?"

"How do you mean?" Mick looked at her, an eyebrow cocked in curiosity.

Of course, she silently fumed. Someone with that eyebrow ability would use it often.

"Say someone jumps ahead of you in line. It seems like it would be hard not to think of how you could kill them with one hand."

"Oh." Mick's smile was growing so Kit forged ahead.

"Or what if the grocery clerk is rude to you? Don't you ever want to shout 'I saved this city from a bomb last week! Show some respect?'" Kit tried to mimic his accent and failed miserably.

His mouth was close enough to a full smile that Kit wanted to cheer. For the first time in months, she felt like her old self. Goofy Kit with her motor mouth trying to make someone giggle. While she didn't really believe he was a spy, it was a fun pastime. And it kept her mind off of the nasty issue of her future.

WHEN THEY REACHED the campsite, Mick was impressed. He had not expected more than a cleared patch of land. The ground was clear of rocks and covered with a layer of dead leaves. There was a stone fire ring on one end that had blackened from use. Tall trees, some evergreen and some beginning to bud, sheltered the site. It was quiet and peaceful, leaving Mick to wish he were not in such a hurry. Now he understood the allure this trip had had for Kit.

Kit slid off her pack, stretched out the kinks in her back, and began removing different bags and sacks from inside. She motioned for Mick to do the same with his repurposed jacket.

"I'll set up the tent." Kit spoke before Mick could volunteer. "If you want to help, you can look nearby for fallen limbs. Anything we can use for firewood. Just make sure it isn't damp."

Mick frowned and snorted. She was just sending him off like some errand boy?

"I can do this much quicker by myself," she said without looking at him.

He stomped off in search of the wood. Yes, she was the expert, but he wasn't a complete tosser in the woods. In fact, he groused as he picked up some downed limbs, he knew that a fire needed kindling. Therefore, he added some small sticks and pinecones to his load, wondering if she would even notice.

Mick took his time gathering the wood, hoping his black mood would vanish. He was being a bastard. Of course, she wouldn't trust him. He refused to tell her much more than his name. He was lucky she let him tag along. Some food and more painkillers should help his foul disposition, he guessed. His body was back to being a chorus of pain now that he had stopped hiking. *Christ*, what he wouldn't give for a hot tub and a bottle of Scotch right now!

Once his arms were full, he turned back toward the campsite. It wasn't difficult to find. His companion had somehow turned on some music. Pausing behind a thick tree trunk, Mick spied a bright red speaker balanced on top of Kit's now-deflated backpack. It was smaller than the pinecones in his load and was tethered to an even smaller device he assumed was a digital music player. It was playing a rather rowdy pop song that intruded on the tranquility of the late afternoon.

Mick continued to watch, and his annoyance faded to amusement. The tent was almost constructed. While working, she sang under her breath until a certain part of the song. Then she would sing along loudly, "I'm alive!" As she moved from one side to the other, tightening ropes that secured the tent to the ground, her body swayed with the music. She executed a spin that was almost flawless, even in her heavy boots. Mick barely dared to breathe. He didn't want to break the spell.

What was it like to be so carefree? To find such enjoyment in music? How was he to reconcile this person with the troubled woman who fled into the wilderness looking for answers? Especially since this might be the true Kit. He shook his head and smiled even though it hurt when the wound scraped against his teeth. What an odd creature.

He waited until the next song, an R&B classic he remembered from school, before striding out of the tree line. Kit met him at the fire ring and helped sort the booty. She nodded toward the speaker.

"I would ask for a request, but it only plays on random. Let me know if it makes your headache worse."

"Or you find it annoying," she added, throwing a worried look his way.

"It's nice," Mick answered, and meant it now that his black mood had passed.

He jumped when she let out a squeal upon spying the kindling he had foraged. He was further shocked when she reached out to squeeze his arm and beam at him.

"Good job, Super Spy!"

Her delectable eyes sparkled and her full lips curved into a broad smile. Mick felt himself smile back, but that was all he could muster. The ability to form words was beyond him.

Christ, was he that hard up? A pretty woman gives him credit for not being a tosser and he wanted to puff up like a pigeon and strut. His savior was quite lovely, and he felt guilty for thinking her face was plain earlier.

When she knelt down to arrange the wood inside the ring, he was finally able to move. *It must be the head injury*, he told himself. It was not like him to get lost in some woman's eyes. Those were just bad song lyrics. He shook his head to clear it and looked around for another project.

Thankfully, it wasn't long before dinner was ready. Kit had shown Mick how to get the fire going while she left to replenish their water supply. He volunteered, but that offer was met with a frown. He nodded, understanding that she needed to go alone to get over the fright from earlier. *Brave girl*, he thought again.

She had selected a hearty chicken chili from the freeze-dried packets, and it cooked within minutes. Mick was grateful since he was hungry and in need of more painkillers. Now that they had sat down, the muscles in his legs were screaming from the day's abuse.

"I do wish to thank you again." Mick glanced up from his plate to the woman across the campfire.

To his surprise, she ducked her head. "For what? Packing awesome camp food?"

He smiled and waited until she raised her head to explain. "For being the type of person who would run to rescue a stranger in the woods. As much as I think the idea was foolhardy, I am grateful you were there."

That made her laugh, and the sound washed over him like a soothing balm. He had never known anyone who smiled and laughed so much. It was genuine, he could tell that much. It was so strange to him; he felt like he was in the presence of something alien. As rotten as he felt physically, his spirit felt lighter than it had in years.

"Of course." She waved her hand and went back to staring at her plate.

AFTER DINNER, KIT insisted upon cleaning the dishes. She needed to keep busy. If she continued to sit across from Mick, she might ask him for more compliments. So she got out the sponge and began scouring.

About halfway through, Mick asked permission to go through her sacks to see if there was anything he could use as a weapon. Kit started to argue, but then remembered the rabid animal. He had protected her. He had even returned the knife to her.

"Have at it," she invited.

Since she was mildly claustrophobic, she had packed a two-person tent. They would both fit and still have a bit of space. She figured she could stack the pack and supplies between them. She was going to be stingy with the lone sleeping bag, though. Mick could make do with the inflatable pad and their jackets. There was no way she could make him sleep outside in the elements. That would be cruel. She would stick the knife inside her sock, just to be safe.

Mick was inventorying her bath bag when she rejoined him by the fire ring. While she knew it was frivolous to pack bathing supplies for a solo trip, she just could not stand going more than two days without a wash. And the nearby stream made it easy. In fact, tomorrow they would be crossing near the waterfall she had made use of during her trip in. She couldn't wait to shower. Her scalp was itchy, and she was afraid her foot odor might knock Mick out if she took off her socks.

Mick's hands suddenly paused as they rifled through the bright yellow bag. "Condoms?"

One of those big hands emerged from the bag with a strip of four. The expression on his face was half curious, half bemused.

Kit blushed furiously and retorted, "Better prepared than sorry! I also brought tampons even though it is nowhere near that time of the month."

He merely quirked an eyebrow and waited for her to continue. Which of course she did now that she was embarrassed and on the spot. Damn her mouth.

"You never know! One day, a hot, non-psychotic beardy hermit could pop into my campsite asking to borrow some coffee…"

Her voice trailed off because the longer she spoke, the wider Mick smiled. *Wow*, she thought, *he must have a great dentist.* His teeth looked blazingly white surrounded by such dark beard stubble.

"How often has such a situation happened?" he asked in an amused tone. "Not just to you, but to anyone?"

Kit bared her teeth in frustration. "It happens…in books."

"Well, I should hope that if a beardy hermit ever does approach you in the wild, you would stab him, not fuck him," he remarked, now serious.

Kit shot him a peeved look. "I neither stabbed nor fucked you, did I? While I am silly, I am not stupid. And just so we are clear, I am not a deprived sex maniac either. Don't get any ideas."

Had anyone gone from capable to silly in such a short time? Not twenty minutes ago, he was lauding her skills. Now she just looked like a ninny.

Lord, why could she not keep her mouth shut? Super Spy barely knew her and now must think she was touched in the head. While she supposed that was for the best – let him keep his distance – she was human enough to despair when anyone thought she was a goofball.

He was just too mysterious and capable. This entire situation was crazy; no wonder she was having issues. Her face still felt like it was on fire. There was no way she could look him in the eye, even after he returned the condoms to the bag. Setting that aside, he sorted through the bag of meal packets.

Mick must have seen how uncomfortable she was because he changed the subject. "You have a striking accent."

She grimaced. "I am from the south. The state of Georgia. To you, it's the part of the US that is associated with slavery, obesity and ignorance. Don't hold that against me."

"I really do not know much American history. The way you speak is…interesting."

Kit rolled her eyes and refrained from sticking her tongue out like a child. Nice of him to be so delicate about her country twang. She wished she could go hide in the tent until her blush lessened. But there was no time for that. They needed to get the camp ready for lights out.

Kit showed him how to make sure the fire was out and explained why she hung the bag containing the rest of their food from a nearby tree limb. For the first time, Mick looked a bit uneasy.

"Have you seen many bears this trip?" he asked, striving for nonchalance.

"None," she answered. "It's just a precaution. This way they stay away from the tent. I told you, bears tend to stay away from people."

After they finished, Mick took the lantern to use the facilities while she ducked into the tent to change clothes. The baggy sweat suit made her look even more unattractive, but it was soft and warm. Not that she was looking for a hook-up. Super Spy was out of her league anyway.

Mick tried to argue with her about the sleeping pad, but she stuck to her guns and made him take it. She was starting to feel guilty about keeping the sleeping bag but he insisted that he had experienced much harsher conditions than this. The look in his eyes when he said that made her uneasy. It was only there for a moment, but it looked…haunted. Stifling an insane urge to hug him, she made sure he had more painkillers and then doused the flashlight and the lantern.

Despite a possibly dangerous man sharing her tent, Kit fell asleep almost immediately. At least all the physical exertion of this trip had returned her sleep patterns back to normal. The turmoil of the scandal had made her sleep restless the past year. Too many worries turned into nightmares when she went to bed. She would never again take a good night's sleep for granted.

It was still dark when something roused Kit. She froze, fearing she had heard a bear – or worse – someone coming back for Mick. She held her breath and listened. The silence was broken by a low moan. It was Mick.

She jerked into a sitting position and peered over the pack that lay between them. Her eyes had adjusted to the moonlight that filtered through the tent walls, and she scanned his prone figure, looking for an injury. Was it his head? Internal bleeding? The moan had been full of pain. The light was too dim to see more than an outline, but she could tell he was still asleep.

She continued to watch him and noticed his legs moving restlessly. He had kicked the jackets off. He shuddered and moaned again.

The deep sound broke her heart. He was having a nightmare, not a medical emergency. Kit hesitated. Should she wake him up? Was it because he was cold? Being over or under heated gave her bad dreams. She sat, chewing on her thumbnail until he moaned again. The sound was muted, involuntary. A pain too strong to bear quietly.

She couldn't stand it. She could try to make it warmer and if that didn't work, she would wake him up. Kit unzipped the sleeping bag and quietly shoved the pack over to where she had been resting. She moved over to him, lay as close to him as she dared, and spread the opened bag over both of them.

Her idea seemed to work. After a few minutes, Mick stopped twitching and relaxed. There were no more moans. Relieved, Kit wadded her discarded jacket up into a pillow and was soon back asleep herself.

This time she did dream. Not surprisingly, her dream starred a beardy hermit who looked a lot like Super Spy. They were inside the tent, and in her dream, she was the one who was cold.

The large man lay down behind her and pulled her close. Dream-Kit sighed in delight because he was so warm. She tried to wiggle even closer, causing the man to gasp as her ass made contact with a rather sizable erection. *Wonderful, filthy dream*, she thought.

The hermit's free hand roamed over the front of her torso in a possessive manner, stopping to squeeze at the sensitive spots. She moaned and writhed in response. It would feel even better without her stupid sports bra, but she was too languid to take it off. She had gone from freezing to overheated in a matter of moments thanks to the dream man.

The questing hand finally slid its way down between her legs. It curved around her, not moving until dream-Kit made a sound of displeasure. She felt the man's chest move with a soundless chuckle before his long fingers began to stroke her through the sweatpants. *Oh, yes*, dream-Kit sighed and rolled onto her back in order to improve the angle.

The dream man's fingers curled and caressed and a hard shiver wracked Kit's body, causing her thighs to involuntary clench around the hand. The movements suddenly stopped and a gravelly voice near her ear hissed, "Oh, shit!"

Chapter Four

THAT PANICKED EXPLETIVE certainly had no place in her erotic dream. Kit blinked open her eyes to see that it was still dark. She was still in her tent. Oh, and Mick's hand was stuck between her still-locked thighs.

"Sorry," he whispered as soon as he knew she was awake. "I didn't mean to molest you in my sleep."

Kit struggled to control her breathing. She wasn't sure which was stronger – her embarrassment or her arousal. Mortified, she relaxed her legs so that he could remove his hand. But she could not stop a whimper of unhappiness at the loss of pressure it caused.

Mick's voice was beside her ear since he was still lying on his side. "Unless…you don't want me to stop?"

Oh, wow, his hand was still there. Not moving, just cupping her as he waited for her answer. Now that she was awake, she could feel how taut his body was. Mick was pressed so close to her side, his shallow breaths were obvious. Was he turned on too?

Such a bad idea, she told herself. Then she considered that she could later blame it on not being fully cognizant.

That was it! There was just no way she was going to pass this up.

"Don't stop," she answered, and was rewarded with a sound of approval from Mick.

The sensual massage continued for a moment before his hand moved to grasp the loose waistband of her sweats. "Need to feel you."

Oh, yes, she thought, so turned on by his deep voice and the urgency that she heard in it. Once the pants and her underwear had cleared her knees, his hand was back. Kit could only whimper as his fingers mapped her carefully.

"Ohhhhh." Mick almost sounded like he was purring. "So wet."

Soon her hips were thrusting in a wanton manner that she refused to be embarrassed about. She needed this. It had been too long.

"I know," he whispered, and she realized she must have said the last bit out loud.

At some point, her hand had become tangled in the fabric of his t-shirt while the other gripped the discarded sleeping bag. His touch was slow and precise. In between gasps, she could hear her voice whispering his name along with other needy sounds.

"Shhh." Mick nuzzled her hair with his nose. "Let me explore first. I promise I will give you what you need."

His voice, his words caused Kit to shiver as if the temperature had dropped to freezing. While in reality, she was burning. When one long finger slipped inside her, she almost forgot how to breathe. Mick hummed in what sounded like agreement, as if he liked the way she felt. As her hips moved restlessly, they encountered Mick's body.

Oh, he was hard. Because of her, because of what was happening. She hadn't just dreamed the erection. Now she knew exactly what she would be doing as soon as she recovered. No way in hell was she going to miss making him wild in return.

"There!" she cried as his thumb brushed the right spot.

Thankfully, Mick was done with the teasing and kept stroking where she had indicated. Her body continued to tighten, and in no time at all, she came with a wail.

"Oh, yes," he murmured into her hair. "That was beautiful."

It felt like hours that she lay there gasping and shuddering. Waiting for the world to stop spinning. Her uterus throbbed in time with her heartbeat. Mick lay still, smoothing his palm in a calming path across her bare hip. His skin was rough against hers, callused spots providing a delightful friction. Perhaps he was really a garbage man. Whatever he did for a living, he certainly had magic hands.

He let out a surprised sound when Kit suddenly sat up and pressed him onto his back. Her body was so loose, yet heavy, and she struggled to unfasten his pants. In the dim moonlight, his hand clasped her wrist.

"You don't have to –" he began, but she cut him off.

"I need to," she growled, and must have been convincing because his hand moved to help her with his pants and briefs.

Kit had to chuckle when she finally got her hand on him. *Big feet don't lie*, she thought as his hips arched up. She squeezed. Now it was her turn.

She lay back down, her head resting on his chest as his arm curved around her back, pulling her close. His soft tee smelled like the forest they had spent all day walking through. She could feel the strong muscles under her cheek bunch as he moved.

Circling her thumb around the head of his cock, she spread the moisture she found. Her beginning strokes were slow and measured as she listened to the groans he made behind clenched teeth.

He was so contained. She wanted to rock his world as violently as he had shaken hers. She tightened her grip but slowed the strokes. It wasn't long before his hips began to move in desperation, and an actual moan escaped his mouth.

Kit grinned in triumph against his side, glad he couldn't see. She then had an insane desire to use her mouth on him. Since she normally was not a big fan of giving blowjobs, that urge was strong and unexpected. How would he react? Too bad, she wasn't that brave.

"Faster, Kit," he implored, and she immediately complied since she was dying for his response.

Mick rewarded her with another throaty groan when she added a twist on the upstroke. She was amazed to realize that she was just as turned on by this as she had been earlier when he had been touching her. Biting her lip to keep from moaning along with him, Kit tightened her grip.

"That's it," he sighed.

Kit shivered at the low tone of his voice. She loved the way his hips began to stutter. Then she felt his release pulse up through her tight grasp. His hand reached over to cover hers, stilling her movement while he came with a massive tremor.

So astounding, Kit thought as she again struggled to catch her breath. That was worth any amount of mortification she might feel in the morning. As Mick quivered in reaction, Kit pulled off one of her socks to clean up his abdomen and her hand.

Now the awkward part. She lay back in order to pull up her pants, grateful it was still too dark to see details. Mick moved beside her, probably doing the same. She sat back up, ready to move back to her original sleeping space.

Should she thank him? Kit had no clue what to do, which meant that she had to babble.

"Uhm. You were restless, having a nightmare. I thought it was because you were cold, so I came over with the sleeping bag and…" Her rambling tapered off when she felt his hand on her head.

"Curls?" His voice sounded surprised as his large hand stroked her hair.

Kit snorted. She had forgotten that a cap had hidden her hair all day. For all he knew, it was also purple, not medium brown. She had a love/hate relationship with her chin-length ringlets. She was again thankful it was dark in the tent. Without a wash and some hair product, it was a frizzy mop.

Mick lay back down and surprised her by tugging her down with him. Tucking her back along his side, he pulled the sleeping bag back over them as if nothing unusual had happened.

Kit felt she should say more, but she was so warm and sated that she fell asleep before deciding on just what to utter.

A PAINFUL THROB in her foot roused her from sleep. Without opening her eyes, she fished around in her sock to pull out the knife that had wedged itself between her ankle and the floor of the tent. *Much better*, she thought, and shifted to a more comfortable position. Then she noticed that her other foot was freezing cold. Why was she missing a sock?

The memory of last night made her eyes pop wide open. A quick look around told her that she was alone in the tent and it was daylight. Trying to make as little noise as possible, she sat up and moved over to peek outside the tent's small plastic window. Mick was outside sitting in front of the fire and rummaging in the food bag.

Kit giggled. He had paid enough attention to her lesson to start the fire on his own. She wanted to celebrate, but when she sat back down, her eyes fell on her discarded sock.

"Augh!" she screamed into her hands, swearing that every inch of her skin was blushing.

What the hell should she do now? Running away or hiding were not options. She would have to leave the tent eventually. In an effort to keep her hands busy, she concentrated on getting dressed and stuffing her hair back under the ball cap. Acting nonchalant was probably the best strategy, she decided. There was no need for him to know last night's orgasm was now in her Top 5 of all time. She needed to remember the "stranger" part. The "alone in the woods" part. The "trusting your gut could lead to disaster" part.

Just pretend it never happened; she told herself and unzipped the door.

Mick looked up, gave her a tentative smile, and held up two packets.

"Cinnamon oatmeal or something called Breakfast Skillet?" he asked.

"Let's do both." She forced herself to smile back. "The rest of our morning hike is uphill. We will need all the energy we can get."

Mick set about boiling the water for their food and coffee while Kit dismantled the tent and repacked. During the meal, they were both quiet, but she did catch Mick looking at her. She didn't point it out, but she could see his fair face turn pink. Good! She wasn't the only one who felt awkward after last night. She exhaled slowly, letting the anxiety leave her system.

They packed up and hiked for an hour or so, the silence filled by Kit reciting her favorite thriller authors and why she liked them. She wanted to act normal but found herself chattering more than usual. Of course. She was far outside her comfort zone, despite knowing Mick was also off-balance. Luckily for Mick's ears, the strenuous hike made constant talking impossible. There were lengthy pauses while she caught her breath.

Kit thought of how he had thanked her the night before and realized something shocking. Basically, he had been grateful that she was impulsive and stubborn. He had thanked her for just being herself. Tears burned her eyes, but she blinked them away before they fell. Could it be that the universe truly had sent her a sign? Either way, she chose to believe it had and that it meant she was alright as she was. She had saved Mick. She could damn well save herself and make a new life. No more avoidance, she decided. As soon as they returned to reality, she would make plans to move. Atlanta was a huge city. Surely, there would be something there for her.

When they paused for a water break, she insisted upon changing his bandage. She had forgotten about checking it earlier. While she was fumbling with the replacement tape, Mick finally spoke.

"My name really is Mick." An embarrassed smile ghosted across his face. "Mick Harris."

"Oh," she said, a bit baffled. "Okay."

At least she knew she had screamed the correct name last night. Her face heated just thinking about it. Okay, and other parts of her heated up, too. Fuck, could they go back to hiking now? Before she jumped on him and begged for another happy ending?

"Nice to meet you, Mr. Harris." She bowed. "I'm Kit Foster and I still need to know why you were dumped out of a helicopter."

Mick heaved a dramatic sigh and shook his head. Oh no. Was he tired of her already? Knots twisted in Kit's stomach.

He placed his hand over his heart, the long fingers spread out on the gray cotton. His vivid blue eyes pleaded as he grimaced.

"I wish I could. I simply cannot and I understand how suspicious that sounds. You seem to hate lying. I could make up a story to satisfy your curiosity or you could stop asking. I know I am asking for your trust when you barely know me. It's your choice."

This time her face heated from shame. Which was worse? But she knew the answer. A lie was the worst. She would have to suffer from curiosity.

"OK." She nodded and wondered how she could salvage the mood. "You win."

The small smile reappeared on Mick's face and Kit wanted to see it broaden. He should smile more, she decided. Ugh, she had it bad. The swelling around his eye had gone down and the skin was a lovely shade of purple today. His lip also looked normal save for the thin scab and was surrounded by the beginnings of a beard. *He must be one of those men who has to shave every day*, she thought. He looked dark and dangerous.

"I will stick with Super Spy then." She grinned. "Or maybe you can't say because the bump on your head caused memory lapse."

Mick hefted her pack and helped her get it back on. "Oh? Then who am I really?"

"Hmmm." She thought. "Maybe a gardener who was caught flirting with the daughter of a mob boss. The dad didn't like his princess noticing the help, so he dumped you out here to die."

Mick snickered. *Bingo*, thought Kit, smirking. It was a wonderful sound. Somehow, she knew he wasn't one who laughed very much. While his worry lines were well-defined, the grooves around his mouth were not as deep.

She saw them only with these rare chuckles. Whatever his secrets involved, it was something grim.

THEIR TRUCE DID make Kit feel more relaxed, so in turn, she talked less for the next few hours. Mick seemed more relaxed until she informed him that they would be stopping mid-afternoon for a wash.

"Is that necessary?" He frowned. "I do not want us to fall behind schedule."

Kit waved off that concern. "We're making great time. Thirty minutes will not make a difference."

When he scowled, she added, "I know you want to get home quickly. Getting clean will help our moods, and it is just healthier. I promise it will be worth it."

She noticed he still looked tense, but she assumed he was worried that she might attack him if he stripped. She was fairly sure she wouldn't...maybe. Lordy, the idea of seeing his chest muscles rather than just feeling them clogged up her imagination. Did he have chest hair? Cute moles? More tattoos? That idea made her knees weak. No, she should act mature. However, if he made the first move, she would not be coy.

Think of something else, Kit's brain scolded. She forced the image of a wet, naked Mick from her mind and launched into a lesson of history of the national park system. The day passed easily until they neared the waterfall.

Kit led them off the path at the spot she had marked previously. As soon as they rounded a corner of fallen boulders, the sound of the waterfall became louder. She could not wait to be clean again. The climb had made her sweaty, and her scalp itched like crazy. She had gone several paces when she sensed that Mick wasn't following.

Curious, she turned around to find him just standing there. Frozen. His face was pale and his expression was one of pure fright. Even his hands were shaking.

"Mick!" Kit ran back to him and grabbed his arm. "Are you okay? What's wrong?"

Nothing happened at first, and then Mick exhaled, blinking his eyes rapidly. He glanced over Kit's shoulder, then turned and hurried back in the direction of the trail.

Kit chased after him, giving him space as they stopped on the path. He threw off his makeshift pack and began pacing, careful to keep his face hidden from her. Easing off her own pack, she pulled out some water and waited. What on earth had upset him so much? Every person was different when it came to triggers, and she needed to tread lightly.

"Want some water?" she asked quietly.

Mick turned but did not look at her. He rubbed one hand across his lower face while the other one he held clenched at his side. She could see perspiration near his hairline. *Panic attack*, she guessed, familiar with the signs.

"Water, the sound of running water," he finally said. "I have…issues with it."

Kit sensed that she needed to stay silent. She held the water bottle where he could see it and then sat back down after he took it.

"The ink," he began, and lifted his tattooed arm in example. "I was in an Iraqi prison. They preferred to use water torture to get information."

After that bombshell, he turned away and drank deeply from the bottle. His hands were still trembling. His shirt stretched across his back as he took deep breaths, trying to calm down.

Kit's mind raced. Iraq, prison, torture, information. He was a soldier! A former POW! That made sense! His cool thinking with the animal, the way he handled her knife, the nightmare. It didn't explain the helicopter, but this was a big piece of the puzzle.

Torture. Kit's lunch rose up, and she forced herself not to heave. Dear God. In her time with the camp, she had heard horrific tales of abuse from the kids. Even though Mick was an adult, it did not make his experience any less awful. He finished the water and slowly turned to her. The look of shame on his face broke her heart, as did the eyes he kept focused on his boots.

"Wow." Kit drew the word out. "How are you so functional? So normal?"

Mick snapped his head up, looking at her sharply. Two spots of color rode high on his cheekbones. He looked furious. This was better than the glimpse of embarrassment she'd seen earlier. Did he think she was mocking him?

Kit went on, her voice low and even. "Mick, it's normal to have post-traumatic stress reactions to triggers. Most of the kids I worked with had some form of PTSD. We can find a bathing place that is less…noisy, okay?"

But Mick didn't move. "You don't think I'm mad, broken, deranged?"

There was a bitter twist to his lips that made her

breath catch in her throat. Did he not have a therapist? Who had made him feel so damaged? They had made his troubles worse, not better. Whoever it was, Kit wanted to hurt them. The vehemence in that urge surprised her. Normally, she was pretty passive. But no one should be made to feel ashamed that they were a survivor.

Kit marched over to him and stood on her toes in order to pull his head down to her level. "Mick, I have seen kids claw their way back out of appalling experiences and go on to lead normal lives. It takes therapy and balls, but you do not have to be defined by what happened. Be proud you lived through it!"

His eyes moved over her face, searching for any signs of dishonesty. Then he nodded, seemingly satisfied with her pronouncement. He straightened and picked up her pack.

"I cannot promise I can go near your alternate wash site, but I will try." He hoisted the pack onto her back and picked up his own load.

"How do you stay clean at home?" Kit knew she was prying, but she needed the information to help pick an appropriate spot in the stream.

"I wash up in the sink. If I let the water slowly run onto a cloth, it does not make much noise. I do my hair and everything. It makes a bloody mess." He set to walking.

Twenty minutes later, the terrain evened out so they were no longer traveling downhill. Kit told Mick to remain on the trail while she explored the nearby creek. She found a spot where the water was fairly still and shallow – only four or five inches deep. The creek bed was patterned with scattered smooth rocks that were large enough to sit on. She hurried back to collect Mick and show him what she had found.

"Will this work?" she asked.

He nodded, even though his face was pale and tight again. Kit pulled out her yellow bag, a couple of thin towels, and fresh clothes. She began unlacing her boots and nodded to Mick, who was still eyeing the water with distrust.

"Okay, strip," she ordered.

"Pardon?" he questioned, actually looking shocked.

Kit had to giggle. "Just down to your underwear so I can wash your hair. I don't want nasty creek germs getting into the cut on your forehead."

When he still hesitated, she added, "It's not like I didn't have my hand in your pants last night. Don't be shy."

Mick looked chagrined and raised an eyebrow at her. "Touché."

Idiot, she scolded herself, *you just had to bring that up! Big mouth strikes again!* But the quip did seem to make him more relaxed. She swiveled around as soon as she saw his tee clear his abdomen. *It would be bad form to get caught drooling*, she thought as she stripped down to her sports bra, her plain black briefs, and her socks. It wasn't as if he was going to be ogling her, even without the water phobia.

Usually, she was comfortable with her body. She was average height and had good skin. Her eyes were a boring brown, but they were big and she had long lashes. While she sometimes wished for straight hair, she liked her curls. Her body was curvy and carried a few extra pounds that no amount of diet or exercise would budge. So she had stopped fretting about it and found that confidence was more important than looks when it came to getting asked out.

Kit was sure that Mick was used to much more beautiful and exotic women. That was okay. Last night had been a wonder and she wasn't sorry it had happened. Their lives were totally different, and she was under no illusions about this fling lasting. Now she was going to help Mick and then go off to see to her own wash. Tomorrow, they would reach the trailhead and part ways. And she would be left with a remarkable experience.

Grabbing her supplies, she waded in and directed him to the rock she had selected. She watched as he gingerly stepped in the water and was proud that her gasp was not audible. Luckily for her, his attention was focused on where he was placing his feet, so she had a moment to gawk.

Good Lord, Kit inwardly sighed, *what a body*. Although his arms and legs were hairy, the furrow on his torso was sparse, narrowing into a line of dark hair between his navel and black boxer briefs. He was lean, toned, and fit. There were stray clusters of bruises on his body. She wasn't sure if they were from his fall or the fight that preceded it. On his upper right arm was what Kit assumed was a tattooed line of barbed wire, but with crosses instead of barbs. Was he religious, or did it have something to do with prison? There were more tattoos on his torso. A warped clock was centered on his chest, the design similar to a Dali painting. Underneath, a string of artistic letters rode on his abdomen. Kit thought the language might be Arabic. They were beautiful, almost like calligraphy in the way the lines were formed.

There was a round, puckered scar on his right side that stood out, even yards away. Kit's stomach clenched. Was it from a bullet? It had to be. She locked her knees and blinked. Of course. Soldiers have war wounds. What had she stumbled into? She pushed all those thoughts out of her head as he reached her spot and sat down.

There were lines of similar letters that ran across his shoulders. Mick faced away from her, tense, his back straight and braced for battle. *Oh, God.* Among the ink were all sorts of scars. Some were faint, but there were more than she had been expecting. So much pain. She blinked back tears and cleared her throat.

"Okay so far?" she asked, carefully laying a hand on his shoulder.

A quick nod was his only reply. Kit handed him a small towel and the bottle of shampoo.

"I am going to tilt your head back so the water shouldn't run into your face or the cut," she explained. "If it does, just use the towel."

Mick nodded again and she bent down to fill her cup with stream water. It was imperative to her that this idea be successful. Knowing she needed to keep him distracted, she started talking. Sometimes her annoying personality trait came in handy.

"So, Mr. Super Spy, are you a dog person or a cat person? I like both but I think I am more in the dog clique." Kit began drenching his hair.

She knew he hated the gasp that he let escape at the first contact with the water, but he soldiered past it and managed to respond. *Excellent*, she silently cheered his bravery.

"I admire a cat's independence and a dog's loyalty." His voice slightly shook. "I've not had a pet since childhood."

"That's a shame," she said. "We had a camp dog. Dex belonged to one of the counselors. He was great with the kids. Little fluffy mutt. Can you hand me the shampoo now?"

Mick's posture eased now that he was having a break from the water. "My family had large dogs."

"Yeah, I prefer big dogs," Kit agreed, and began lathering the shampoo in his short hair.

She had to grin when Mick tipped his head further back. Everyone loves a scalp massage. She was enjoying her part. His hair was so silky. The biodegradable shampoo wasn't very sudsy and would easily rinse out.

"Almost done," she announced. "What instrument do you play?"

Stunned, Mick looked back at her. "And how did you guess that?"

She moved his head back into position and started the rinse. "Your hands. The way you move them. I've known a lot of musicians. C'mon, what instrument?"

"I played violin in school. Bravo, detective."

Kit quizzed him about his favorite pieces to play while she made sure all the shampoo washed away. It was almost hypnotic to watch the water slide over the tattoos. Stylized letters spread out into three lines along his upper back.

She wanted to lick them. Follow the water's path with her tongue instead of a towel. What was it about this man and her mouth? She had never had such a reaction. Must be due to the bizarre situation they were in. And the earth-shattering orgasm. That would turn anyone's hormones on high.

"Done!" she exclaimed, and then asked before she could censor herself, "What does this mean?"

She lightly touched the lines of ink that sat between his shoulder blades.

"Common prison tattoo where I was," he explained and moved to stand. "'I suffered, I learned, I changed.' It's written in Arabic."

Kit blinked back sudden tears. "Ouch."

Mick gifted her with a small, grateful smile. "It's not as bleak as it sounds. Thank you for the wash."

Instead of responding, Kit sloshed back to the bank, disconcerted at how proud of him she was. She gathered her clothes, a towel, and half the bar of soap. The other half she handed to Mick.

"I'm going upstream to wash. I have some extra socks you can squeeze into, but… uh, not underwear. In case you wanted to clean yours."

"I can go without while they dry." He smirked, more confident now that the water only reached his ankles.

Don't go there, Kit warned her libido and practically ran back upstream where the water was deeper. *And stop mooning over how remarkable he is*, she added. It was mind-boggling how someone could endure what he did and still be so confident. And HOT.

Of course, her hormones refused to calm down, especially when she was nude in the water. Her imagination was full of what-if-Mick-were-here scenarios. Of him walking up to find her like this, naked and wet. This made her imagine him, naked and wet.

But with his aversion, it was just a fantasy. How could she still be so turned on after last night's explosive orgasm? Quickly scrubbing herself and her undies down, she discarded the notion of trying to get off by herself.

It was too dangerous to be that distracted while alone. She was still aware of how close to death she had come with the rabid animal. She hurried to dry off and slip into clean clothes. She wanted to moan in ecstasy when she felt the clean cotton next to her skin. It was pure bliss after wearing the same clothes for almost three days. She left her cap off after the shampoo so her hair could dry in the sun. Because that was practical. It had nothing to do with wanting Mick to see her looking somewhat girly and put-together. Gathering her wet clothes, she hurried back to where she had left Mick.

While she had been away, Mick had taken it upon himself to pump fresh water to refill their supply. It was nice to be with someone who pulled his own weight automatically. She also realized that he had not treated her like a helpless female like many of the men on trips she had led. The wilderness was her element, and Mick had no issue with letting her run the show. *Ugh!* Yet another attractive feature about the mysterious man.

He had redressed and stashed his wet underwear and socks in the waterproof bag she had left. Kit added her own wet clothing and tried not to look at Mick's crotch.

It wasn't obvious he was going commando. *Mercy!* Who was this hussy in her head? Kit desperately hoped that after this trip was over she would go back to her previous, non-sex-maniac self.

Thinking that he would be more relaxed away from the stream, Kit waited until they were back on the path before changing the bandage on his forehead. Positioning him on a rock so that the top of his head was even with her chin, she carefully removed the old dressing.

"Nice and scabby!" she pronounced. "Another day and you can go without the gauze."

As Kit gingerly daubed the antibiotic gel on the gash, she was aware of Mick's breath on her throat. It was light and smooth, unlike her own. Being this close to him caused her lungs to seize up. She forced herself to inhale and hoped he could not see her hands trembling. He was tilting his head forward so all she could see was his eyebrows and the straight slope of his nose.

She suddenly realized that he reminded her of someone. The cartoon movie version of Snow White. Not that he was remotely feminine, but he had the same coloring: jet-black hair, big blue eyes, and pale skin. She swallowed a snicker as she realized he had also tangled with a villain, gotten lost in the forest and been somewhat rescued. Which made her one of the dwarves! Oh well, maybe one day she could be Prince Charming and get a kiss from Super Spy.

Even with his dirty clothes, he smelled clean. She brushed his bangs aside in order to apply the adhesive. His short hair was even sleeker now that it had dried. Wanting to feel it again, she needlessly repositioned the bandage before stepping back. When had she regressed into a teenage girl? Next thing, she would be writing his name inside hearts in her non-existent diary.

Chapter Five

DESPITE HIS ISSUES with water, Mick loved being clean. Bathing opportunities had been rare during his three years in that foreign hellhole of a prison. Back then, he had been grateful to stay dirty, since he was never sure how a shower would end. He might be crouched in a panic attack, unable to move or passed out on the chipped concrete floor. Those outcomes had been less than ideal.

After the escape, he had found a therapist and was making progress, but improvement was slow. He knew that was normal and recovery would just take time. Luckily, he was able to hide his weakness from most people. He kept physical encounters casual and had no mates outside of work colleagues. One day, he promised himself. Miracles took longer than six months.

At this moment, he was feeling better than he had in weeks. He was clean, away from the water, and Kit was fussing over the cut on his forehead. He held still, enjoying her hands on his skin. The bonus was that he could stare at her chest without being caught.

As he had noticed back at the creek, her sports bra secured her assets with no hint of cleavage, but that did not make her any less beguiling. He only wished his phobia had let him commit her scantily clad form to memory. He would have liked a longer look at her legs.

Had she truly been honest about how she perceived his panic? He had been in bits after his reaction to the waterfall. Gritting his teeth, he prayed that shame was not again flooding his face with color. She seemed sincere, and her background spoke of experience. He had let himself believe her, and the feeling had been wondrous, freeing. When she had been massaging the shampoo in, he had almost forgotten he was sitting in water.

Kit secured the bandage and stepped back. He swallowed his disappointment and reminded himself they were on a tight timeline.

"Okay." Her smile was over-bright. "Ready to go?"

Mick gave her a curious look but said nothing as they set off on the last leg of the day's journey. She seemed off-balance, but who wouldn't be?

He glanced at his watch, grateful that the bathing debacle had not taken too much time. When she had mentioned it, his first thought had been his mission and staying on course. It was better to stick to the plan. If his intel did not reach DAG by Friday, the results would be disastrous. He was grateful that Kit was willing to stay on schedule and keep walking until they reached the planned rest stop.

By the time they reached the next campsite, dusk was approaching, so they divided the work. By the time full dark fell, the tent was up and water was boiling for dinner.

The night's meal was reconstituted beef stew with wheat crackers. Since the temperature had fallen, Kit made some hot tea, apologizing for the lack of cream or honey.

Mick smirked. "We British are not all that picky. I prefer tea with just a bit of sugar."

He glanced pointedly at her own cup, where she had just dumped several heaping spoonfuls. Kit stuck out her tongue and giggled. Mick chuckled. He was on schedule and mildly sore from exertion. He was clean, fed, and in the company of a beguiling woman. What could be better?

He shifted, trying to hide the beginnings of an erection. His thoughts were crowded with steamy fragments from the previous night. She was so uninhibited, so alive. What would shagging her be like? She took such enjoyment out of little things. Did he have the skills to make her lose her mind? Mick knew he should not be letting his thoughts wander there, but he was too curious.

He reached over and tugged at one of her curls. She gave him an odd look when his lips quirked as it bounced back into shape. Fascinating. He tried again with another strand. Dark ringlets surrounded her face, hugging her sun-kissed cheeks.

"It suits you," he remarked.

"So people have told me." Kit grimaced. "Sassy hair, sassy mouth. I'd love to cut it shorter," she rambled on, trying not to stammer as his hand returned to play with another curl. "But then it looks old-ladyish. If I let it grow past my chin, it becomes a tangled mess."

KIT WAS MORTIFIED. Damn, he was only touching her hair. She sat her cup down, afraid it would spill. Even sitting in front of the fire, she felt shivery. Was it just him, the situation, or had she just gone mad?

Perhaps she was mental but she thought it was mainly him. Her reaction to him. When his blue gaze latched onto her, she could feel her knees weaken. It was pure lust. Animal attraction.

She needed to keep her mind on that and not think of him as an actual person. If she dwelled on all that she had learned today, her heart would melt. Such a strong man to have survived and kept going.

But she could not consider that. The last thing she needed from this adventure was a broken heart. She would accept what the universe had gifted her and not be greedy. One mega-orgasm was plenty. Even if she dearly wanted another.

Mick brought her back to the present by stretching his legs out and leaning back on his elbows. He looked up at the piece of night sky visible through the trees.

"I had forgotten how bright the stars could be," he mused.

Kit shook her head. "You should take more vacations."

From behind her, Mick snorted, making her laugh. They sat in silence for a moment, enjoying being full and watching the fire burn down.

"So." Mick finally spoke. "What are the chances of

breaking into your condom stash tonight?"

Kit was grateful that he was behind her and could not see the giant smile that erupted on her face. *Thank you, universe*, she thought. She tried to compose herself before she replied.

"Well, that depends on one thing." Kit still did not turn to look at him.

"Oh?" His deep voice sounded amused.

"Yes. You must apologize for laughing at me for being prepared." Kit continued, speaking in a lower tone. "'I am so sorry Kit! If not for your foresight, I would be spending the night as a lonely, celibate Super Spy.'"

Mick managed to repeat the apology, although he did chuckle near the end.

"Speaking of the super spy." Mick's voice turned serious, and he moved to sit alongside her. "I hope you do not expect me to live up to Mr. Bond. No mere man can compete with that."

"Oh good," Kit said in relief.

His head snapped around to look at her in surprise. She smiled back, worried that he thought she was being a smartass.

"That means you will not count my limited experience against me. I mean, I'm not a prude, just picky." Kit was glad when Mick's posture relaxed even more.

Mick volunteered to put out the fire and hang the food bag. While he tended to those chores, she snuck inside the tent. Her anticipation made her awkward, and she kept fumbling simple tasks.

She tripped while trying to arrange the sleeping pad and jackets into a bed. The zipper on the sleeping bag snagged, and she scratched her hand forcing it open. Kit stopped to take a couple of deep breaths and then pulled out the condom and a towel. The tent was toasty warm, so she started unlacing her boots.

Should she undress completely? She was still puzzling over that when Mick crawled inside and zipped the flap shut behind him. After sitting to pull off his own boots and socks, he took one look at her anxious face and jerked her into his lap. Kit gasped in surprise but wasn't about to protest as he lowered his head.

She expected a hot, urgent kiss but this was measured and precise. Although she was consumed by heat inside, his mouth was oh-so warm. Their lips would meet for a moment and then he would pull back for another angle. Only when she relaxed did he add his tongue. Even then, it was just quick swipes, not an assault.

It was just what she needed. At first, her body melted onto his and her fingers scraped against the stubble on his cheeks before sliding into his hair. It was hard to find purchase in the silky strands, so she made do with just running it through her fingers. She teased him back, nipping at his lips before surrendering to the most thorough kiss she had ever experienced.

It wasn't long before the cozy feeling was replaced by need. She began to fidget in his embrace, her body unconsciously rubbing against his. As breathtaking as this was, she ached. She needed more. More touching, more contact, not just his hands leaving hot trails along her back.

She pulled back to find Mick's face dazed with lust, probably matching her own. His lips were damp from her mouth. With a fingertip, she stopped to trace the upper bow shape before pulling off her shirt with one quick yank.

He followed suit and then bent to kiss the skin above the edge of her sports bra. His stubble scraped erotically against her chest as he dragged his mouth up to her neck. His breath ghosted across her skin, causing Kit to shiver in delight. But suddenly she pulled back. This was still not enough.

"Close your eyes for a minute," she gasped.

He looked at her in confusion, and Kit flushed. She did not want to turn off the small lamp in the corner. She had spent all day trying not to look at his body and wasn't about to skimp on the chance to do so now.

"Getting out of a sports bra is messy and very unsexy," she explained. "I'm not modest. Just close your eyes until I get it off."

Understanding dawned on Mick's face, followed by a smirk. He complied, and Kit began her struggle. She stared at him while she contorted to get the bra off. His face was...perfection. Even bruised and scruffy, even with the large nose. And those tattoos! She was definitely going to lick each and every line.

"Okay," she whispered after throwing the offending garment in the corner.

She tried to appear nonchalant as his long eyelashes fluttered open and he looked down at what she had uncovered. His eyebrows rose in surprise as his big hands covered and lightly squeezed.

"I had no idea," he murmured, his warm fingers moving on her skin.

Kit's awkward chuckle ended in a moan as he flicked his thumbs against her nipples. Like most sports bras, this one squished her almost flat. In reality, she was a curvy girl. Watching for her reaction, Mick pinched the peaks between his thumbs and index fingers. He hummed in appreciation as she arched into his touch with a louder moan.

"Gorgeous tits, Miss Foster," he breathed as he raised her up so that he could reach them with his mouth.

Kit was sure the noise she made sounded suspiciously like *"gah,"* but she was beyond caring. Her hands were now free to roam over his strong shoulders. Lord, his skin was so warm.

Trying not to disturb the contact of his mouth on her, Kit wiggled around until she was sitting astride him, her ass between his spread legs. She scooted forward and they both stopped to moan when her center came in contact with his erection.

Mick's hands moved around to her ass so he could grip it and rock her against him. Kit locked her arms around his back so that their bare torsos made contact for the first time. Fuck! She was so turned on she was almost panting like a dog.

Helplessly sighing his name, Kit's head fell back as he continued to masterfully grind them together. His teeth nipped at her neck and jaw. *Damn, I could probably come like this*, she thought as his hands slipped into the loose waistband of her cargos to access the bare skin of her ass.

"You are really good at all this but I can't take much more," she gasped against his chest.

Mick pulled back to look at her. Even heavy-lidded,

his eyes were wild. Spots of color showed high on his cheeks. They were both gasping for breath. The knowledge that he was just as excited as she was caused Kit's insides to clench, dying to feel him inside her.

"Pants off then."

The low order made her shiver in excitement. She rolled off his lap and somehow rid herself of the cargos and underwear. She turned to see Mick flat on his back, working his own clothing down his legs.

This time her shiver was bone-rattling as she looked at him lying on the tent floor. He was gloriously aroused and finally completely naked. It was all she could do not to fall on him like a horny beast. Thank goodness, she had no experience being such a beast and held back.

His magical hands reached for her, pulling her alongside him on the mat. Soon they were roaming all over her. Her own hands slid down his abdomen to grasp his cock.

"Seriously, Mick, I'm ready," she clarified by squeezing him in both her fists.

He muttered some choice foreign curse words against her cheek and slid his hand between her thighs to check.

"Oh, fuck, you are," he groaned as his fingers found her wet and hot. "Where's the condom, love?"

Kit positioned her legs so his nimble fingers would not stray and grabbed the condom from beside her head. Her own hands were shaking too much to manage the packaging, so she reluctantly freed his hand.

His hands were steady as he ripped it open and put it on, but he was breathing even harder now. He lay back and tugged on her arm.

"On top. Ground's hard," he ordered, his deep voice strained.

Kit could have argued. The inflatable pad was quite comfortable, but his chivalry made her feel gooey inside. So she uncharacteristically kept her mouth shut and swung her leg over his hip. She wanted him inside her now. This very instant.

She rose up, hands braced on his shoulders so he could guide himself inside. Mick's head came up off the floor so he could watch where they were joining.

Such a guy, Kit grinned. But she was glad because it meant she could watch his face while she worked herself down.

When he slid in the final inch, she had to laugh in delight at the look of rapture on his normally stern face. Mick looked at her and raised that eyebrow, his face suddenly guarded. Horrified that he might mistake it for something negative, Kit rushed to explain, tripping over words.

"Oh, no! You just looked so …happy." She blushed.

Mick rewarded her with a slow and full smile. Kit swore her heart stopped for a moment. *Dear Lord.* Then his large, magical hands cupped her hips, urging her to move.

"I could be much…happier." He smirked.

A delighted laugh burst out of her chest. Knowing she should make a snarky reply, all Kit could do was moan and swivel her hips as she went up and down. The fit was perfect. She felt full and stretched. It was heavenly but it wasn't enough.

Sitting up, she smoothed her hands down his abdomen to the tops of his hips. Mick sucked in air through his teeth as she began to raise herself higher on his thrusts. Each time he filled her, Kit wanted to cry out at how astounding it was. Even better than all the dirty fantasies that had been in her head since they met. She wanted to tell him, but could not seem to form complete words. A heretofore unknown state for her. All that came out were gasps, needy sounds, and his name.

When he moved a hand between her legs, she did manage to add, "Oh, please."

Circling her clit with his thumb, his hooded eyes found hers. "You never have to beg, brave girl. Just tell me what you need."

"That. There," Kit gasped as his touch became firmer.

After that, she was back to making nonsensical noises as his other hand moved up to twist her nipple. She faintly heard Mick crooning her name and urging her on. Abandoning her breast, he switched out his hands and raised the one that had been playing in her wetness to his mouth. Kit could not stop moving, but she did gape as he sucked his thumb and smiled wickedly.

"Delicious," his voice rumbled. "But then I already knew that."

The naughty grin grew as she looked at him in confusion. He began to massage her clit with both thumbs and then answered, his voice deep and growly.

"Last night after you fell asleep," he confessed, "I licked my fingers."

Kit froze for a moment, dozens of thoughts buzzing through her head. Had he been thinking of this all day too? Did he really want to go down on her? She honestly made him that hot, really?

Everything collided within her then. The thoughts, all the ways he was touching her and the way he was gazing at her with such lust-filled eyes.

The orgasm slammed into her like a tornado. She knew it was messy and loud. She thrashed around, wailing his name in a way that probably looked unbecoming. But her body had taken over and she was helpless. It was just so wonderful to let go. To have to let go.

"Yes!" Mick grunted. "Come for me, Kit."

Falling on his sweaty chest, she continued to shudder as she came down from the unbelievable orgasm. Mick chuckled in her ear, but the sound was smug and satisfied. As was the look on his face when she finally managed to raise her head.

Feeling his hips twitch under her, she moved his hands from her back to her hips. "Move me," she whispered, "take what you need. I won't break."

His eyes darkened and he kissed her, his lips and tongue urgent. He then guided her hips in a hard and fast manner, his own hips twisting and thrusting up to meet her. Kit watched him in wonder. His eyes lost focus and he was gasping.

It wasn't long before he started to lose his place as she had. His hips began to stutter. Soon, he threw his head back and groaned through a long climax as Kit marveled at how passionate he looked, even with his eyes closed. The cords in his neck stood out and his lips pulled back in a grimace before relaxing with a sigh.

He appeared so primal, so sated that her channel involuntarily clenched around him. His next moan came from behind lips that were smiling as he felt it.

He opened his eyes then and they just looked at each other. Kit smiled back, hoping she looked as contented and replete as he did.

"Wow, Mr. Magic Hands." Kit finally found her voice and grinned. "You're good at that part too."

A surprised snicker erupted from Mick. "I cannot remember laughing during sex." At her wary look, he added, "Thank you. Laughter made it different...joyful."

Kit blushed and carefully moved up and off him. She handed him the small towel so he could dispose of the condom and clean up. There was no way he enjoyed their encounter more than she did, but it was nice to know she had given him something new.

"We should probably get dressed," she said in a voice that did not sound at all enthusiastic about the idea.

"Soon." Mick pulled her back against his chest like he had the previous night.

Kit snuggled closer, not needing the sleeping bag since they were both still heated and sweaty from exertion. She forced back a giggle when one of his hands came up to play with her curls again.

In front of her face was the clock tattoo on his chest. She traced the Roman numerals with a fingertip. Lower on his abdomen were more foreign words written in the same elegant script as the ones on his back.

"The clock signifies that I was imprisoned for life. That is why there are no hands on it to tell time." His voice rumbled underneath her ear. "One of my fellow inmates was an artist. Giving tattoos took his mind off his incarceration and the pain involved helped to take my mind off of my situation."

"How long were you there?" she asked before remembering their pact.

"Three years," he answered, giving her another bit of his story.

"What does this say?" Kit touched the letters below his navel and smiled when he shivered.

"Determination," he translated.

"Official super spy motto? I'm glad you fell into my forest, Mick." She lightly nipped at his pec.

Mick breathed a sigh that she chose to see as relief. When he hugged her closer and kissed the top of her head, she knew she had been right. So many layers to such a complicated man. She wished they could have more time together, but they would part ways soon. This was a fun fairytale adventure, but not real life.

THE NEXT MORNING, the horrified look on Mick's face made Kit pause as she exited the tent. What the hell? He should be used to how awful she looked after waking up. Why was he scowling at her now? She stopped and bit her lip, embarrassed at how bad her feelings were hurt. Well, fuck him. He'd had a damn good orgasm thanks to her.

Before indignation could erupt out of her mouth, he marched over and lightly trailed a fingertip under her bottom lip. That baffled her even more. Her fingers uncurled and relaxed.

"I am so sorry." Mick still looked dismayed as he

continued to stroke the skin around her mouth. "You have whisker burn," he explained, now looking pained and guilty.

Kit's heartbeat eased up and she laughed. That was it? Some minor skin irritation was a small price for his amazing kisses the night before.

"It was worth it." She blushed.

Kit glanced at her watch and tried to calculate if they had enough time for a round two. The lot where she parked her truck was roughly five hours away. She started to float the idea to Mick but was interrupted by the sound of a helicopter. They both froze and listened as the noise faded.

"It sounds like it was near the trailhead," she whispered. "Probably just the forestry service."

Mick nodded. "Yes, but we need to pack up and get started."

Kit was disappointed, but readily agreed. The sooner they reached her truck, the sooner Mick could notify his mysterious employer. Then perhaps they would both feel safe. The thought of that black helicopter coming back still make Kit's skin crawl.

Luckily, the day was clear, bright, and cool. They set a faster pace knowing civilization was close. The light wind kept them from getting overheated. Kit took as many deep breaths as she could. She knew she needed to move to a city where it would be easier to find a job. She wanted to remember the smell of the woods for as long as possible.

The once-narrow trail had widened and showed more signs of being traveled. Kit would not be surprised if they were to encounter other hikers soon. She knew Mick had a secret reason for wanting to hurry, and she respected that. If it were up to her, she would have asked for a slower pace. The thought of letting him go was just as bad as facing her future. And now she would be handling both hurts at the same time.

Don't waste these hours, her brain cautioned, and she gladly obeyed. Perhaps she could drag a few more tidbits out of Mick.

"Did your family push you into working for the charity?" Mick asked after she finished retelling a funny camp incident.

"No!" she responded forcefully, then flushed. "Before I went to college, my dad asked me what my dream job would be. I told him I wanted to work with the charity, with the kids, but that I also wanted to be outdoors as much as possible. He built the camp for me, essentially."

Mick looked at her in sympathy. "It must have been brutal to lose the camp and have him fade at the same time."

She blinked back tears and answered with a choked voice. "Thanks. That's why I cannot forgive my mother. Not yet, maybe not ever. We were not that close to begin with."

"I stopped visiting the facility he's in," she went on. "I feel awful, but it hurts too much when he doesn't recognize me. He…has violent episodes. The doctors say it is normal for someone in his condition, but that is not my dad. My father rarely raised his voice. I am just grateful his care was fully funded before the fucking embezzlement happened."

Instead of speaking, Mick reached out and squeezed her hand. Kit squeezed back before she let go. It felt nice to have someone acknowledge her pain. After her dad stopped knowing who she was, she had thrown herself into work. Then that had been ripped away. She needed to remake her identity, and that was a scary prospect.

"Are your parents proud of their Super-Spy-slash-mob-enforcer?" She tried to brighten the mood, but her words had the opposite effect.

Mick's face closed up so fast she could almost hear the snap of the lock. She rushed to apologize, but he cut her off with a tight smile.

"Sorry. Bad subject that is best left for another day."

"Okay," she whispered, and racked her brain for an innocuous topic to bring up next. When nothing came, she decided it was a good time to take a break.

"How far away are we now?" Mick asked as they packed up after lunch.

"Just two hours or so. We'll start seeing more hikers soon."

"I cannot wait to find a hotel and sleep in a real bed again," she added with a grin.

As much as she wished she would be sharing it with him, she knew Mick had to get back to his job as soon as possible. Her grand adventure was almost over. Kit was aware of this and was determined to act like a sophisticated adult. She was so enamored, though, that Mick's quick smile looked wistful to her. *Don't go there*, she cautioned herself. It's just your imagination. Stay sunny.

"Ah, well then." Mick looked uncharacteristically unsettled. "I'll just use the loo and we'll be off."

"Okay." Kit hoped the fake smile on her face wouldn't crack.

As he disappeared into the bush, she let out a breath. *Crap*. She really liked this man. Her luck this past year was abysmal.

And it was getting worse, she realized, as a man suddenly dropped down from a tree branch above her. He wore tactical gear and, most importantly, had a gun in his hand...pointed at her. Kit's heart stuttered as she found herself actually looking down the barrel of a gun. It was worse when she actually looked at the man's face. There was no life, no soul in his flat brown eyes. How had she suddenly fallen into one of her books? This could not be real!

Chapter Six

"HANDS BEHIND YOUR back," he ordered in some sort of accent that she could not place.

Kit remained seated on the fallen log and slowly moved her arms behind her. Her lungs, vocal cords, and brain were…frozen. Numb. She did not want to die, but she could not seem to think.

The awful man pulled out some zip cuffs and had her restrained in seconds. In fact, he was standing beside her, very nonchalant, when Mick reappeared.

The instant Mick saw the man, his entire demeanor changed. It was like when he killed the rabid animal. His eyes hardened and his body tightened. His chin dipped lower as his gaze quickly surveyed the area around them. His stance became arrogant, dispassionate. To Kit they looked like two alpha wolves sizing each other up. This could not be happening.

"Who are you?" Mick barked, his eyes narrow.

"Dumping you in the middle of nowhere was an inventive, yet idiotic, plan. Peck now knows not to let his son make decisions. He sent me to make sure you did not make it out." The man's smile was cold, anticipatory. "Although I had not counted on you getting help from a dirty urchin."

Kit managed to breathe again. Good Lord, he was here to kill Mick! Even worse, he looked like he was going to enjoy it. Now that she had someone else to worry about, Kit felt herself begin to thaw. What could she do? Mick was the pro with the knife.

THE KNIFE! She had the knife sheathed onto her belt. Her long t-shirt had hidden it from view. Kit slowly moved her bound arms to the side before realizing there was no way she could reach it. The knife sat against her right hip and, short of dislocating her shoulder, there was no way she could grab it.

She wanted to cry but also scream in fury. Then what the man said reached her brain. He'd called her a *dirty urchin.* How dare he.

"Thanks, fucktard," Kit rejoined before she could think better of it.

Her voice surprised both the man and Mick. When the man shot her a scowling glance, she saw Mick nod. He wanted her to keep talking? That she could definitely accomplish.

"An ugly mouth as well," the man sneered, his attention back on Mick.

"Geez, that is rich coming from a guy who sounds like he pays someone to wipe his ass." Kit could hardly hear her own voice over the sound of her pulse pounding in her ears.

She was trying to thicken her accent in hopes of confusing him. Praying she did not sound terrified, thinking that might make him pause. Kit could see Mick out of the corner of her eye. His attention was fully on the gun. She kept her gaze away from his face, not wanting to see how cold and vicious it had become. He had morphed into someone else. Now he truly was the man in black, a super spy soldier. But this was who he was and his skills were their only hope.

"Just get on with it, douche-nozzle." She projected an air of boredom into her voice, forcing it not to shake. "Or is this your first time, honey bunch?"

"Will you keep quiet?" The man thundered, and aimed the gun at her.

For a tall man, Mick was brutally quick. Kit could scarcely follow his movements. Instead of going for the gun, he simply grabbed the man by the elbow. One quick twist and he broke his arm before Kit could even exhale. Mick caught the gun as it slid out of the man's now limp grasp.

She had always imagined that the sound of bones cracking would be louder. More dramatic. Clearly, she watched too many movies. The man's scream of pain was cut short when Mick knocked him in the back of the neck with the gun. All she could do was blink as Mick pocketed the gun and searched the unconscious man's pockets. He pulled out some sort of electronic device that he crushed under his boot before throwing the remains into the woods.

He marched over and cut her bindings with the knife he pulled out of her belt. Mortified at her inability to have helped, she sat and watched as Mick dragged the body off into the brush. Shit...he had just overpowered a man in two seconds.

I must be in shock, she thought. *Again.* Twice in one week. It was a record. Her movements were sluggish as she forced herself to stand. She had never thought of herself as squeamish or frail. But she could not seem to pick up her pack or control the sudden rush of nausea that pushed up through her gut. *Shit,* why weren't her arms working?

Mick came back and within seconds had both packs on. Kit stood there, looking around in bewilderment. They were just going to leave? As if nothing had occurred?

"Let's go," he ordered and grabbed her wrist, pulling her along after him.

His touch burned away some of the fog in Kit's brain. Jerking her arm from his grasp, she shook her head in confusion.

"We're just leaving him here? And going on like nothing happened?" The more she spoke, the higher her voice rose.

Tremors replaced the former lethargy in her body. She felt like she was vibrating. Kit wasn't sure if it was shock, a panic attack, or just a normal reaction to watching your lover brutally hurt someone in front of you.

"Yes," Mick answered dispassionately. "We need to be long gone when he comes to."

"Stop!" She cried, trying desperately not to throw up or cry.

It didn't work. She turned and stumbled away from Mick before being sick. Fuck. She hated being sick.

Puking always made her cry. But her recent lunch came thundering up after she'd gone two steps. After her stomach was empty, she remained bent over, her hands braced on her knees for balance. All she could do was sob, gasp, and spit.

A water bottle appeared under Kit's nose, but thankfully, Mick did not try to touch her. She could hear him move away as she washed out her mouth. Not bothering to wipe her tears, Kit turned to face him.

"I'm not going anywhere until you change back to the other Mick," she announced, her voice raspy from retching.

Mick kept his face ice-cold and simply raised his eyebrows to show that her request was ridiculous. Kit growled in frustration and hurled the now empty water container at him. He moved slightly to the side so it sailed past him into the bushes.

"I know you're the same guy!" Kit was now furious at his patronizing. "But I also know you can turn it off and on! It happened when you saved me from that animal!"

"And I just saved you from another type of animal," he pointed out. "I gave my word that you would be safe, and I kept it."

Kit's anger fled, leaving her tired and sagging. "I know. You saved my life and I *am* grateful to be alive."

Tears threatened to start again as she finished, "I am really freaked-out right now and simply need the Mick I know to be here. Please."

Right before her eyes, he softened. It was good that he shrugged out of the packs so fast because within seconds, Kit had her arms around him in the tightest hold she could manage.

She felt him sigh deeply as one arm banded around her and the other hand came up to dislodge her cap and tangle in her hair. His fingers rubbed her scalp as she tried to stop shaking. Somehow, she would have to get this day to make sense…later. Currently, she was too overwhelmed, and they still had a hike ahead of them. Kit locked her knees to keep from collapsing and welcomed the warmth coming off of Mick's body. Although his heart was racing underneath her cheek, his breathing was even and steady.

At 5'8" and a size ten, Kit was not used to being so physically overwhelmed by a man. But Mick was big enough to make her feel sheltered. His hand covered the entire back of her head. His other hand rubbed comforting circles along her back.

There was one last part she had to confess. "I'm sorry I couldn't reach the knife."

"What?"

"I had the knife but I couldn't reach it," she mumbled against his shirt. "I could have cut myself free and helped you."

"No!" Mick gasped in horror and pulled back to look at her face. "That would have been too dangerous, Kit! You did exactly what I hoped you would do, brave girl. The distraction was all I needed."

Kit nodded, relieved yet still embarrassed. She had not totally fucked up. That confirmation gave her the impetus to dry her tears and pull herself back together.

"I'm sorry you had to witness that," he said. "I know you must be terribly confused. But we need to hurry."

They both took a step back and reached for the packs. Since the trail had narrowed again, Kit followed Mick as they made their way toward civilization. She could hear the forest noises again and feel the breeze on her cheeks. The strong smell of pine and dirt made the inside of her nose tingle. Her brain was awhirl. In order not to think about what had just happened, she started to identify the trees and shrubs they passed. Mick was silent as she relayed the names and any trivia she could remember.

"That is a hickory," she waved in the direction of a tall tree in front of them.

"It's common. It can live to be hundreds of years old. One of our Presidents, Andrew Jackson, was called 'Old Hickory' because he was considered so tough."

THEY PASSED A few more hikers before they reached the parking lot where Kit had left her vehicle. Right away, she retrieved her cell phone from the glove box and handed it to Mick. As he waited for it to power on, he looked pointedly at the side of the older model truck. What had been the camp logo was now covered with messy black globs of paint that stood out against the white door.

Kit blushed and shrugged her shoulders. "The truck is mine so it wasn't considered a camp asset. One night I was drunk and upset and found a can of spray paint."

A small smile appeared on his face before he became all business and dialed. As much as she wanted to see a broad grin on his face, she was growing fond of these barely-there smiles. The edges of his lips seemed to curl up, though it was surely a trick of his facial muscles. Whatever the reason, the effect was enchanting.

While he spoke to whoever he had called, Kit pulled her suitcase out of the cab and threw it into the truck bed along with the packs. After the camping trip, she had planned to take her time driving back home, staying at a couple of cheap hotels along the way. One last treat before resigning herself to whatever job she could find now that she was no longer welcome in her profession.

Mick moved the phone from his ear to ask her for their exact location. He relayed this and listened to the response. He then asked Kit if she could get them to a hotel in a nearby town. When she nodded, he started reciting what sounded like clothing sizes to the person at the other end.

"Do you need a change of clothes?" he asked Kit.

Shaking her head, she pointed at the bright green suitcase next to her backpack. Mick exchanged a few more words and then ended the call. They climbed into the cab, and Kit was grateful when the engine turned over. It was old and rickety, but reliable.

Kit pulled out onto the highway and almost sent the truck into a ditch when Mick announced, "I have clearance to explain myself to you. To answer some of your questions."

Well played, she thought. Since she was driving, she could not devote her full attention to him and his story.

"The truth?"

"After university, I became employed by Security Services. I had a head for finance and they needed someone to work undercover in an Iraqi bank."

"Wait!" She stopped him. "You weren't a soldier?"

He looked at her, confused. "No. Never."

So much for her powers of deduction. Clandestine math nerd. Wow.

"I was in a relationship. I'm still not sure how she guessed, but my girlfriend was more of a patriot than I realized. She turned me in. That's how I ended up in the prison."

"How did you get out? What is your job now? Why did you get dumped out of a spooky helicopter?" Questions rushed from her mouth.

"One of the founders of the company I now work for liberated me. We do contract work, information gathering for companies and the government. Not quite so top secret and usually not that dangerous. I do believe none of my co-workers have been abandoned in the wilderness before." Mick tried to be clever, but Kit was too intent upon getting answers.

She made the turn onto the next road. Luckily, this one was not as curvy. She took one hand off the wheel to chew on her thumbnail.

"What about the helicopter? The guy you…" Kit swallowed down more bile.

Mick sighed and grimaced. "We plant bugs, install hidden devices on computers, that sort of thing. Sometimes we go in undercover. It is not as dangerous as being an agent, but there are hazards if you are caught. I was bloody sloppy on this job. I thought I had lucked out, being nabbed by the second in command. Obviously not."

Kit was quiet, trying to process all of the bombshells.

The helicopter had held "bad guys." And that team included the man who'd pointed a gun at her. Mick had saved her. Tears pricked at her eyes as relief swept through her body.

In about five minutes, they arrived at one of the quaint, country towns that populated the mountains. There were few cars about. Early April was still considered off-season because of the chance of snow at higher elevations. As they pulled into the lot of a cabin style motel, Mick hopped out to haul her suitcase out of the back. "I hate to ask, but until my contact gets here, you are the only one with money and ID."

"No problem." Kit smiled, thinking the embarrassment that heated his cheeks was adorable.

Luckily, it was not the height of tourist season and there were plenty of rooms available. Kit didn't know what to expect once they were inside. Her nerves were raw and she was grateful the room included a mini fridge stocked with water. The thought of food was nauseating. She was halfway through gulping down the bottle of water when it hit her.

For a moment, all Kit could do was gape at him in shock. Slowly it dawned on her what he meant. Then she dropped the water and began to jump around in excitement.

"Yes!" She shouted with glee. "I was right!"

"You are a Super Spy!"

Mick chuckled and shook his head at her antics. Kit didn't care. She had been so wrong about so many things the past year that she was going to celebrate this one success. Triumph surged through her, making her giddy.

Her instincts had made a wild guess and it had been correct. It made sense now. Not a soldier, but a spy.

"Oh no." She froze, looking anxious. "Now that you've told me, do you have to kill me?"

She had meant it as a joke, but apprehension slid up her spine. He could kill her without even blinking, she knew. This man was an experienced, trained killer. One with whom she'd had sex and was now in a room alone.

"No!" Mick looked horrified. "It appears I made the situation worse. I will not harm you." He repeated what he had vowed the day before.

"Okay." Kit took a deep, calming breath. "I appreciate that, Super Spy."

They looked at each other, and the mood shifted to awkward. Kit picked up the discarded bottle and used some paper towels to wipe up the spill. He would not hurt her. She believed that down to her bones.

Mick motioned to her suitcase. "Why don't you shower? I'll wait until after my supplies arrive."

Kit agreed, grateful for some alone time. The inside of her mind felt like a tornado had blown through. She pinched her wrist, hoping the pain would take away the unreal mist surrounding her. Now that she knew what he did for a living, why wasn't she running for the hills? He no longer needed her, so her conscience would be clear.

You know why, her inner voice whispered as she stood under the hot water. *You're fascinated with him. You're greedy and want another orgasm.*

No, she thought, and roughly scrubbed her scalp. Logically, this adventure – however brutal – was better than her dim outlook for the future. She just wanted to draw the fantasy out. That was an acceptable reason, she decided as she dried off. In addition, she did indeed want another orgasm from Super Spy Magic Hands.

Kit grabbed her cell and texted her friend Kerry, letting her know she was safe and sound back in civilization. Should she mention Mick? It was the safe thing to do, she told herself, and texted before she could change her mind.

> **Kit:** *Back in the real world! Met a guy during trip. Former spy. Sex was great.*
>
> **Kerry:** *Great fanfic idea! Bourne or Bond????*

Kit didn't reply, just chewed on her lower lip.

> **Kerry:** *Wait. Are you fucking serious???*

Kit had just started typing a reply when the ringer on her phone started playing "Dancing Queen," the ringtone she had picked for Kerry's number. Not wanting Mick to hear, she turned on the sink faucet to cover her voice and answered the phone.

"What the fuck, Kit!" Her friend's voice was loud enough to make her wince. "Are you crazy? Did you get knocked on the head?"

Kit whispered, "It's not as exciting as it sounds. He's just a government worker now. I am being very cautious, taking things slow."

"Why are you whispering?" Kerry screeched in panic. "Is he nearby? Are you in danger?"

"No!" Kit growled into the slim phone. "I'm fine! This is a private conversation between you and me."

"This is just like that time you decided to learn paddling and went for the Level Five course! You could be hurt or worse! What happened to the new-not-impulsive-Kit?" Kerry asked.

"I told you, I am being careful. It's not like this is more than a fling," Kit hissed back, embarrassed that her friend was right.

She had fallen back into her standard way of living. Leap and then learn to fly. It had been a great lifestyle until the scandal had taught her caution and suspicion.

Kerry sighed, and her voice returned to normal. "Well, okay for now. A fling could be just what you need. Text me your location in case he is a serial killer. Stay in touch! Often!"

"I promise."

BY THE TIME she was dressed and had her damp hair under control, she could feel the past few days catching up to her. Her arms were lead weights, and she was sure she could sleep for days. The muscles in her legs were jumpy from a week of intense use. She would need to look into scheduling a massage soon.

She wasn't the only one who was beat, she noticed as she opened the bathroom door. Mick had fallen asleep sitting up on the bed. The bathroom door hinge squeaked, and he opened his eyes.

"Sorry." He smiled ruefully.

"Don't be." She yawned and flopped on the bed beside him. "I think a nap is a great idea."

Mick scooted down until he was lying beside her. "If you insist," he murmured, and laid his hand on top of Kit's leg that curved beside him.

Kit wasn't sure how long they slept before a loud banging on the door woke them. Despite any aches and pains he might have, Mick sprang from the bed and cautiously looked through a break in the room's orange plaid curtains, the pilfered gun in his hand. Kit watched in fascination as his body relaxed and he opened the door. Wow. He had reacted before she even had time to be afraid.

The smell of hot pizza distracted her for a moment. Now, she was hungry. Oh, and there was even a six-pack of beer in their savior's other hand. The mysterious co-worker handed the bounty over to Mick before picking up the large, black duffel that was at his feet. Only then did the men move into the small room.

"Hello, ma'am," the man beside Mick greeted as Kit managed to stand.

The man standing by Mick smiled at her, flashing a dimple on one cheek. She wanted to chuckle, for here was a man she knew how to deal with. A good-old-boy. Southern, polite, and cute.

Thick hair swept back from his forehead. At first Kit thought it was dark brown, but as she got closer, she could see the auburn strands. Sharp cheekbones kept his face from looking too round and a dimple divided his chin. Bright blue eyes twinkled merrily, but she found she preferred Mick's darker hue. The man was not as tall as Mick was, but broader. He also looked younger.

"Kit, this is Archie," Mick made the introductions after frowning at his friend.

Jealous? Kit allowed herself to be thrilled for a milli-second before coming to her senses. *Of course not.* Maybe his friend brought the wrong beer or something like that.

"Hey." She smiled back.

"Oh, Mick," Archie laughed. "I should have known the woman that saved you was a southern belle."

Mick looked confused at the description but didn't ask Archie to explain. He sat the food on the small dresser and motioned at Kit. Too hungry to demur, she grabbed some paper towels from the top of the mini fridge and helped herself. Mick did the same, and they returned to their seats on the bed, letting Archie have the sole chair. He joined them in eating dinner but went with a bottle of water rather than alcohol.

When the first bit of greasy cheese hit her taste buds, Kit groaned and rolled her eyes in bliss. After a full week of camp meals, this was the most delicious food in the world. She closed her eyes and chewed the first bite, sighing in delight. Had any food been this tasty before? Doubtful.

Archie's snicker prompted her to look in his direction. She was used to making people laugh, but was surprised to see that he wasn't looking at her, but at Mick. She turned her head to find Mick sitting with his uneaten slice, his focus completely on her. All the air left her lungs at the look on his face. He looked ravenous, but for her, not the pizza. She was pretty sure that if Archie had not been there, he would have jumped her. Which would have been wonderful.

She swallowed and offered him a tiny smile. He relaxed, shook his head, and began to eat.

"I have clearance to fly back out at 8pm," Archie announced.

"Archie is a pilot," Mick explained. "He'll be flying the three of us to DC tonight."

"Us?" Kit asked in shock.

"Well…you'll need to come to Washington with me," he said, almost nonchalantly. "My superiors will need to interview you, have you sign some confidentiality documents, debrief you."

"What?" Kit exclaimed. "You want me to fly to another state with two strange men?"

Oh, no. She could tell Mick felt insulted by the way his mouth thinned. Too bad. Her safety was more important than his feelings. While she still felt secure with him, jetting off to DC was a different matter. While she would rather continue this adventure rather than face real life, she did not want to act like an idiot again.

"Do I really have to sign papers? Do you think I am crazy enough to tweet about what happened? 'OMG peeps! I rescued a spy during my camping trip!'"

Well…she had told Kerry. But they had been friends since college. She could keep a secret. Oops.

"And I do not sign anything without my lawyer's approval," she added.

"Smart girl," Archie broke in. "We can have the papers emailed to your lawyer if you'd like to give me the address. We will include our company's physical address, where you will be interviewed. DAG is a legitimate company, and not all of our dealings are top secret."

Kit frowned at him. Part of her was happy that he was assuaging her concerns, but the other part was peeved that that he made it sound so simple.

"I am unemployed! I cannot afford to go!"

"They will take care of it, Kit," Mick finally spoke, his smile faint. "Consider it a free holiday."

She opened her mouth to argue and then a thought hit her. She had her suitcase and a little extra money, and the truck would be safe in the airport lot. This would mean more time with Mick. At least another day. Something he seemed to have an interest in.

Did she want that? Despite everything she had seen recently, she did, idiot that she was. The man himself seemed to be holding his breath, waiting for her decision. One look into those blue eyes and she was a goner. He had ensured her safety so far.

Archie watched their exchange with a smirk that Kit managed to catch out of the corner of her eye. When Mick turned, his friend's face was blank.

"Okay." Kit turned to Archie. "But send the forms to me. I'll email them myself. My Gmail is outdoor-chick05."

"Smart lady." Archie nodded at the duffel. "I need to head back to the airport and get Darcelle ready. Why don't you shower and meet me there in an hour?"

Mick nodded and clarified for Kit, "Darcelle is his plane."

Kit managed not to laugh. Men were just weird sometimes. Archie finished his dinner and stretched. After jotting an address on a paper towel, he handed it to Kit.

"The airport is easy to find using GPS." Archie shook Mick's hand and waved in her direction. "See y'all in a bit."

Mick locked the door after him and came back to sit

by Kit's side on the bed. He grabbed her and gave her a blistering kiss that left her gasping. His beard stubble abraded her chin, but she leaned in, returning the kiss.

"Do you always make sex sounds when you eat pizza?" he ground out.

"Not always," she whispered.

Mick shook his head and stood. "It's a pity we are short on time. Be warned that next time, I will immediately fuck you for teasing me like that."

Next time. It was all she could do not to moan. Pizza was now her all-time favorite food in the world.

Mick grinned and stood to retrieve clean clothes out of the duffle bag. He turned toward the bathroom, but paused before entering. Kit sat up straighter as when she saw his shoulders tense.

"I should explain the water," he said, still facing away from her.

"My girlfriend let them believe I was important, that I knew secrets. They tortured me for intel that I didn't have. When the beatings and electric shocks didn't produce answers, they shackled me in a tank, filled it with water. They would wait. Let me drown. Then bring me back with CPR. I lost count of how many times. When that didn't work, they threw me into the work prison where I was to remain until I died."

"How long?"

"The torture was just a few weeks. The prison was three years." His answer was quick and quiet.

Kit could not stop the gagging noise that left her mouth. She tried to mitigate it by wrapping her arms around Mick and laying her cheek against his back.

"No wonder you hate the sound of water," she hugged him tighter as he smoothed a hand over his arm. "Can I help?"

"I will be fine," he answered and pulled one of her hands up for a soft kiss. "Thank you for understanding."

AS SOON AS the door clicked shut, she collapsed on the bed, struggling not to cry. The hot tears burned her eyes, but she locked her jaw and forced them back. Dear God! She tilted her head back and blinked rapidly. He would be out soon and she did not want him to see how affected she was.

How betrayed he must have felt! She could empathize there, but she had only lost her job and her family, not everything. He could have easily died! Unable to be still, she jumped up and paced the tiny room. Suddenly, she was happy that he wanted her to travel with him. Whatever she could do to make him happy the rest of their time together, she would do. By the time she heard him open the door, she had calmed down.

She tried not to gawk when he exited the bathroom. He had obviously washed up using the sink. He was freshly shaven and dressed in a nice blue shirt and jeans, along with his wiped down boots. Jeans that fit him well, she noticed with a leer. Jeez, he had an amazing ass.

Kit had chosen a similar outfit. Mick nodded in approval at her jeans, flat boots and hunter green sweater. It seemed everything he needed was in the mysterious duffle Archie had brought. Not only were there credit cards and an ID for Mick, but a sleek black gun that fit in the matching belt holster. The gun he had recovered from the woods, he placed into a plastic bag and stowed inside the duffle.

"Did you let your friend know you'll be traveling again?" Mick asked.

A warm glow bloomed inside Kit at his concern, "Yes. She's dying of curiosity. I promised to bring her up to speed in a day or so. I forwarded the email with the papers to my lawyer. He'll get back to me by the time we land."

Mick smiled in approval and snatched their luggage off the bed. They loaded up the truck and set off. For such a remote town, it had great cell service. Kit had a strong signal as they headed into the night.

"So," she began, "you two make quite an odd pair."

Mick almost snickered. "He is a character, but bloody good at his job. A good man, too."

"So he's a coworker?" Kit knew she was being nosy, but after all they had gone through the past few days, she didn't feel restrained.

"Yes. It was he who convinced me to switch employers," Mick explained.

"So you knew him before?" she asked.

"No." Mick looked over with another small smile. "And to answer your next question, Archie was put in the same prison I was in. He was placed there to organize a jailbreak for another inmate, Daniel. Daniel is one of the founders of DAG. They graciously allowed me to tag along."

Mick thought about telling her the whole story, but didn't think they had enough time before reaching the airport. Nevertheless, he fondly remembered every aspect of that day. How could he not? He had gone from despair to hope so fast, his head had spun.

IN PRISON, MICK had not minded being assigned to the machine shop. The hot, back-breaking work kept his mind off the fact that while he might never get out, he was still alive. And there was Daniel. The older American had joined them a few months ago. He and Mick operated the lathes, a job that gave them small breaks in which to talk. While Mick had never been chatty, he could tell Daniel had a similar undercover background. Not that Daniel ever gave up much about his own past. He was crafty enough, however, to wrangle Mick's story out of him. Mick blamed it on the fact he was able to speak his native language with the man.

"Which do you prefer Yankee?" Daniel asked one day, using his nickname for Mick "Being covert or being yourself?"

They were standing side by side and Mick looked down at the man's thick, white hair while the question pinged around his mind. Daniel was a good foot shorter than he was, but with a strong, stocky body that belied his obvious age. Mick was silent until Daniel eyed him sharply for an answer.

"Being myself, even as a prisoner." Mick admitted. "But I don't know if I could live without the thrill."

At that, Daniel let out a big belly laugh and just clapped him on the back. The inmates working across the room looked over in fright at the sound. Daniel shot them a look and they quickly went back to their jobs. The guard near the door purposefully ignored the exchange since there was no physical contact.

Daniel's right arm pulled a lever; the keloid scar that covered the back of his hand looked shiny under the bare bulbs that lit the room. Daniel had all manner of scars and tats, but that one disturbed Mick the most. The physical pain that it must have involved. It had been treated to scar in the most horrific way. He could not quite decipher the image and could not bring himself to ask. In here, secrets were protection.

The next day was even more peculiar. They were joined by three new inmates, which wasn't out of the ordinary. While Daniel usually ignored anyone but Mick, he did smile broadly as one convict swaggered toward them. Mick saw murder in the man's eyes and stood ready to fight. He flinched as a light hand made contact with his arm.

"Stand down." Daniel murmured then turned to the new person. "Took you long enough!"

The man's head whipped around in panic until he saw that no one had heard Daniel's comment. Still scowling he turned back to Daniel, completely ignoring Mick.

"Jesus-fucking-Christ Daniel! This prison doesn't even officially exist! Why can't you stick to the ones in the states where we can just get you out with a lawyer?" the man delivered his words through clenched teeth.

Mick stepped back, totally confused. The man was obviously American like Daniel. They knew each other? The situation grew even stranger when Daniel gestured back at him.

"Archie, meet Mick. He's coming with us." the older

man grinned like a lunatic.

"What? Where?" Mick sputtered in confusion, but the other man just rolled his eyes and held out his hand.

"I'm Archie," he said. "And it seems you are DAG's newest recruit. Or will be, as soon as I break us out of this hellhole. Welcome to the team."

"What the fuck is DAG?" Mick asked, still confused.

"Data Acquisitions Group," Daniel laughed, "You'll love it."

Chapter Seven

KIT WAS THANKFUL for her phone's GPS because she would have never found the small airport without it. She slid into a parking space in front of the main building and helped Mick gather their luggage. Even though she was not crazy about flying, Kit was excited about having another adventure with Mick. Rather, she was until they rounded the corner and she saw Archie's plane.

"Grphlm," a strangled noise left her throat as she stood still in alarm.

Mick looked back and raised an eyebrow. "Kit?"

Kit nodded to the green and white plane and found her voice. "My truck is bigger than that thing! Shit! It doesn't look like we'll even fit inside!"

Mick dropped their bags and squeezed her arm. "I've flown with Archie dozens of times. He treats Darcelle better than most people treat their pets. He's a crack pilot, Kit."

Shooting him a look of disbelief, she managed to walk closer when she saw Archie appear from inside the hanger.

"She's a Cessna Corvalis TTx." He ran a hand lovingly along the wing and came to grab Kit's backpack.

He and Mick stowed the luggage, then Archie placed a textured rug up on the wing. He gestured for Mick to go first. Kit watched in growing horror as Mick had to flip the front seat up in order to climb in behind it. Really? These crazy men expected her to FLY in this? To leave the ground and go up thousands of feet?

Archie helped her up onto the wing and then Mick pulled her inside. Kit tried to breathe evenly. It would be too embarrassing for her to pass out. The interior of the plane was surprisingly posh. The beige leather bucket seats put a regular airline seat to shame. One glance at the cockpit showed Kit an array of computer screens, dials and buttons that made her feel more at ease. At least Darcelle was modern.

"Wait!" Her voice squeaked again as Archie climbed in and shut the door. "Where's the steering wheel?"

Archie laughed and popped on the headphones. Mick pointed to the joysticks next to the front seats. "There are two if you'd like to try your hand at it."

Kit glowered at him and fastened her seatbelt. She kept her eyes on the window as Archie radioed the tower and began to speed down the runway. Thank heavens it was dark outside. Her stomach bottomed out when the wheels left the land, but she was proud that she didn't make a sound. She could do this. It was pitch black outside once they were in the air.

If she could see land outside, she might panic and that would be too embarrassing. She tried to read an old newspaper that she found in the seat pocket as Archie effortlessly evened the plane out at the correct altitude. She had to admit it was a smooth ride so far. Archie looked thoroughly competent as he went about all his piloting activities.

She took a deep breath and melted back into the leather cushions. Mick pulled a magazine from a door pocket and flipped through it. Kit watched his hands under the small spotlights as he turned the pages, marveling over how graceful they were. Resting her head on his shoulder, she ran her index finger over the fabric of his sleeve that hid the tattoo on his arm.

"Why were you there for so long?" she whispered, knowing her voice sounded sad.

Mick put down the magazine and held her hand in his. "I was too low level to rescue. I knew that going into the undercover mission. I was just too arrogant to think I would ever get caught. So I was lax and my girlfriend caught on."

Fury from earlier swept through her. Back in the hotel room, she'd imagined doing all sorts of awful acts to his betrayer. She had not realized how bloodthirsty she was. The idea of breaking bones was appealing in this instance. Or at least pulling her hair out, strand by strand.

"That's awful!" Kit gasped. "I want to kill her! I can't imagine how abandoned you felt!"

"It wasn't so bad," Mick said.

"Liar," she challenged but without any heat. "I'll let that pass since you swore you were seeing a therapist."

"As I said, I see him when I can but it has made a

difference thus far." Mick gave her another of his small smiles. "Try to rest some more. When we land, there will be a car waiting to take us straight to the office."

Consenting to his idea, she leaned the seat back but refused to let go of his hand. She watched through her lashes as he went back to the magazine. However, he now folded it so that he could read it one-handed. A sloppy warmth suffused her body. Yeah, she was pretty sure he liked her.

After her very short nap, Kit argued with Mick about not getting any sleep himself. Even though he insisted that he was used to going without for long stretches, he looked tired. There were more lines around his eyes. But she could only get him to agree to close his eyes for about twenty minutes. She knew he didn't sleep but at least he had relaxed.

THEY ARRIVED IN DC before midnight. Kit tried to look sophisticated but could not help but gawk. She was in the capitol! Having never been, she felt like an ungainly tourist. Archie helped her and Mick grab their luggage and exit the small plane. Mick picked up their bags and turned in the direction of the waiting car. Halfway there, Kit stopped.

"Oh!" She exclaimed. "I forgot something. I'll meet you at the car."

Mick flashed her a quizzical smile but continued toward the car. Kit waited for a moment to make sure he wasn't watching and then ran back to the plane. Archie was outside checking the right wing and turned when he heard her approach. Without thinking, Kit flung herself

120

at him and wrapped her arms around his torso in a bear hug.

Big mistake, she thought when he stiffened and held his arms up and away from her. Ooops. His friendly persona hid a man who was not comfortable being touched.

She pulled her arms away and stepped back. "Sorry. I just wanted to thank you."

"No problem, darlin'." He smiled, covering his discomfort. "Always happy to give a pretty lady a lift."

"No." Kit frowned. "Thank you for saving him. For rescuing Mick."

Archie's face softened and he bowed gallantly, his hand over his heart. "My pleasure. We're lucky to have him aboard."

A young man in a suit stowed their luggage in the trunk of a dark sedan. Kit and Mick slid into the backseat, grateful for the warmth. The air was cool and neither of them had coats. Thanks to the lack of sleep, Kit was fidgety. It didn't help that she was also nervous about the next few hours.

Mick placed one of his large hands on her thigh and squeezed. "There's no need to be anxious. You'll be asked to recount what happened, not interrogated."

"I don't have to tell them about what happened with us, do I?" Kit's heart stopped. She could not bear that. It was much too private.

"No." Mick looked amused. "Just about when you found me and yesterday's events. Relax." Mick's hand slid down to her knee. "This time of night, there will be few people about."

Kit hated feeling off-balance. But she had no clue what to expect. They were heading into a business district. Dark windows of the tall buildings they passed reflected the street lights.

"Like who?" she pouted, hoping Mick could help her feel more at ease.

His big hand squeezed again. "Daniel is usually out in the field. He's a recruiter of sorts for the company. My direct supervisor, Peter, could be there. He runs the operations, and his hours vary. His daughter, Vivienne, is a lawyer who acts as the go-between with the government. The other company head is Malachai, who is in charge of tech. I swear he lives there in his computer cave. Peter will have arranged for a couple of operatives to de-brief us."

Kit fidgeted in her seat. "Is Daniel the man you met in prison?"

Mick's white teeth flashed as he smiled in the dark car. "Yes. He likes to infiltrate prisons to find new recruits. He has a knack for finding a diamond in a pile of shit. Someone who had no other choice. But not everyone was once incarcerated. You will be safe, Kit."

He laughed when Kit threw him an incredulous look. "I promise," he said. "These are good people."

Kit relaxed a bit as he gave her a quick sketch of his employers. "The legend goes that Peter and Daniel were CIA agents who busted Malachai for hacking back when computers were first being used. Something clicked and they formed Data Acquisitions Group. They could do things, go places that the government couldn't."

"And they could get quite wealthy from doing it," he

added with a grin. "It fulfilled their sense of patriotism and their need for danger."

Kit wasn't sure she could handle much more danger. She desperately wanted to grab onto his hand again, but forced herself to appear composed. Luckily, she had no more time to fret because the car turned onto a side street lined with older brick buildings. At the corner of a three-story structure, the driver took a sharp left into an underground parking garage. After a security guard raised the barrier, the driver parked in front of an elevator. Mick arranged for her luggage to be held before they proceeded upstairs.

"The first two floors are home to the part of the company that deals with business contracts. It also houses marketing, HR and the like," Mick explained. "Third floor is for black-ops. But the rest of the company doesn't know that."

The elevator opened into an atrium with two armed guards who checked them for weapons and issued Kit an ID badge. She tried not to stare as Mick escorted her through the labyrinth of hallways. Although it looked like a historic building on the outside, it was sleek and modern on the inside. Glimpsing the inner workings of such an enterprise was going to be fascinating, she thought, even what little she would be exposed to.

BY THE TIME they reached his floor, she was feeling under-dressed, but there had been no elegant clothes in her bag, or in her entire wardrobe, for that matter. Even in the middle of the night, the few people they passed looked to be wearing suits or designer denim. At least Kit had thrown some make-up on, and her hair was behaving. *Get a grip, girl,* she silently chastised herself. *Enjoy the trip down the rabbit hole.*

Mick led her through an unmarked door into a room full of chrome and computer stations. People at desks paused to glance up, and a few others filed in from other doorways.

Kit was even more apprehensive under the scrutiny. Was she going to be dissected?

She turned her head to Mick and whispered, "I haven't had this many people gawk at me since I was five and yelled *Shit* when I messed up during a dance recital."

Mick chuckled and squeezed her shoulder. This seemed to make the people stare even harder. Kit frowned and started to call out the bad manners. But as soon as she opened her mouth, an older man spoke up.

"How impolite we are!" He came forward to shake her hand. "I'm sorry. It's just – I don't think we've ever heard Mick laugh. I'm Malachai."

Kit smiled back, liking him immediately. This was the systems guru, a former hacker. He was much older than she had assumed a tech-head would be. About mid-sixties, with graying hair that brushed the shoulders of his sweater and a goatee that was completely white. If not for the tailored clothing, Kit would have thought he was a hippie throwback to the 1960s.

Kit looked on in confusion as Mick undid the metal watch on his wrist and handed it to Malachai. Long fingers moved over the segments of the band until something popped out and landed in Malachai's hand. He returned the watch to Mick and plugged the small piece of metal into a tablet he fished out of his pocket.

"Excellent work, as always." The man beamed at Mick. "Only two hours until deadline. Sorry you had to fall from a helicopter to get this."

Mick shrugged and looked uncomfortable. Kit had dozens of questions about what might be on what was obviously a tiny flash drive. Now his urgency made sense. She started to look back and recall all the times he had not wanted to dawdle, but another thought took precedence.

"Wait!" she cried, and all eyes were on her again. "You're the tech guy and your name begins with M!"

She started laughing, but it died off when no one but Malachai laughed along.

She swatted Mick on the arm. "James Bond! You're the super spy and you have your own M!"

Then the room erupted into chuckles. Malachai shook his head and gave her a thumbs-up.

"Peter said that it was a sign that our company would be successful." He smiled and moved back so she could meet the others.

Mick had given her a bare-bones sketch of his coworkers so she would be less anxious. She wasn't sure what to make of his next colleague, Del. Mick had cautioned Kit not to use her full name – Delilah. "Hates it," he had informed her with a smile. The tall ebony woman looked like she could snap Kit in half without breaking a nail. Now she *did* look like a spy...and a model. Fuck. Kit really felt like an unattractive lump now. The other woman, Amy, was much more personable. Her blonde hair was pulled back into a loose knot, and Kit guessed her innocent-looking face came in handy. Her lavender t-shirt and ripped jeans were more casual than her co-workers clothing were. Kit liked her even more after she offered her coffee.

The women wanted to speak to Kit first, so everyone except Malachai and Mick moved to a conference room. Another man was inside waiting on them. Amy introduced him as Whitaker. He was short and stocky, and his handshake was like holding a cold fish. Kit struggled not to show her revulsion. It wasn't fair to judge a person based on their handshake, but she hoped he didn't see how she scrubbed her palm along her jeans afterward.

Kit straightened her shoulders as she sat down. It must be the late hour or the unreal situation because the daughter of Ben Foster was not normally so off-balance. *Suck it up,* she scolded herself. She could fake confidence.

She caught Del suppressing a grin when she announced, "Ask me anything! Or do I need to swear on a bible first?"

Amy did chuckle but Whitaker just blinked. There was always one tough nut in every crowd.

Del launched into the technicalities – the session would be recorded, and Kit needed to sign a sheaf of papers that dealt with rights and secrets. Her lawyer had assured her that there was nothing suspicious in the documents. Still, Kit leafed through them to make sure they were a match to the ones her lawyer had seen. Only then did she sign.

Once the preliminaries were out of the way, Del asked Kit to start from the beginning. Kit almost described the day she was born but thought better of it.

Now was not the time to be a clown.

The women in the room nodded in approval when she recounted how she had tied up an unconscious Mick before tending to his head wound. Whitaker was quiet until she was at the part where Mick killed the rabid animal. At that point, he groaned and rolled his eyes.

"You have something to say?" Del asked him coolly.

"James Bond strikes again," he replied with a smirk.

Lips tight, Del turned back to Kit. "Please continue."

Kit condensed most of their time together down to, "We would hike all day, then camp, eat and sleep. Mick kept with my pace, despite his injuries."

Recounting the time with the hit man, however, required more detail. Kit wrapped her hands around her now cold coffee mug and stared into its depths as she talked.

"It's okay. I know…it's a job and I am not going to wail about it. He had to do it. It was just so…brutal. I was grateful and repulsed."

She looked up to see Whitaker finally smiling. The sight made her stomach clench even tighter. It was a shark smile, full of teeth and ill-will. Del shot him a displeased glance, and his flat expression returned.

Kit was glad that Mick had someone like Del on his team. She was an unflappable leader that obviously did not take any shit, even from her own group.

Amy yawned and stretched her arms above her head. The movement caused her messy bun to cant to one side.

"Do you have any questions for us?" she asked with an open smile.

"Millions." Kit laughed. "But I think it is safer if I

remain ignorant."

Del chuckled, showing off a set of teeth as white as Mick's. *Really good dental plan here*, Kit mused.

"Good," Del said and nodded to Amy. "We need to de-brief Mick. Malachai will need to get some info from you. I promise we won't keep you here all night."

Whittaker snorted. "Yeah, we're in a hurry because Amy is due for her yearly penance trip."

Amy froze for a moment, halfway out of her chair. Kit was impressed that her expression gave nothing away. She wanted to snicker at the look of repulsion Amy threw his way, but forced herself not to. What was the story with this dude? There was obviously dislike on all sides.

AMY ESCORTED KIT back out to the main room where Malachai and Mick were watching a soccer game on one of the desktops. Kit smiled and gave Mick an OK sign in response to his worried face.

Malachai found her a fresh coffee and escorted her down to his office. Of course, it was full of computers. His desk held three monitors larger than Kit's TV. Shelving units held all manner of equipment that blinked, chirped, and pulsed.

Malachai pulled out a chair for her. "While we found your basic info easily enough, we need to do a more thorough background check on you. Where should we start?"

Kit sighed in dread. "Just type in my name and The Foster Foundation."

She explained the story behind all the inflammatory

articles that filled the search page. Malachai made her feel better when he became indignant at what she had gone through. For a man in charge of a sophisticated technical department, he was nicer than she expected. Most of the geeks she knew had abysmal social skills.

Kit gave him the website address for the camp. "Now you can see me back when my life made sense."

Malachai finished his web search and then found Kit a bottle of water and a doughnut. It turned out that he was a bit of an outdoorsman himself. They were comparing brands of hiking boots when Mick finally emerged from the hallway, followed by Del.

"You two look dead on your feet. Go get some sleep." Del ordered with a small smile.

Mick nodded, and Kit noticed how exhausted he appeared. There were circles under his brilliant eyes. She was alert until the caffeine wore off. Which should be in less than an hour. A nap had never been so appealing.

They rode the elevator back down to another floor of the garage that held a row of almost identical snazzy, black sedans. One chirped in response to the fob in Mick's hand. As he helped her into the front seat, she noticed their suitcases in the back.

"Company car," he explained. "Another job perk considering this is far above my pay grade."

He hesitated before starting the ignition. "There are several nice hotels nearby."

"Anything is fine," Kit managed to reply over the lump in her throat.

She was so tired and now so disappointed. She had been counting on more time with him, but now they were back in the real world. He had a job to get back to and a life that didn't include her. She forced back tears and ground her teeth together. It was just exhaustion and the caffeine and sugar crash. She absolutely did not care that much about a man she barely knew. Fuck.

It wasn't that she would not cherish the experience. Intrigue and hot sex? What an adventure! She would never regret it. She simply had not prepared herself for this abrupt ending. She had assumed they would have another day or so together.

Mick stopped the car at the exit and blurted out, "Or you could stay with me."

He nodded and tossed her a grin before turning the car left. Kit relaxed back into the plush seat. Relief flooded her body, leaving her boneless. Yes! She would get one more day!

By the time they reached his apartment, or "flat," as he called it, they were both sluggish from fatigue. He had the bottom corner of an older building that sat on a tree-lined street with small shops and offices. The apartment itself was a blur as Mick showed her the bathroom and the bedroom. Kit managed to wash her face without looking too closely at her red-eyed and fatigued face in the mirror. She texted a quick update to Kerry and turned her phone off.

When she exited, she found Mick had used the half bath and was pulling back the comforter. He dug out a t-shirt for her to sleep in and then they practically fell into bed. The last thing Kit remembered was Mick drawing her close.

A FEW HOURS later, Kit was awoken by Mick pulling on her leg. "Wake up, Angel. I have food."

Kit snickered as her stomach growled before she could speak. "You are wonderful."

She dragged herself from the bed, her body stiff from the past day's inactivity. She stopped to pull on her jeans but didn't bother with a bra or socks. She was far too hungry. Besides, Mick knew well what she looked like first thing in the morning. Although from glancing at the clock, she realized that it was early evening.

She found the kitchen where Mick was dishing out pasta from take-out containers. It smelled wonderful, the spices making her stomach growl again. Other parts of her growled after getting a good look at Mick. He was dressed in black track pants that cupped his ass nicely and a black tank that showed off his ink and muscles. Lord, if she weren't starving, she would attack him right where he stood.

Attempting nonchalance, she placed the water glasses on the small table and helped him with the plates and cutlery. Everything coordinated. There were no souvenir glasses or mismatched forks. *Of course*, she realized with a shattered heart as she looked over the perfection of his cutlery drawer. After prison, he'd started over from scratch. Thinking of her own collection of cast-offs and hand-me-downs, she was grateful for their variety. Each piece had some sort of story. She hoped she would have an opportunity to add some diversity to Mick's kitchen. Even if it was only a china plate from a thrift store.

Shaking off the melancholy, Kit resolved to make the next day count. Time was almost up with her super spy.

As they sat down, she felt Mick's leg brush hers. She tried not to shiver.

"I hope I chose well with the food." He gestured to their loaded plates. "This café is just down the street and delivers."

Kit took a bite and moaned in delight. "It's wonderful. Thank you."

They were both quiet while they ate their first real meal in days. Mick produced a bottle of red wine and Kit gratefully accepted a glass. Maybe it would help her feel less keyed-up.

"I have to check in with Peter every day," Mick announced. "But I am on restricted duty for two weeks."

Kit was scared to breathe. "Oh? Is that a hint?"

Was she dreaming? Still asleep? She carefully set her glass down, not breaking eye contact with his blue gaze.

Mick flushed and grinned. "Would you like to stay and let me show you what I know of DC?"

"Yes." She was impressed that she did not squeal the word in delight.

Then she turned solemn. "But why me? Seriously, Mick. Don't feel obligated."

Mick looked incredulous before jerking her into his lap. Kit yelped in surprise and clutched at his shoulders. His mostly naked, muscled shoulders.

"Kit, you astound me." He peered straight into her eyes. "When I came to in that meadow, the first thing I saw were your eyes. Utterly beautiful. Moreover, you are unbelievably brave. You were ready to take on that animal and that assassin. But beyond that you are so full of life it's almost blinding to look at."

"Oh?" was all she could manage over the lump in her throat.

"The last few years." He paused. "My life has been so dark. And it's not just my job or the years in prison. I have always been too serious, too aloof."

His blue eyes lit up with affection. "But you didn't care. You blasted through all of my barriers with the simple intent of making a connection. Few people have ever bothered. It's more than that. I happen to find you utterly fascinating and alluring."

Kit felt as if her face was on fire. "Oh. Well...I would be beyond happy to spend more time with you."

Mick smiled, and Kit shifted in his lap, causing his eyes to darken. This time, she initiated the kiss. His freshly shaven cheeks felt different, but his lips were oh-so familiar. His arms were tight around her as the kiss turned hungry. Kit yelped in shock when he stood up with her in his arms.

"This time we have a bed," he announced with a cheeky leer and carried her back into the bedroom as she laughed in delight.

Chapter Eight

THEY SPENT THE next few days wandering through the city, hitting all the tourist spots. Mick also made sure to stop at as many unusual restaurants as possible. Kit was adventurous and only refused one meal at an Indian café.

"I can't breathe. Too much curry," she hissed to Mick.

His apartment was furnished with items he had selected on a single trip to a furniture store, she learned. There were few personal touches. Mick scoffed at the idea of decorating by saying, "It should just be comfortable." However, a framed photo held a place of honor on a bookshelf by the overstuffed leather sofa.

The image was in full color, yet grainy. As Kit picked it up, she felt Mick come to stand behind her. The couple was older, smiling at the camera rather formally, even though they were casually dressed.

"It was taken at a work function." Mick explained, his warm hands coming to rest on her hips.

"My father was a maths professor. He expected me to

follow in his footsteps. The subject came easy to me and I was somewhat lazy, so I didn't make waves until after my second degree."

He rested his cheek on the side of her head. Kit's heart clenched, remembering the way he had closed up in the woods. Something bad had happened. Something that still pained him. As curious as she was, she almost asked him to stop. How many ways could this man's story break her heart?

"They abhorred violence, so I didn't tell them about my recruitment for months. I wanted adventure, something they did not understand. I wanted to make a difference. Save the world. Needless to say, they were disappointed."

She leaned back into his body and felt the deep sigh that came up from his chest. "They were on holiday...there was a leak. Carbon monoxide. Everyone in the inn died in their sleep."

It was so quiet inside the flat that Kit could hear the ticking of the kitchen clock. She waited, but he seemed to be at a loss for words. She covered his hands with hers, squeezed and waited for him to collect his thoughts.

"I moved their belongings to storage and volunteered for Iraq. I paid rent for an entire year, thinking I would be better able to deal with it when I returned. There was no one to keep up with the fees after my capture. So the contents were sold or thrown away."

"I am so, so sorry." Kit's voice was thick with tears.

She felt him shake his head. "Thank heavens for the internet. I found that photo in the university's archives. It is all I have left of them."

Kit whirled in his embrace so that she could look into his eyes. The light blue orbs were murky with grief and guilt.

"No! Mick, please! Don't hate yourself!"

She smoothed her hands over the cotton fabric covering his chest. "Saving the world is a wonderful ambition! They would have seen that, given time. Feeling guilty won't bring them back. I doubt they would want you to feel this way."

"Perhaps, angel." He engulfed her in a giant hug.

Kit tightened her arms around him and confessed, "After my mother admitted her guilt, I snuck into their house. I didn't have time to take much."

She pulled back and held up her left wrist. The large black watch slid to one side, too loose for her arm.

"I took this. He wore a nice one for every day. This one, he wore whenever we went camping. I also nabbed some pictures."

"Aren't we a pair?" Mick murmured, and bent down for a kiss before pulling on one of her curls.

"Come now. Enough of this melancholy. Let's procure some dinner."

SHE HAD FOUND out that Mick ran on his treadmill every morning. There was such a nice park nearby, that she convinced him to exercise with her there instead. During the few hours that Mick spent at work or with his therapist, Kit shopped for some extra clothes or read a book in the coffee shop that was down the street. Before she knew it, two weeks had flown by.

The city was much more charming and exciting than

she had expected. Kit had always been sure she would hate living in a city. Now the thought of moving to Atlanta didn't seem so bad. Except that Mick wasn't there.

Being around him so much was easier than she had hoped. He had loosened up considerably. She loved nothing more than when he laughed. He also seemed to enjoy the cheesy sightseeing spots she made him take her to. He was almost playful, especially in bed. There were days when Kit expected to find scorch marks on the sheets.

"I have tickets to a play tonight," Mick announced as they shopped for fruit at a roadside stand.

Kit rolled her eyes. "It's Shakespeare, isn't it? I told you I cannot understand those plays."

"It's one of his comedies." Mick started to reach for an apple, but Kit's hand landed on it first.

She playfully held it just out of his reach. "I think you need to beg for it."

Mick froze, and she was amazed at the anger that filled his face and then just as quickly disappeared. He turned on his heel and walked to the nearest streetlight. Kit put the apple down and hurried after him.

"Oh, shit," she said as tears filled her eyes. "I said something really wrong, didn't I?"

Mick pulled her into his embrace, wrapping his opened jacket around her. "You didn't know, Angel." He stroked her hair.

"Begging to stop the torture did nothing except make me feel more beaten and powerless," he explained in a quiet voice. "So I swore I would never do it again. There is nothing that I need that much."

"I'll never say that word again," Kit swore fiercely and hugged him. "And I will go see a boring play with you and not complain. I'll even eat Indian food with you!"

Mick smiled against the top of her head. "Thank you for understanding, brave girl. And I think you might enjoy tonight."

ALTHOUGH SHE HATED to admit it, she did. However, her favorite part wasn't the performance; it was seeing the look on Mick's face when she emerged from the bedroom in her new dress. It was a deep red sheath that flared out from her hips to her knees. The stretchy fabric hugged her in all the right places. It was a dress designed for a woman with shape, not some skinny twig.

Mick's mouth was actually hanging open. Kit giggled in delight, feeling beautiful. Even her hair looked stylish for once. She would have gawked herself, but she had seen Mick in a suit and tie two days earlier. There had been some sort of important meeting he'd attended. He gallantly held his arm out and escorted her to the waiting cab. *So this is what it must feel like to be a princess*, she mused.

"I can't believe you made me like Shakespeare," Kit teased as they browsed the souvenir area after the play.

"I could not let you visit and not see one. I am British, remember?" Mick smirked.

Kit giggled. "I love the way you refrain from pointing out when you're right."

Mick's smirk turned into a grin. "It's enough that

you notice."

Kit laughed and turned to peruse the poster section. Her time was almost up. While they had not discussed when she would fly home, his time of light duty was almost up.

Desperate not to dwell on reality tonight, she pushed the thought away. She was going to enjoy whatever time she had left with her super spy.

"Let's stop for a glass of wine," she suggested. "And you can gloat some more."

Mick tipped his head to the side in confusion. "Didn't you want to purchase a poster?"

Refusing to glance back at the display, Kit shook her head. "Nah. Too hard to fit into my suitcase."

His eyes narrowed, sharpening in on her face. His expression turned from teasing to serious. Kit was suddenly anxious that she had ruined the mood, but she had no idea how she had done so. Before she could draw in a panicked breath, Mick uttered just one word.

"Stay."

Kit sagged in both relief and despair. Grabbing his arm, she pulled him away from the crowd and into a hallway.

"Mick," she sighed over the lump in her throat. "My savings are almost gone. I have to get settled and find a job."

Mick turned his head away, scrubbing his palm over his mouth and chin. "You're not happy here?"

Kit tugged his hand down, her eyes wide.

"Are you insane? I've loved every minute, but I can't keep putting off the real world. And don't you dare offer me money again. I don't care that you have three years of back pay languishing in a bank."

Mick nodded at the fierce tone in her voice. His expression relaxed, but he still would not look at her.

"What if you tried to find a job here?" he asked softly.

Kit's heart paused. Did he mean it? Of course, that was her secret fantasy, but could he really be asking her to stay? Her heart pounded and she swallowed. Was she dreaming?

Pulling on his arm again, she made him turn to meet her gaze. "You truly want me to stay? Stay and be your roommate...your girlfriend? I'm confused."

She must have looked desperate because Mick took pity on her, framing her face in his magical hands. God, she loved those hands and the way they moved on her skin. *Please let this be real*, she prayed.

"I think we've made a go so far." Mick smiled. "You make me laugh, think..."

He bent his head so his mouth was at her ear. "And you are brilliant at making me moan and sweat."

Nipping at her neck, he raised his head. "Why on earth would I want that to end?"

Kit was speechless, a rare state for her. She just looked at him for a moment with eyes full of tears. Mick simply smiled and patiently waited for her answer. She cleared her throat and covered his hands with hers. She needed an anchor. The world was spinning around her.

"So it would be you and me exclusively?" Kit was embarrassed that she needed so many assurances, but this would be a big step for her.

"Absolutely," Mick answered but then turned grave. "But one thing I cannot promise is that I make it home every day. Some assignments are sudden. And while this line of work is much less perilous, there are still dangers."

"I know." She sighed and smoothed the lapels of his jacket.

"I'd love to stay," she managed to get out before launching herself into his arms. "Let's buy that poster and then go home. You'll need to clear out more closet space for me."

THE SECOND THEY were inside the flat, Kit pulled off Mick's tie and went to work on his shirt buttons. Her dress was soon a heap on the floor. They managed to make it to the bedroom, laughing while undressing. Mick snagged a condom while Kit untied his shoes.

Soon they were on the bed and joined. Once inside, Mick paused and dipped his head to give her a kiss that was so thorough, it made her dizzy. When he pulled back, she panted, "I could…uhm…go see a doctor. Get tested, get on the pill. Unless you would rather stay with condoms."

Mick's eyes lit up as he exclaimed, "Christ, no! The thought of having you raw with nothing between us…Yes. I would love that!"

His sentence trailed off into a full body shudder. Kit locked her legs around his hips and gasped her approval when he started to move. It was almost embarrassing how quickly she orgasmed, but he had such a strong effect on her.

When she finally came back to herself, Mick was

looking down at her. His face made her want to snicker. He looked so smug yet so adoring.

"You're mine," the words slipped out before Kit could bite them off.

However, her worries were short-lived for he growled back, "Yes, brave girl. And you are all mine."

His thrusts then became more powerful, as if he was trying to mark her, claim her. This was just fine with Kit. Soon, she could actually feel Mick begin to lose control. His gasps interspaced with moans, and his thrusts became disordered as he started shivering. He was completely unrestrained and it thrilled Kit.

"That's it. You're mine," she crooned. "Let go. I've got you."

"Kit," he cried her name helplessly.

"I want all of you, Mick," she encouraged. "Let go."

He threw his head back and groaned through a shattering climax. Afterward, he collapsed on top of her, his head by hers on the pillow. She stroked his back as he shuddered and struggled to catch his breath.

"Angel," he breathed into her ear.

"Shhh," she cut him off, not wanting to hear anything that resembled an apology.

"My ego is huge right now," she continued. "Let me enjoy my contribution to that magnificent orgasm, Mr. Harris."

Mick chuckled weakly. "Gloat away angel. It *was* magnificent."

Kit relaxed, letting his deep, satisfied voice wash over her. She wanted to pinch herself to make sure the night had not been a dream.

THE NEXT DAY, Kit arranged to have her meager possessions put in storage until she could have them shipped. She also sold her truck to a former camp staffer with hardly a pang. She didn't need a vehicle living in the city. Mick went to see what strings he could pull to help her get interviews. After that, he was due for another appointment with his therapist.

Kerry responded to this news by texting, "Well, fuck you, Ms Romance Novel. I am so happy for you!!! Will visit soon to check up on you. Congrats!!!!!"

They finished the evening with a quiet supper and a rented movie. Full of hope and excitement over the future, Kit could not recall having a better day. It was sappy, but she was sure she fell asleep with a smile on her face.

THE BEDSIDE CLOCK read almost two a.m. Kit wasn't sure what had woken her. But a quick check of the bed showed Mick was missing. Listening closely, she could make out faint noises coming from the adjacent dark bathroom.

This is going to hurt, she guessed as she rolled out of bed, taking the comforter with her. While Mick was periodically plagued by nightmares, none had been severe until now. His doctor had warned him that the toughest parts were yet to come.

Kit needed to be strong, both to help Mick and to not let him know how much she cared. Not now. He was not ready to hear the three words she longed to blurt out. She had always thought falling in love took months. Yet here she was, willing to walk through fire for a man she had known for mere weeks.

Luckily, there was enough light coming in from the small window so she could make out his form. He was curled into a ball in the corner, gasping and shivering. He must have bolted straight from bed, she guessed by the fact he was clad in only what he wore to sleep.

Her feet moved across the cold tile floor. She tried to make enough noise so that he would not be startled. It must have worked, for he didn't jerk as she carefully tucked the comforter around him.

"Do you want me to stay?" she whispered.

He didn't look at her, merely shook his head. The movement was sharp and absolute.

She ached with the need to touch him. Just to brush her fingers through his hair or press her palm against his cheek. But her instincts said to just back away. She managed not to whimper as she pulled back her hand. At least he would be warm now, she consoled herself.

She went back to bed, still listening, forcing herself not to cry. He would hear her and feel worse. But it felt like her heart had broken open and was sending shards of pain throughout her body. Just breathe, she told herself. Listen to see if Mick needs you. She finally drifted off when the flat became quiet again.

WHEN SHE NEXT opened her eyes, it was morning and Mick was asleep beside her. Good, he had come back at some point. Trying not to disturb him, she slipped out of bed and tiptoed out. She could use the guest bathroom and see to breakfast.

Kit was on the sofa sipping her second cup of coffee

when he finally entered the kitchen. He was visible through the breakfast bar opening, and Kit stifled a grin. He always looked so disheveled and cuddly in the morning, so unlike his usual stoic, super spy self. Today, his hair was sticking up in the back and he had a pillow crease on one stubbled cheek.

However, the rest of him looked formidable. Dressed in thin sweatpants and a tank top, his muscles and ink screamed dangerous and lethal. *What a badass hunk*, she thought, as she did every day. *MY badass hunk.*

She could tell by the time it took him to fix his cup of coffee that he was nervous. It was also in the way he moved and the fact that he had yet to speak to her. The torture he'd endured was bad enough. Now he had to relive it in order to break free. To top it all off, he was embarrassed. It broke Kit's heart.

Silly man, she thought and marched into the kitchen to put a stop to the foolish behavior.

"I'm glad you were able to get some sleep," she said, stopping beside him.

Mick nodded and continued to stir his coffee. She could tell that he wanted to appear aloof, but his eyes were haunted, his lips tight. Something cracked inside her.

"It's not fair that you have to go through this a second time!" she cried, slapping the countertop. "I wish I could rip those fucking monsters to pieces with my bare hands! You did nothing to deserve this sort of pain!"

She realized she was crying when Mick touched her wet cheek. Taking it as a positive sign, she wiggled her way between him and the counter and flattened herself along his frame. He returned the embrace hesitantly at first, resting his cheek on her head.

"No one has ever cried over me," he murmured in wonder, pulling her closer with one arm, his other hand making soothing swipes up and down her back.

Because you had shitty taste in women before, Kit thought, but would never say it aloud. She clutched him tighter and tried to stop crying. This man who thought he was so broken still had such a tender soul. It was a miracle.

She sniffed, and her lungs filled with the fragrance of dried sweat on his skin from the night before. There was also the scent coming off his tank top, or singlet as he called it. The cotton material smelled like their bed. It calmed her anger.

"But I also want to taunt them with the fact that they failed to destroy you. You are so brave, so strong. You will get past this. One day the nightmares will stop." She spoke fervently because she believed it was true.

"Oh, Angel. They didn't know me. It wasn't personal." His deep voice was soft. "Emotionally, your pain is worse."

"It's not the same at all," she protested, not raising her head.

"Pain is pain. It's easier with you here, Kit," he said, and her heart soared. "I am so grateful you understand."

They stayed that way until Mick finally pulled back and smiled down at her. The shadows in his eyes had retreated again. The warmth coming off his body made Kit feel drowsy. She wanted to continue the snuggle, but Mick had another plan.

"Come here." He tugged her hand and led her into the entryway of the flat. Confused, Kit watched as he dug through the coat closet to pull something out of the pocket of the leather jacket he'd worn yesterday.

"I'm not good at such things," he began, and awkwardly shoved a wad of tissue in her hands. "I was going to get it wrapped today. Anyway, it made me think of you."

He'd actually bought her a gift! Kit squealed in excitement, carefully opening the white bundle. Oh, it was jewelry. Gold glinted up from her palm. She could not remember the last time a man had bought her something like this. Her past boyfriends had assumed she didn't like such feminine things. They had been wrong.

But Mick had guessed and that made this precious. She straightened out the delicate chain to see that the ends held a small gold circle. It was gorgeous. But why did a loop remind Mick of her?

He must have seen her confusion because he explained, "I found your halo, Angel."

Oh.

"It's beautiful," she managed to get out over more tears. "But you're the angel. The one who fell out of the sky."

"I am in no way angelic," Mick protested as he helped her fasten the necklace around her throat.

"Well, Lucifer was an angel once," she pointed out jokingly as the pendant rested in the hollow of her throat. "I don't have the words to tell you what this means. Where did you find it?"

For the first time that she had seen, Mick blushed a

deep red. What in the world?

"Ah...well." He actually shuffled his bare feet and kept his eyes on the floor.

"A woman on the Metro was wearing it. She could not remember where she had purchased it...So I convinced her to let me buy it," he finished, finally looking at her with discomfort.

He sagged in relief when a big belly laugh escaped Kit's chest. Now she was crying and laughing. She kissed the lines of ink visible above his tank.

"Mick, that is the best story!" She wiped her eyes. "Did you convince her with your charm or lots of cash?"

Mick blushed again but was now smiling. "A bit of both, I think."

Kit touched the necklace in wonder. He might not be ready to say the words, but this showed he did care for her. And for that reason alone, she would never take it off.

Chapter Nine

THE WEEK BEFORE, Kit had convinced Mick to let her wash his hair as she had in the woods. The idea involved him sitting in a few inches of bathwater for as long as it took to wash and rinse his hair. Even though she knew Mick wanted to overcome his water issues, she realized he had agreed mainly to please her.

The first couple of times were tense. Kit had tried to keep him occupied with conversation, but he had kept drifting off into the past. Then a brilliant idea struck her. Instead of sitting outside the tub, she would get in with him…naked.

Even though he was in water, Mick had to smirk when she climbed in the tub. He was sitting sideways with his legs crossed. She settled at his side, shampoo and rinsing cup ready. She chattered away like before, but couldn't help noticing how his eyes kept cutting aside to watch her breasts bounce as she worked the shampoo into his hair.

Luckily, he did not see her grin. Her idea was working. While he was still tense, he definitely wasn't having a flashback. The next part was trickier, since he had to tilt his head back as she rinsed.

"Give me your hand," she instructed and then placed it on her breast. "There. Hold on until I'm done."

Mick actually barked out a laugh. While in water. Kit suddenly felt ten feet tall.

They continued to make progress, and soon Mick could stay in the bath long enough for a quick wash, too. Kit was certain they would someday graduate to showering.

THE WORLD WAS even brighter the next day. Kit's professionally-done resumes came in the mail, along with digital versions. She started to phone Mick but then decided to wait. He would be home soon. In the meantime, she could cook up a nice meal and get started on more job applications.

When Mick wasn't home by the time dinner was ready, Kit began to fret. He hadn't texted to say he would be late. She resisted the urge to call and check on him, not wanting to be seen as a worrier. But then again, it wasn't as if he was a banker or a lawyer. His lateness could have serious implications. Another hour passed with no news. She absently began to chew on her thumbnail, but a sudden pain had her jerking her hand from her mouth. The nail was topped by a bloody crescent of flesh. There was nothing left to nibble. She sighed and went to work on the thumb of her other hand.

"You signed up for this," she reminded herself.

She had just picked up her phone to triple-check that

there were no messages when there was a knock on the door. Heart in her throat, she ran over and looked through the peephole to see Mick's coworker, Malachai.

Jerking the door open, Kit gasped, "Is he okay?"

Malachai put a hand on her arm. "He's fine. Deep breaths now."

Kit sagged with relief and managed not to hyperventilate. After a moment, she stepped back to let him enter.

"I'm sorry." She blushed as she relocked the door. "He's late and seeing you…"

"You thought the worst," Malachai finished with an understanding smile. "Mick isn't here because he was sent into the field. He asked me to let you know in person. He was afraid you might panic."

"Oh?" The nervous knot was back in Kit's stomach. And yes, she was panicking.

"It's routine," the older man assured her. "He can't communicate until he returns. It should only be two or three days."

Kit nodded, disappointed and alarmed. How was she going to get through this without giving herself a heart attack? She knew he was brilliant at his job and could just as easily be killed crossing the street. She knew those facts. It just didn't help her anxiety.

"You'll get better at it," Malachai said and pulled a cell phone out of his pocket. "But I think I can help."

Kit looked at him, confused and hopeful.

"The cell is secure and encrypted, but still, only turn it on once a day," he explained. "I'll send a message each day after Mick checks in. After you read it, delete it and turn the phone off."

Kit looked at the phone he had placed in her hand and then back at Malachai. "Is this standard for all agents' girlfriends?"

Malachai shrugged and cleared his throat. Kit was enchanted at the sheepish look on his face, but still curious. He sighed heavily before he spoke.

"You make Mick laugh. For the first time since we met, he's truly happy." Malachai grimaced. "I was appalled by how his government lost track of him for years. I can tell it damaged him."

He looked at her and shrugged. "So, now I can help him by assisting you. Because you are good for him."

Kit blinked back tears and engulfed the man in a bear hug. He started in surprise but returned the embrace.

"Just keep this between us," Malachai added. "Neither Mick nor Peter know I'm doing this."

"Thank you." Kit hoped her voice was fervent enough to convey her emotions. "Would you like some dinner? I made enough for two."

Malachai smiled. "Food someone else cooks! Now you know my weakness."

While they ate, Malachai shared some stories about Mick with her. Silly, office-related things. She now knew he always nabbed the chocolate ones whenever Amy brought doughnuts. And that Malachai had won an office pool that concerned Kit and Mick.

"After you left that first night, we bet on how long it would take for Mick to ask that you be vetted."

"It's unfortunately a standard and necessary process that has to be done when an agent enters a relationship.

Sort of a secret background check," he added with a frown that turned into a sly grin. "My pick was the next day."

Kit giggled in delight. "Really? It still boggles my mind that he likes me."

The mock frown on Malachai's face made her giggle again. He shook his head.

"Remember, working undercover involves suppression, secrecy. You seem quite the opposite to me."

The idea that Malachai knew Mick wanted her sent a thrill through Kit. The fact that her crazy-self fit perfectly with him made her want to sing. By the time Malachai left, she was feeling much less apprehensive. She could actually breathe again. She would know daily that Mick was safe, and she had made a new friend.

MALACHAI WAS TRUE to his word, and for the next three days, there was a message waiting for Kit. By the fourth day, she had applied to dozens of jobs, read two books, washed all the towels and sheets in the flat, planted an herb garden in the kitchen window, and installed curtains on all the windows. Anything to keep her hands and mind busy.

Malachai had helped, too. Last night he had whisked her away to a movie, making sure to pick a comedy. Since Kit's father used to do the same thing, Malachai's concern made her feel more at home in the big city. She was doubly grateful because he let her chatter on to work out the nervous energy.

Kit was in the kitchen making banana bread when she heard the front door open that afternoon. By the time Mick had called her name, she was in the entryway, jumping into his arms.

Laughing in delight, he lifted her up and kicked the door shut with his boot. Kit wrapped her legs around his waist and buried her head in his neck. She blinked back relieved tears. He was home. He was safe.

"Welcome back." She leaned her head back in order to kiss him.

Mick growled low in his throat and kissed her back. It was ferocious. His slight beard stubble scraped her face, and his arms were like steel bands around her back. It was heavenly, Kit thought. It showed he missed her, too.

They finally broke apart to gasp for air. Mick had dropped his keys when he'd caught her and now kicked them out of the way. He hooked one arm under her butt and strode toward the bedroom.

Kit rocked against his erection, and he stumbled with a snort. His next kiss was desperate. Spots of color rode high on his cheekbones and heavy lids hid most of his eyes.

"I am full of adrenaline and lust," he warned her. "I need it hard and fast. And then I'll need it again."

He looked down, waiting for her response before proceeding. Kit shivered and almost came on the spot.

"Hurry," she moaned, and he happily complied.

Over the next few days, Kit became obsessed with checking her phone and email for responses to the positions she had applied for. Mick had insisted on not letting her help with any bills until she had a job. While she knew it wasn't a financial hardship for him, it still grated on her. She had been on her own for so many years, it was difficult not to be able to at least contribute.

Plus, she was bored. She missed working. Getting satisfaction from a job well done, making a difference. At least Mick understood her frustration and was supportive. He, too, was preoccupied. There was something big happening at DAG, but of course, he could not share much with Kit. She knew it involved an old case and that everyone was on high alert.

"I know it will be inconvenient," Mick told her over dinner, "but just stay inside the flat the next two days."

Kit made a face. "Two days? Is it that serious?"

"I am just being cautious. Humor me Angel. Do this for me and we can go back to that cabin we rented last month at the lake."

Kit agreed, but grumbled over it. Luckily, she had just visited the bookstore for new reading material. She could always spend a couple of hours searching for positions on her laptop.

The weather was nice so she was able to sit on the terrace and read. And she found two new online career sites. While running on the treadmill was not her favorite, at least it helped to pass the time until Mick came home. Halloween was just weeks away, which meant that Mick's birthday was approaching. Kit had been wracking her brain for gift ideas, but kept coming up empty. She hoped to put in some browsing time at a cluster of quaint shops on the other side of town soon. The gift had to be unique.

THE SECOND DAY was a mirror of the first until her

phone rang. Kit answered and the female caller identified herself as the director of a veterans' charity. Kit's heart seized in anticipation.

"I saw your resume, and while we will not be inter-viewing for this position for another week, I had hoped you could help with some freelance work," the woman explained.

They needed a grant proposal written immediately. The staffer who had been working on it was down with food poisoning. The director named a fair wage considering it was a rush job. Kit could hardly contain her excitement.

When she agreed, the caller added, "I am thrilled! If you can pop by before noon, I will have everything ready."

Kit's heart sank. She tried to find a way out of having to go to their offices, but the director was adamant. She needed someone who could pull the needed files off the staffer's computer. Kit needed to speak to Mick first so she offered to call back in a few minutes.

The problem was that Mick didn't answer her call or text. She didn't want to bother Malachai. Surely, it would be safe. The charity office wasn't too far away. She could even take a cab instead of the Metro. Mick himself had admitted he was being overly cautious.

She waited another few minutes and when there was no reply from Mick, she called the charity back to say she was on her way. Instead of calling a cab to the flat, she snuck out and called from the coffee house down the street. Kit thought even Mick might approve of her stealth. Living with a super spy was rubbing off on her.

She smiled as she sipped her latte. This covert stuff was actually fun. She could not wait to tell Mick about her day and her upcoming paycheck. Surely, if she aced this project, she would be first in line for the upcoming open position. Seeing the cab approaching, she moved toward the street, trying to avoid the crowd walking by. The last thing she wanted was coffee spilled all over her outfit.

That was her final thought before someone pinched her arm and everything went blurry then black.

MICK WATCHED IN awe as Malachai worked his magic on his glitchy cell phone. The damn device had been giving him fits all morning – cutting off by itself and displaying odd error messages. DAG used state-of-the-art equipment that was unfortunately fragile when manhandled. Personal phone usage had changed drastically while Mick was incarcerated, and he often forgot to treat his device with care.

The offending item dinged, and Malachai handed it back with a mock frown.

"Press the buttons gently instead of stabbing."

"Of course," Mick agreed and started to exit the workroom.

The phone buzzed, and he glanced down to see he had several missed messages. Blasted machine! He thought longingly of his time in the forest with Kit. No internet, no phones, just them. He was looking forward to their lake trip. When he saw the messages were from Kit, his heart beat faster. Damn, she always brightened his day.

Kit: *Can you call? Job opportunity wants me to come by today.*

The text was dated an hour ago. There was no follow up. Not wanting to panic, he dialed into voicemail. As he listened, his heart began to pound for a different reason. He heard her lay out her plan and end the call by promising to text him when she arrived. He tried calling her number and waited in horror as it rang and eventually flowed into voicemail. *Oh no.*

"Shit!" Mick raced out of the repair room and down the hall to Peter's office.

On the way, he fumbled with his cell, calling up the website to the charity. He heard Malachai following, calling his name, but he didn't pause.

Daniel looked up in shock as Mick burst through the door without bothering to knock. Peter was in Brazil, nailing down an important contract. Daniel was in charge during his absence. Since he disliked being tied down to an office, he took over Peter's or Malachai's when he was in town.

"Kit." Mick tried to pull air into his lungs enough to speak. "She went out. She won't answer."

He held up his cell with a shaky hand. Malachai came in behind him and shut the door. Daniel jumped out of his seat and pushed Mick into it.

"Give us the details. I'm sure it's nothing."

As Mick relayed the basics, Malachai jumped on Peter's computer and soon had a call into the charity. The look on his face as he talked to the director stabbed Mick like a knife. She had not made it to the interview.

"Where is she?" His voice was full of anguish, but he

didn't care.

Where was she? The phone dropped from his hands, and he scrubbed his fingers along his face. Panicking would not help Kit – he knew this. He closed his eyes, taking deep breaths. He heard Malachai call someone to gather data from CCTV cameras near the coffee house. He opened his eyes to see Daniel holding out a glass of water.

"We will find her," his mentor promised. "This guy, this Marius Weber, is a businessman. Not a terrorist. We will find her."

Surely it was a mistake. Perhaps her own phone was buggy. But Mick knew, he just knew something bad had befallen her. His leg muscles tightened, ready to run save her.

After the first few days of torture in the prison, he had stopped believing in any sort of benevolent deity until landing in that meadow. Such a perfect meeting must not be random, he mused. Willing to do anything he could, he silently prayed for Kit to be safe. Unharmed. If he were just granted this one thing, he would never ask for more.

It was all his fault. He had brought her into his life despite his job. Not wanting to frighten her, he had made light of Peter's warnings about Mr. Weber. Whatever happened, it was on his head.

ROUGH HANDS SHOOK Kit, and an accented voice demanded, "Get up!"

Something wasn't right. Was she drunk? Had she been ill? Kit struggled through the fog in her brain.

When she opened her eyes, the interior of a van swam into her vision. That explained the rocking movement that made her want to heave. The van was driving on a smooth but winding road. The carpeting in front of her face was ragged, and a half-empty soda bottle rolled back and forth along the dented wall. Why was she lying down? She raised her hand to push back a hank of hair and found that her hands were bound together with nylon rope.

"Get up! Now!" the man beside her shouted.

Swallowing back the acidic taste of bile that rose in her throat, she slowly managed to scoot until she was sitting up along the metal wall. Kit blinked her eyes and counted to ten, praying that she would not puke.

The man stooping in front of her nodded in approval. Checking to make sure her hands and feet were still bound, he retreated to the passenger seat.

It was obviously a work van, Kit noted. There were no back seats, just an open area with smelly brown carpeting. There was nothing else in the back but her and the soda bottle. No tools, no weapons, not even a window.

The fog in her brain was slower to clear than the last time. After she had been abducted outside the coffee shop, she had come to rather lucid. There must have been something different in last night's syringe. Fear had her gritting her teeth, frantically trying to think straight. Her vision undulated, and she forced back a whimper. *Shit*, her head hurt.

She couldn't see anything other than daylight out the front window from where she was sitting. The driver had dark hair and the passenger was one of the men from before. Was that just last night? Or days ago? How long had she been unconscious? What had they done to her after they knocked her out? But deep inside she knew. *Don't go there yet,* she told herself. Concentrate on getting out of this mess. Then you can revisit that nightmare.

While she wasn't drunk, the nauseous feeling was similar. Although this was much, much worse. Parts of her body throbbed and stung with pain. Kit tenderly touched her face and found the left side swollen and crusty with what she assumed was dried blood. The image of the man who had punched her came to mind, and she firmly pushed it away. *Not now.*

She should have listened to Mick. She had been snatched in broad daylight on a busy street. She knew he would be angry, but he would also feel guilty. But this was all her fault. And now she had to find a way out of this fucking mess. This time, Mick was not here to save her. She needed to be strong. Steely calculation overtook her earlier fear. She refused to let them break her. She had fought back last night and would continue to do so.

The van stopped and the men got out. She heard other doors opening and closing outside. The echo was odd. She realized why when the back doors opened to reveal that they were inside some sort of large brick building.

"Get up!" the blond man again demanded, yanking on her arm and cutting the rope on her ankles.

When Kit didn't move as fast as he wanted, he grabbed her arm again and pulled her out onto the concrete floor. Unsteady, she almost fell, but his hold kept her upright.

She swayed on her feet at first, then gritted her teeth and locked her knees. She knew better than to appear weak. Pushing a clump of matted curls out of her face, she looked around for a way to escape.

The building seemed to be an old warehouse. *How cliché*, Kit thought, and had an insane urge to laugh. It was so old that parts of the walls had fallen, letting in daylight and a strong fishy odor. While there was all sorts of debris in the corners, the cracked cement floor was clear where she was standing.

That was lucky since she noted that her shoes were missing. She was still wearing the black pants and nice burgundy blouse that she had chosen for the charity interview. At least she wasn't naked. A damp breeze blew past, making her shiver. Since yesterday had been sunny, she had not needed a jacket. Fall weather along the Atlantic coast was fickle, however, and it was just her luck that today was chilly.

Glancing to her left and right, she saw that the blond man and a bearded man, who must have been the driver, had flanked her. There were also two other men in the line, one tall and one husky. Kit quickly averted her eyes and tried not to gag. They had been with the blonde man last night...in the dining room from hell. The older tall man had been in charge. He had watched, expressionless. Revulsion bubbled again in Kit's stomach, and she prayed for it to go down. *Not now*, she reminded herself. *Focus*.

She wanted to ask what was happening, even though

she knew it would probably earn her another punch. Before she could open her mouth, however, another van entered and parked alongside the first one. Two men emerged from the front seat, and Kit wasn't surprised when they pulled another hostage out of the back.

Kit thought it was a young man. The figure stayed balled up even as one of the men pulled on his arm and then kicked him in disgust.

Punches be damned. Kit moved to go help the boy but the door on the far side of the building opened and in strode Del and Mick.

Mick's face was set in stone, but she saw his eyes widen when he looked at her. Her face must be pretty horrific. Hating the tears that sprang to her eyes, she tried to convey what she felt through her expression. This was all her fault. If only she had listened to him.

She kept mouthing, "I'm sorry" until she saw his chin dip in acknowledgement. Then his focus switched to the men around her and she let his attention go.

The tense silence was broken by an anguished cry from the other hostage.

"Li-yah!"

The boy was kneeling now, trying to crawl over to where Mick and Del stood. He flipped his head so that his shaggy blond hair fell back from his face and Kit gasped in horror. These monsters had kidnapped someone with Down's syndrome! How horrified he must be! She had to help him.

A massive hand on her arm held her back as two men corralled the slight man back by the van. He was sobbing now, and the sound broke her heart.

"It's okay, John." Del's voice shook. "We'll get you out of here soon."

Though they looked nothing alike, the boy was obviously someone special to Del. She was struggling to get her emotions under control, judging by the deep breaths she was taking.

The tall man with the graying beard stepped forward. "Where is Peter Pierce?"

"Out of the country," Mick answered. "You'll have to deal with us."

Full of arrogance, the bearded man continued, his voice bearing a trace of a German accent. "I want his heart on a plate! He owes me for my brother's life!"

"Your brother was an international arms dealer." Del spoke calmly. "He chose to commit suicide rather than go to prison. That is hardly Peter's fault."

"Peter broadcasted his contacts to intelligence agencies! He looked like a traitor! He owes my family for his death!" He breathed heavily. "Now I believe we can come to terms," he continued and gestured to Kit and the boy, who again curled into a ball on the broken concrete.

"I told you we were just a hook-up!" Kit finally found her voice and protested.

"She's right," Mick played along, his voice as arrogant and unconcerned as the tall man's. "Keep her for all I care."

"Do not insult me!" the man screamed, his face turning red with fury. "She lives with you!" He then took a deep breath and laughed. "I have no need for a chubby *Hure* or a retard. But I do need a test subject for a traceless poison I have developed."

The short man handed over a syringe. Kit swallowed hard. She didn't want to die. The vile man near her waved the syringe at Mick.

"You two can choose." He smiled, and Kit was thankful she could see it only in profile.

It wasn't like cartoons of her youth. A wicked smile, full of teeth and power, exposing a devious mind full of all sorts of evil ideas. No, this smile was full of crazy, capable of turning your spine to liquid terror. He covered his insanity well. The pristine suit and well-groomed façade gave no clue to the slimy contents of his brain. This man was completely batshit and proud of it. Coupled with the way he had simply watched her struggle last night…he was truly a monster.

"No!" Kit gasped. "Don't you dare pick me, Mick!"

Everyone turned to look at Kit, mostly in shock. Mick just looked bleak. Del still looked furious. Perhaps she had a plan? If not, Kit had to act.

"You know I could not bear it if someone died in my place! Don't do it!"

Suddenly, all her aches and pains fell away, and she stood up straighter. It wasn't that she felt brave. In fact, she just wanted to cry. But she had spoken the truth. She could not live with such a burden.

She saw by Mick's expression that he believed her. He looked haunted, the way he did after a nightmare. But there was something else there. The glint gave her hope that there was a rescue plan.

There was a noise from outside and everyone froze. Everyone except the tall man. Barking an order to his men, they began to pile into one van as he grabbed Kit's bound hands. He dragged her backwards toward the waiting vehicle.

Mick and Del had their guns out, but the man was holding Kit as a shield. At the very last second, before he jumped into the van, he plunged the needle into Kit's neck and emptied the contents. The needle pricked as it entered her skin and she realized what had happened. *Oh, fuck no.*

Almost immediately, she started to sag and then the man dropped her as the auto sped off. Her shoulder hit first, but she didn't feel any pain. She heard an anguished roar come from Mick. She faintly heard others yelling for emergency services and backup. Mick's face came into view as tires squealed in the background. She tried to speak, but she couldn't seem to make her mouth move. Was the boy okay? *Dammit!* She just wanted to say goodbye. Mick cried her name, horror all over his face, and then Kit lost consciousness.

Chapter Ten

WHAT ODD DREAMS she was having. Kit felt untethered from her body, as if she was floating from dream to dream. In one, she imagined Mick the way he had been in the woods, with almost a beard from not shaving for three days. Of course, she made the black eye and busted lip disappear so his face was again perfection. In another dream, she was in a white room and Mick was looking out a window, even though there was nothing outside. She tried to get his attention, but he never turned around.

The scenes continued to fade in and out. She visited her childhood school, the camp, and even the bowling alley where she'd had her first date. But she always came back to Mick and the white room. Kit tried to hold on to the latest one. Mick was asleep in an armchair. She wanted to smooth his untidy hair and guide him to bed. Although the image soon faded, the next time she heard his voice breaking through the darkness.

"Time to wake up now, brave girl," his voice was so insistent, she tried to comply. "Come on now, open your eyes."

Her eyelids were heavy weights and it took so much effort to lift them. But she wanted to see Mick. She knew he was there from not just the voice, but also the hand she felt stroking her arm.

The room was dim, but her vision adjusted enough so she recognized a very tired Mick. He had the almost-beard from her dream, and his eyes were red and bleary. The room was shadowed, the only light coming from behind his head. Her hero had a real halo.

"Really?" Kit managed to smile. "This is Heaven and you really are an angel?"

A similar smile coasted across his face. "No love, you're not dead."

He moved closer and Kit saw the lamp behind him. From what she could see, she was in a hospital room. How long had she been here? Her head buzzed and ached. Her throat was so dry she could hardly speak.

Mick kissed her forehead. "I'll let the doctor know you are awake. Perhaps they will let you have some water."

He pressed a button near the bed, and in seconds, a nurse appeared. She raised the bed a bit, took Kit's vitals, and approved a small cup of ice chips until the doctor arrived.

"Shit," Kit cursed hoarsely when she was unable to lift her arm to hold the cup Mick offered.

"Just temporary," he assured her. "You were given painkillers along with poison antidotes. You've been unconscious for four days. Relax. The men who hurt you have been caught."

He spooned up a small bit of ice and filled her in on what had happened. John was safe. He was Peter's son, taken from his care home. There had been a secondary plan, but she was injected before the rescue team could move in. Luckily, there had been a medic standing by and they were able to get her to the main governmental hospital. A hospital stocked with dozens of poison antidotes.

"Thank you for doing what I asked." Kit squeezed his hand. "If things had gone awry, I really meant what I said about not being able to live with the guilt. I know it was hard for you."

Mick's eyes shone with what Kit could not believe were tears. "My brave girl, I don't think I could go through that again."

Kit wanted to protest that it was all her fault. She had been stupid, impulsive, and now she knew better. She had not listened to him. Mick also needed to know what had happened the night before the incident at the factory, but she did not want to confess. Perhaps it was better if he heard that from the doctors. She was suddenly too exhausted to think anymore.

"Sorry," was all she got out before going back to sleep.

IT WAS MORNING when Kit next awoke. While her body felt like it was made of lead, her mind was clearer. In the daylight, Mick looked both gorgeous and awful. He obviously had not slept much, judging by the lines on his face and his bloodshot eyes. While the fact he had stayed at her side made her all mushy inside, he needed to take care of himself now that she was recovering.

"You should go home and rest." Kit spoke after she downed two glasses of water.

"I will," he conceded, leaving a lingering kiss on her brow. "I need to wash, shave and check in with DAG. But first, let's see about some breakfast for you."

Mick arranged for Amy to come sit with her while he was away. Kit protested, feeling guilty about using so many of the agency's resources. But Mick assured her that his colleagues were chomping at the bit to help. And that there would always be a guard at the door no matter who was inside the room with her. Kit rolled her eyes but was secretly glad. Anything to ensure her safety at this point.

MICK KEPT HIS expression placid until the door to Kit's room shut behind him. Then he let the fury he'd kept in check flow freely as he stalked downstairs to where a car was waiting for him. Peter was back and Mick needed answers. As the driver quickly pulled away from the hospital, his head swam from the lack of sleep, too much caffeine, and four days of fear. He had almost lost her. He could have lost her. If the poison had been stronger, if there had not been a crack doctor on standby…IF.

He was so grateful that she was alive, but she wasn't unscathed. Someone had taken their anger out on her face. The bruising looked worse today. It had progressed to purple, the color highlighting the bandages and small stitches. When he had first seen her in the warehouse, he'd almost fallen to his knees. He had lied to Kit. A few of the men did escape. He would find them.

Once in the building, Mick stormed into the conference room, ready to tear flesh. The fact that the weighted door refused to slam behind him only aggravated his fury.

He faced the three seated men, his fists clenching and loosening as he tried to form words. He wanted to growl, to howl, to snarl like a wild beast. He should calm down. These were his superiors, after all. Instead, he took a deep breath and roared, "What the bloody hell happened?"

His deep voice thundered through the room. Peter's face was pained as he rose from his chair. He made a move toward Mick, but Mick waved him off.

"You said nothing of a potential kidnapping! Or any physical harm!" His voice became choked. "Kit could have died! He pumped her full of poison! They beat her!" His voice cracked and his shoulders slumped.

Daniel moved back in and held Mick by the shoulders. Any other time, this man's gesture would have been calming. But not now.

Mick broke away and moved to the other side of the table. Not wanting to sit, he leaned against the wall, willing his legs to hold him up. *Christ,* he was exhausted. He was ready to keep blasting out his frustration, but Malachai's voice stopped him.

"It was our fault," he admitted, his face lined with pain and guilt. "We had no idea what Marius had planned. There is no record of kidnapping…"

He sighed and turned his attention back to the laptop on the table before him. Within seconds, he was frantically typing, searching for the hole.

Mick looked from him to Daniel to Malachai.

Christ, did he look that bad? All their clothing was sweat-stained and wrinkled. Red eyes looked out from lined faces. Daniel's gray hair was standing on end, thanks to him pulling on it. Normally immaculate Malachai had coffee stains on the front of his light blue shirt.

"We should have been more vigil," Peter admitted. "As soon as we found out our data had been compromised, we should have moved our families to safe houses."

Mick wanted to feel sympathy for Peter. His son had also been taken. But John Pierce had made it through the ordeal without a scratch, while Kit was bruised, bloodied, and poisoned. Unable to remain still, he pushed off of the wall and began to pace. He rubbed his jaw and felt the beginnings of a beard under his hands. He had remained by Kit's bedside for the last four days, waiting and praying for her to wake up. Memorizing every contusion on her lovely face, committing his sins to memory.

He should have been a better protector. He could rail at the DAG founders all day, but in the end, he had to face his own guilt. He had failed her.

Instead of trying to downplay the danger, to not frighten her, he should have been firm and ordered her to stay put. Made her too afraid to leave the flat.

His head dropped as the weariness returned with a vengeance. He felt Daniel's hand on his shoulder again, this time pressing him down into a chair. It was spot-on timing, because Mick's legs gave out halfway down and the chair squeaked as it took on the sudden weight.

Daniel pulled over another chair, sat down, and looked Mick in the eyes.

"There's more."

Mick shook his head, unable to comprehend what Daniel meant. Kit was fine. He had been assured by the doctors that she would fully recover. What else could there be?

"The CIA let Russia take custody of Marius." Peter spoke from the other side of the table. "He escaped."

"What?"

Mick wanted to jump out of the chair, but his body would just not cooperate. What the fuck? When had this tits-up event happened?

Daniel put a steadying hand on his arm. "You know the exchange of gunfire at the site killed his son."

Mick nodded. "Yes. Get on with it!"

"He blames Kit and has offered a multi-million dollar bounty on her."

I must look ridiculous, Mick thought. *Sitting here with my mouth open.* However, nothing Daniel had said made sense. His sleep-deprived brain wrestled with the words and came up empty. Marius was crazy, obviously. But he was also very, very wealthy. Now Kit had a target on her chest.

"I have to get back to her!"

This time, Mick's legs did assist him long enough to stand. Daniel blocked his way. The man was shorter than he was, but stockier. Mick respected him too much to push him away.

"She's fine. There are guards all over the building and Amy is inside her room."

Mick grabbed Daniel by the arms, digging in his fingers to make his point. "We have to protect her! She asked for none of this!"

Peter gently pulled Mick back, steadying him when he wanted to collapse. He tried to wrestle out of his grip, but he was just too tired. All he could focus on was that this was his fault and Kit might once again be hurt.

"You know people," he challenged Peter. "Get her somewhere safe, under a new name. Make him think she died."

"We will explore all avenues after you are rested," Peter promised. "Whittaker is waiting to drive you home."

"Go home. Get some rest. Real rest," Peter urged. "Del is available if Amy needs a break."

Mick knew that was the prudent choice. He needed to be sharp in order to wrap his head around this new development. What was he thinking? How could he send her away? But what if she stayed and was found?

"We have everyone on this," Peter added.

"I *will* find out how they got in, how they found the addresses," Malachai snarled, still typing away.

Mick looked at him in shock. What on earth was he talking about? His systems were impenetrable. The other founders looked at Malachai in sympathy. Daniel sighed and explained, "It could have been a hack. Or there is a small chance it was an inside job."

Mick managed a weak laugh in disbelief. Not his team. Someone in another division, perhaps. But no one in the field team would do this. There was too much respect. Why risk harm to your co-workers' loved ones?

"Whoever it is, wherever they came from, their heads are mine," Mick vowed, his voice pitched low.

Daniel sighed as Peter frowned. "I understand you want blood right now. Rest and we'll talk."

"Go home." Peter's voice was stern. "I'll be stopping by to apologize and thank Miss Foster soon."

Mick paused on his way out of the room and addressed Peter. "Have a plan for her. Keep her safe. You owe her that much. She was ready to sacrifice herself for your son."

KIT EXPECTED TO be awkward around Amy since they had met only once before. But it turned out that Amy was just as chatty as she was. After the first hour, Kit was feeling much more like herself and was thrilled to be distracted.

The day became even better when the nurses unhooked all her tubes and wires and approved a short shower as long as she used a chair. As much as she desperately wanted to get clean, Kit dreaded seeing her reflection in the mirror. Her face felt stiff and puffy, so it must look awful.

While she allowed Amy to help her to the small bathroom, she wanted to be alone when she assessed the damage done from the last few days. She hesitated, her bare feet glued to the chilly tile floor. Taking a deep gulp of antiseptic-tinged air, she toddled to the mirror above the sink and grimaced at what she saw.

"Ugh! You look like shit," she told the girl in the mirror.

Her matted and greasy curls actually looked better

175

than her face. The bruises left by the blond man's punches had turned a dark purple. At least he had missed her eye. The florescent colors ran from her temple across her cheek to her chin. Butterfly bandages covered the places where he had broken the skin. Her bottom lip was inflated, and she could feel the cuts on the inside of her mouth.

"Least you didn't need stitches." She tried to be up-beat, but tears clogged her throat.

Taking a deep breath for strength, she untied the hospital gown and let it fall. She looked down and must have made an audible sound of distress because Amy suddenly opened the door, her gun in hand.

All Kit could do was stand there and cry. Amy wrapped a towel around her before leading her to the toilet for a seat.

"You survived." Amy squatted on the floor and held Kit's hands. "It will be okay. I learned the hard way that it's better to break down and work through it than to try to pretend it never happened."

Kit choked out a laugh through her sobs. Exactly what she had told Mick. Keeping their hands clasped, Amy shifted to sit cross-legged on the floor.

"Get it all out," she encouraged. "You've had a hella-cious bitch of a week."

Kit did not want to keep it inside anymore. The story of the last few days came pouring out of her, the words rushing out between whimpers. By the time her tale was finished, she was exhausted and out of tears. Or so she thought until it was Amy's turn to speak.

"I understand," Amy said quietly and proceeded to

tell her own story of being taken that contained all the same horror, powerlessness and fury that Kit's had.

"I used to be a cop. Narcotics." Her voice was soft and void of emotion. "I worked with a couple of informants. One became so in debt to his supplier that he sold me out. The problem was that when they picked me up, they also took my sister."

Amy sighed. "We had met for lunch. We were taken to an empty house and raped before my squad found us."

Amy started to tear up, and Kit squeezed her hands. "My sister never recovered. Even with therapy and support…she committed suicide a year later."

"Oh no!" Kit whispered, and then remembered something from their first meeting. "You do some sort of penance every year?"

Amy nodded. "She left behind a husband and a daughter. After…he banned me from their lives. But once a year, I check in on them."

A wet laugh escaped. "I spy on them, let's be truthful. Just to make sure they are okay. And to see Claire. She looks so much like her mother."

"I am so sorry, Amy." Kit's heart was full of knots. So much pain, horror, and powerlessness in both of their lives.

By the time they finished talking, crying, and hugging, it was lunchtime. Kit had a quick shower and pulled on a modest nightgown that Amy had graciously brought for her. Thanks to the shower and the cry, she was cleaner inside and out and felt less like a helpless invalid. She was back in bed, waiting for her tray to be picked up, when Amy's cell buzzed.

Amy's brows rose in surprise as she read the text. "Del says Peter is coming to see you."

"Why?"

Amy snickered and put the phone down. "Maybe to thank you for saving his son's life? The rest of us had no idea he existed. I thought Vivienne was his only child."

He knew Del, Kit wanted to point out, but held her tongue. It wasn't her place to share what might be a secret.

Kit watched in envy as Amy pulled her long blond hair back into a ponytail. Her hair would end up as one giant tangle if she tried to grow it that long. At least she was able to shampoo it during the brief shower. She now looked somewhat presentable. She couldn't wait for Mick to return. Besides how much she missed him, they needed to talk about what happened.

"What's Peter like?"

Amy laughed. "The best explanation is something Whittaker thought up. If DAG is a family, Daniel is the Dad who left to go find adventure. Malachai is the worried Mom, and Peter is the strict new Stepdad."

"Adventure is getting thrown into different prisons?" Kit asked with a shudder. "Not in my book."

"You'll like Daniel." Amy's eyes twinkled. "Mick is his second favorite, after Archie."

"Really? Why? Does that make his coworkers jealous?"

Amy rolled her eyes. "Only Whittaker is jealous. That is because, unlike the rest of us, he wasn't voted in."

"Anyone new to DAG gets put to a vote by the other agents," she explained at Kit's confused look. "It helps us work better as a team. Whittaker is the son of Peter's first partner. Sort of a 'legacy' hire."

That explained his behavior at their first meeting, Kit realized. But enough about that jerk. Kit wanted to hear more stories about Mick.

"How did Mick get to be the teacher's pet?"

"Daniel infiltrated that work prison due to intel that several CIA agents were held there." Amy shifted to get more comfortable in her chair. "The only former intelligence agent he found there was Mick. They were assigned to the machinery room. Daniel was impressed by the stamina and strength it took for Mick to survive his torture and three years in that hellhole. So when Archie came to break him out, he brought Mick along."

"Oh." Kit blinked back tears. Now she could not wait to meet Daniel and thank him like she had Archie.

"Does Peter think highly of Mick? I don't want my stupidity to be a black mark on his record."

"Don't worry." Amy patted Kit's arm. "Peter is a good man. He blames himself for this episode, not you or Mick. Relax. He just comes across as stiff and professional."

After the past few months, Kit wasn't worried about handling Peter. She was pretty sure she could handle anything now. Her family's disgrace seemed so minor and so far away. She simply did not want to make a bad impression on Mick's boss. There was no way she could take back her stupid decision to go to the job interview, but she could at least mitigate it by not looking so foolish today.

PETER PIERCE ENTERED her hospital room a few minutes later. Kit had expected him to be similar to Malachai. Peter was older, taller, and gave off a dangerous air, totally opposite of Malachai the teddy bear. His face was thin, but not gaunt. A faint hairline scar bisected his left eyebrow. The bald man was dressed in a suit so tailored that Kit had no idea there was a gun strapped under his arm until he removed the jacket.

"Miss Foster," he began, "there is no way I can thank you enough. I know you volunteered yourself in place of my son. I...I have no words. I hope you will accept my regrets about what happened. I am sorry that you were involved in such a way."

"It was my fault," Kit repeated. "I should have listened to Mick. Is John okay?"

"Traumatized, but thankfully he remembers very little of it. He was only in their clutches for an hour."

"May we have a moment, Amy?" He asked the agent, and she left the room after shooting a curious look at Kit.

Peter approached the bed to look at Kit face to face. "The man behind your kidnapping has held a grudge against DAG for years. He was also wanted by the Russian government in connection with a bank fraud case last year. In order to balance out a debt, our government let them take custody of him. I regret to inform you that Marius is no longer under their watch."

Dread formed a giant knot in Kit's stomach. "You mean he's loose? He escaped?"

"I'm afraid so," Peter replied, and he did look uncomfortable. "I am here to offer you protection."

"What? Why?"

Peter sighed. "When we moved in to capture them before they could leave the factory, his son was fatally wounded. For some reason, Marius has placed all the blame upon you. We just learned there is a ten million dollar bounty on your head."

Kit had the urge to heave, but there was nothing left in her stomach. Ten million dollars? It was mind-boggling that someone could hate her that much. She looked at Peter for confirmation and saw his hazel eyes softened. He was telling the truth.

"What can I do?" She asked weakly, envisioning some sort of underground safe house that she would hate.

"Witness Protection. The FBI owes me quite a few favors. They can give you a new name, papers, and set you up with a home and job somewhere far from here," Peter clarified.

"I can't do that!"

It was preposterous. What about her friends, her family? Her life here with Mick?

"Isn't Witness Protection where everyone thinks you are dead? I cannot do that to my friends!" Kit's voice rose in panic.

Peter nodded in understanding. "I believe we could contrive a story where you fall off the grid instead of die. It would also serve to send Marius on a wild goose chase."

There had to be an alternative. But from Peter's point of view, there was nothing else. The choice was bogus either way, she thought. Mick had a career. He could not be her constant bodyguard. Surely, he could help her think of an alternate plan. One that would keep them together.

Kit's head pounded from the lingering headache and all this new information. *Don't panic*, she scolded. Mick will be here soon, and he will have better ideas.

"I am truly sorry, Miss Foster," Peter added before leaving. "I will do everything in my power to fix this. We take safety very seriously. We have no idea how Marius found Mick's apartment and John's location. Would you like me to send Amy back in?"

"No." Kit's voice was faint. "I'm very tired. I would like to rest."

There were no tears left in her body to weep, but Kit was swamped with hopelessness as Peter shut the door behind him. Mick would have another strategy, she just knew it. He would be back soon; she just had to hold on until then. Together they could find a way out of this new nightmare. She just had to remain calm and rest.

SOMETHING WAS OFF with Mick, Kit noticed when he arrived back at the hospital that afternoon. It was hard to discern exactly what because her pain was disorientating. They had scaled back her meds, and she was in a good deal of discomfort. But she wanted to be discharged so she had to show the doctors that she didn't need to be doped up.

"Guess what went on sale today?" Mick asked and pulled a thick book from behind his back.

"You remembered!" Kit smiled and eagerly accepted the newest hardback by one of her favorite authors.

Her earlier feeling of worry was obviously just a by-product of the drugs or leftover unease from Peter's visit. She and Mick could come up with a proposal to keep her safe. The issue of catching Marius could be left to the government. Surely, it would be over in no time, and they could go back to the way things were before.

Mick stood near the edge of the bed, facing her, but made no move to touch her. The bedside lamp glinted off the face of his watch as he folded his arms across his chest. The first icy brush of unease whispered along her spine.

"I know about Peter's offer. Are you going to take it?" He asked, his eyes scanning everywhere but her face.

"No," Kit answered, confused. "Why would I do that?"

"Marius knows who you are!" Now his eyes bored into hers. "Do you have any idea of his resources?"

Kit drew back at his vehemence. "I'm not that important. He'll move on to some other bad guy scheme and forget about me."

"You lived. He blames you for his son's death." He shook his head. "To him, it's a matter of vengeance now, not reason or business."

Kit shifted on the bed, causing a streak of agony along her lower abdomen. She must still be under the influence of some of the pain meds because Mick was not making sense. She touched her necklace with fidgety fingers. He was acting as if he wanted her to leave. That was ridiculous, right?

What if he thinks you're tainted? She dismissed the vile thought. Surely not…But more frost moved through her veins.

"Mick, I lost so much this past year. Now you expect me to just toss everything and start all over a second time?" Kit hated the pleading note in her voice.

What she was too afraid to ask concerned them as a couple. Surely, he did not want her to take the offer. His guilt must be blinding him to the reality that they would be apart...forever.

Mick crammed his fists into the front pockets of his jeans. His demeanor was calm and his voice was even. But his stunning blue eyes were distant as he finally met her gaze.

"Take the offer, Kit."

She gaped at him. What? Was she still unconscious and caught in a nightmare? No. She could feel the slick paper of the jacket on the book that she had clutched in her hands and hear the muted hospital sounds from outside the closed door.

No, he couldn't mean this. Not after all they had gone through together. She needed him now, more than ever. No, he couldn't be urging her to go away, never to see him again. The doubts kept circling in her head until she was dizzy. It *had* to be a misunderstanding. It just had to be. ....

"But." Her voice went soft with fear. "But...you love me."

Instead of softening, Mick's expression remained impassive. Not one flicker of warmth touched his eyes. He shifted his weight and folded his arms again before speaking. His head canted to the side, making his next statement even more condescending.

"I never said that."

The declaration came out flat but adamant. *I must look ridiculous*, Kit thought absently. She could feel her eyes bug out and her jaw drop open. Mick looked like he had just delivered her tax bill, not ripped her heart out. It wasn't a joke, a hallucination? All he had to do was reach out, touch her with one of his magical hands, and break the spell. Moments passed and he didn't.

Weeks later, when she was able to look back on the incident, Kit would realize that all her romantic ideas about a broken heart had been wrong. In that moment, her heart had not cracked or shattered.

It brought to mind a cheesy sci-fi movie she'd once seen. One moment, a planet had been there, whole and thriving. The next moment, it was gone. It had imploded into nothing. It had ceased to exist, sucked into a void. No explosion. No fanfare. It and all its parts simply no longer survived. That was what it felt like.

"Get out," she demanded hoarsely, not bothering to hold back the first few tears.

When Mick didn't move, she began to repeat the two words as loud as she could. Perhaps if he left, the room would stop spinning and the world would right itself. All she knew was that she could no longer bear to look at him. *Righteous bastard.*

The weight of the book in her hands registered and before she could think, she hurled it at his head. The anger felt good, just as cleansing as her previous cry had been. It burned away the fog in her brain.

The book struck his mouth, busting his upper lip. He stared at her in shock, trying to stem the blood with one hand.

"Get out!" she screamed, the anger helping center her.

Mick didn't move until she began to repeat the words, her voice rising with each sentence. As he pulled open the door, Amy rushed in, her gun out and ready. Glancing from him to an obviously distressed Kit, Amy approached the hospital bed in confusion. Kit watched Mick disappear through the opening.

It seemed the loss of her heart had affected Kit's lungs, for she found it hard to breathe. Gasping for air, she grabbed Amy's arm in panic.

"Can't..." Kit got only one word out before black spots began to swim in front of her eyes. She struggled to inhale, but her body would not cooperate. Once again, the darkness swallowed her. This time, however, she welcomed it.

Chapter Eleven

W HEN KIT CAME to, the room was quiet and dim. She turned her head to see Amy sitting by the bed reading a magazine. She tried to speak, but only a cough came out. Her throat was on fire and her eyes felt gritty.

"You're awake!" Amy exclaimed, and handed her a glass of water from the bed side table.

Kit drained the glass and was able to ask, "What happened?"

Amy's expression was concerned. "You had a panic attack and passed out. Before that… I'm not sure."

The memories filled Kit's brain like a tidal wave. Mick didn't love her. She could either disappear or be killed. Mick wanted her gone. Once more, things she valued had been ripped away from her. Only this time, she truly would be left with nothing. How could she have been so wrong?

While she had come to terms with not visiting her father, the thought of never being able to see him again was horrific. What if she eventually found a way to forgive her mother and cousin? They would never know.

What an awful mistake she had made by remaining in DC.

"Mick wants me to take Peter's offer. To disappear," Kit explained, her voice raspy and discouraged.

Amy looked at her in shock. "I thought…"

"Yeah, me too," Kit agreed, and swallowed back stray tears.

She was through crying for today. She needed to be angry. That would get her through the next bit. How dare he decide her future for her! There had been no discussion, no compromise. Well, he would get what he wanted. Even though part of her wanted to, she would not beg. She would do this and he would be sorry.

"Tell Peter I'll take the deal under three conditions," she announced. "I want to get some of my things from the apartment without Mick being there. I want it to happen as soon as possible. I refuse to pretend to be dead. He said he could come up with an alternative."

Amy nodded. "I am so, so sorry. I thought things would turn out differently. I'll call Peter right away."

It turned out there was no need to worry about Mick showing up. According to Malachai – who Amy spoke to when she called the office – Mick was out on assignment and not expected back for weeks. Of course. Kit wanted to laugh. How convenient. For someone she had been sure was a strong, brave man, this was a cowardly finish.

THE NEXT DAY, Malachai came by before she was discharged. After engulfing her in a big hug, he set his laptop up on her bed tray. He was the one who had devised a brilliant explanation for her soon-to-be disappearance. Kit wanted to cry again because it showed that he understood her. And now she had to give up that friendship.

He turned the computer toward her. "In your own words, tell your friends about the opportunity. Then write the updates. I'll make sure they are sent out every few months. Then write the final one where you decide to stay."

"Don't forget to send it to my mother's lawyer, too," she reminded him.

"I have all the emails." His smile was crooked. "I also set up the fake charity so your financial manager could transfer your trust fund. In a few months, I'll move the money over to you."

He then left her alone to compose the emails. The first one was the roughest. Kit sobbed as she typed.

"Hey guys. Remember that saying, 'when one door closes, another opens?' My big romance fell apart. But I was just offered a job I cannot pass up!!! A charity is rebuilding a school in a part of Africa recovering after a civil war. I will be working with traumatized kids again!!! I hope you understand why I need to go so far away. I need to get my life and my heart back in order. There is no cell or internet where I will be. I promise to check in periodically. I understand I will be able to when we do supply runs to a nearby city. I will miss you all terribly!"

She finished the other emails and called for Malachai. When he opened the door, she saw that Amy was with him. It was really happening. While it felt like a boulder had lodged in her chest, part of Kit was relieved to be actively participating in life again. She never wanted to see the inside of another hospital room again. And she wanted to be as far away from Mick Harris as she could.

Amy and some other agents had a decoy scheme set up to get her from the hospital to the apartment and then off to her new life. Peter had accomplished all she had asked for. Her new identity was in a folder in a plain cloth grocery bag on the bed. It was all set up.

"You will always be my friend, Kit." Malachai hugged her and handed her a small envelope. "It contains instructions on how to hack into the security cameras at your father's rest home."

Kit was speechless with gratitude. She grabbed the man with all her might and held on for a long moment. She rubbed the undamaged side of her face against his tweed jacket, trying to commit him to memory. *Fuck*, she would miss her new friends. It just wasn't fair.

Malachai, looking a little misty-eyed, kissed her on the cheek and quickly left. Kit cleared her throat and nodded to Amy. She was ready.

The agent who was driving got them to the apartment in no time. As they stepped out of the car, other agents pulled up, and all four of them went inside. Kit carried the cloth bag, and Amy slung a large black messenger bag over her shoulder.

Don't stop to look, Kit cautioned herself. She had only a few minutes to get the items she wanted. The waterproof jacket that she took on every camping trip. The colorful quilt lying on the couch that she had picked up while shopping with Mick. The photos of her family and of camp she kept in a shoebox along with small souvenir items she had accumulated while in DC.

She ignored the closet. She could buy a new wardrobe. Averting her gaze from the bed, she moved to the bathroom. Grabbing her bottle of insanely expensive hair product, her eyes fell on one of Mick's tanks lying beside the hamper. Before she could stop herself, she added it to the box.

Catching her reflection in the mirror, she paused. The woman looking back at her was older, more somber than she had ever believed she could be. Christ! Why couldn't she just go back and erase that one stupid decision from her past? From now on, she had to be different. No more rushing into situations, following her instincts. Look where her past behavior had gotten her. It was past time she learned her lesson and changed.

One last thing, she thought, and unhooked the necklace from around her throat. She carefully laid it on the bathroom counter, along with her broken heart, and walked out.

She and Amy exchanged outfits and donned wigs that made them look like the other. Luckily, they were similar heights. While Amy was thinner, they had both picked loose clothing to hide their different shapes.

"One last thing." Amy stopped her after a quick hug.

She pulled off the plain silver band she always wore on her left hand and slid it onto Kit's finger. "Don't ever give up. Know that I am always cheering for you."

Before either could say anything more, the other agents whisked them off in opposite directions. The messenger bag contained all of Kit's belongings, and Amy had the decoy cloth sack with her. The car with Amy headed to the train station while the car with Kit drove off to a distant airport and her future.

TWO WEEKS LATER, Mick paused outside of his flat. It was late, and he was exhausted from the six-hour commercial flight. He needed to sleep. However, he could not seem to put his key into the lock. A faint light shone through the front window, but it was only the lamp that was set to a timer whenever he was away. Despite the glow, the flat gave off a black gloom. He knew it was just his mind expanding on the truth that Kit was no longer there and never would be again. The center of his chest burned, and he reached for the almost empty tin of antacids.

As much as he ached for rest, he could not open the door. There was a bar down the street. A couple of shots might put him past the point of caring. Then he would be sure to sleep. He put the keys back into his pocket and turned on his heel.

His constant companion for the last two weeks had been the replay of the scene in Kit's hospital room. He could not banish it. It looped, repeatedly.

The lie he had practiced stuck in his throat. Normally, lying came easy to him. For a spy, it was as natural as breathing. But the agony in Kit's eyes had almost brought him to his knees.

His expression must have remained frozen, for tears had welled in her brown eyes. Still, the lie would not leave his lungs, so he had struggled to find an answer that wasn't a fib but would still push her away. She had to be safe, and for that, he had to be cruel.

"I never said that."

After the attack, he hurried past Amy and the nurse and locked himself in the closest restroom. He grabbed two handfuls of paper towels, one for his busted lip and the other for his eyes. He was careful to make sure his sobs never made it past his gritted teeth.

Dear God. He'd known it was going to hurt, but this was beyond what he had expected. It was difficult enough to send her away, but to also break her heart? He felt gutted.

It's the only way she can stay alive, his conscious chimed in as he managed to stop crying. He obviously was not enough to protect her. Look what had happened. The condemnation had filled his head the last few days. She had been hurt because of him. Had almost died because of him. The first words he had ever said to her had been a promise to protect her. But he had failed.

He knew she would be better off this way. It wouldn't take her long to bounce back. Even if she had thought she loved him, it hadn't been real. Right? She was too bright and he was utter darkness. It was better this way. Ending it before she realized her true feelings.

Yes, after Kit calmed down she would see reason. Perhaps even one day thank him for ending it. And maybe one day she would pull out the necklace and think back fondly on their adventure.

He hoped so. That gift symbolized all the feelings he had but were too afraid to say. That he would never forget her. That she had saved his soul and helped him begin his trek out of a nightmare. That he loved her.

It took more than just a couple of shots to give Mick the courage to re-enter his flat. Somehow, he had managed to stumble home and undo the locks. He lurched to the bedroom and almost retched at the sight of the empty bed. No, he just could not do it. He'd sleep on the couch, no matter if it was too short for his height. The dim hallway whirled around him as if he was inside a kaleidoscope. Moaning, he slid down the wall and decided to lie on the carpeted floor until the spinning receded.

HE ENJOYED THE oblivion until someone's voice intruded and a cool cloth touched his face. He cracked open his eyes to see a frowning Archie bending over him.

"Jesus, Yankee. I'm gone for a few weeks and everything goes to hell."

"G'way," Mick slurred and shut his eyes.

"Sorry, no can do. I'll make some coffee and be back to pull your sorry ass up."

Archie was one of the last people Mick wanted to see. His accent was too much like Kit's. Now that he was mostly sober, Mick knew he would have to force his teammate to leave and he was just not up to it. He rolled onto his stomach and slowly moved to a crouching position.

So far, so good. The hangover was not as bad as he had feared. His head pounded and his gut churned, but he was not in danger of chundering. Using the wall for balance, he made it onto his feet. Instead of heading for the kitchen and the enticing smell of brewing coffee, he headed toward the spare bathroom and a wash.

For once, his mind was too crowded for any flashbacks to happen. Still, he muffled the sound of the hot water flowing into the sink by covering his ears with a towel. Trying to keep his mind blank, he started reciting algebra equations under his breath. Thoughts of prison, Kit, and death wanted to crowd in, but he was determined to resist. He was wiping off soap when he heard tapping at the door.

"Clean clothes just outside," Archie shouted.

As much as he wanted to tell his friend to fuck off, Mick was grateful that he hadn't had to enter the bedroom in search of something to wear. *What a pussy I am,* he thought as he dried off. Archie had left him a pair of sweatpants and a t-shirt. No underwear, but macho male friendship did not extend that far. Mick shuffled toward the smell of coffee, determined to thank Archie, then get rid of him so that he could avoid mourning in private.

The man in question was lounging against the sink, but Mick had eyes for only the large steaming cup on the table. Next to it was a plate of toast dripping with butter and a bottle of painkillers. His memory flashed back to his first meeting with Kit and how stunned he had been at her concern for his head injury. Since then, he had kept the same brand stocked in his cabinet.

Archie raised his eyebrows at Mick's glare, unaware that he was contemplating murder over the reminder. Luckily, Mick was too knackered and ill to do anything other than collapse in the chair and down some coffee. Archie turned his attention to the window as soon as

Mick started in on the toast. He did not speak until Mick had finished eating.

"What the hell happened?"

Archie's voice was soft and confused, not accusatory, as he poured Mick a second cup. While his colleague looked better than he did, his face was pale and there were shadows under his eyes. He was normally upbeat and energetic, but this morning his eyes were shadowed and his skin was pale. The change did go with the job. Whatever assignment he had been on must have been a tough one. Sometimes agents came back looking as if they had seen a ghost.

Usually it meant they'd had to kill someone. The past few weeks, Mick had killed three men, and they made no mark on his soul. They had deserved death and should be grateful he made it quick. *Bastards.*

"I get back and everyone is worried because you haven't checked in. I come to check and find your door unlocked, and I fear the worst."

Mick shrugged.

"We could protect her, Mick. There was no need to send her away."

"You were not there!" Mick snarled. "You did not watch her die. You did not pray over her for days. Her face…they *hurt her*!"

Archie was silent.

"No one can locate Marius," Mick added, rubbing his aching head. "Every bounty hunter on earth is after her. This was the only way."

"I can't see her buying into this idea." Archie's eyes narrowed. "What did you say to get her to agree?"

Mick just shook his head and didn't take his eyes off the mug in his hand. It was none of Archie's business how he had virtually stabbed her in the heart. It had been the only way. As much as he wanted to confess, to hope for some sort of absolution, the words burned in his throat. She deserved life and happiness. That was just not possible with him.

Archie sighed. "I am so, so sorry, Yank. What can I do?"

"Keep an eye on Marius and anyone he hires. Peter will not give me access. Keep her safe. And leave me the hell alone with my hangover."

Archie nodded and stood up. "Of course I'll watch him. Again, I'm sorry. You two seemed so…happy."

Mick watched him leave, contemplating adding some Scotch to his coffee. No. He needed to be sober. He was at fault and deserved every bit of agony the day could deliver. Once he finished the coffee, he would tackle the bedroom. Thinking of how he had hurt Kit made him look forward to the pain. On the off-chance she left anything behind, he should just leave it as a reminder of how at fault he was. He had chosen this career, again and again. He should have never pulled her into it. Thank Christ he had been given the opportunity to rectify his mistake and to keep her from any further harm.

What was she doing right now? He knew they had placed her out west, after he had requested that she be near mountains. Somewhere with forests and new trails to explore. He could just imagine her there, after the hurt and anger wore off. She would explore the area armed with books to identify new trees and unusual birds. In his mind, she was excited by the new challenge. She was alive and getting on with her life. He was nothing special. She would be over him in no time.

Chapter Twelve

Part Two

"HOW LONG ARE you going to stare at that computer screen, Yankee?"

Mick jumped, irritated that he had not sensed Archie's approach. He knew better than to zone out at work. However, it was late and the office was almost deserted. He closed the file he was working on, jabbing the keyboard hard enough to make his annoyance clear.

Archie came into view, smiling. Mick wanted to growl and tell him to fuck off, but Archie was sporting his "I have an outrageous plan" grin. So instead, Mick leaned back in his seat as Archie, followed by their teammate Mateo, pulled over two chairs.

Heaven knew he needed a distraction, and the more dangerous, the better. The times when he could disappear into an op were what had saved his sanity the last few months. Those precious hours when he could forget Kit. In the office, he wasn't so lucky. His mind would wander, and all thoughts eventually led to her. And how he had hurt her.

"How's the arm?" He asked Mateo.

"Still a bitch," the other man joked as he settled the sling against his chest.

Mick frowned. Mateo was still pale from his recent surgery. Since he had joined DAG, he had been undercover in a Hispanic gang that was involved in drug and arm sales. The same gang he had been a member of before joining DAG.

Part of his cover included short-term prison sentences. Mateo would soon instigate a brawl in order to be confined to solitary. At that point, he would rejoin the team, relay all of his information, and get a short break from his undercover life. Only this time, he had picked a fight with the wrong inmate. Recovering from a compound fracture had made the normally quiet man cranky and vocal.

"I have a plan," Archie announced, his blue eyes twinkling.

Mick smiled back, except his expression was feral, full of teeth. "I am all ears, mate."

But his smile vanished when Archie added, "It's about Kit."

"Fuck off." Mick pushed away from his desk and rose to his feet.

Mateo started to rise to play peacemaker, but the movement made him grimace in pain. With his free hand, he flipped his long, straight hair over his shoulder, exposing the gang tattoos that decorated his neck. Archie remained seated and just shook his head.

"Jesus, Mick!" He said without heat. "Sit your ass down and listen to me."

Mick glared at his teammate and started to walk out, until Mateo added, "It's a tight plan. Just hear him out."

"Kit is safe, there does not need to be a plan." He forced the words through gritted teeth.

Archie sighed. "She's temporarily safe. Don't you want to get rid of Marius once and for all?"

Mick froze and gauged the honesty in the other man's face. Of course, he wanted the bastard dead. That would mean Kit was forever free. Not that she would come running back to him, but she could at least rejoin her friends. He had no doubt she had recovered from his deceit and was happy. If Marius were gone, there would be no more hiding. Mick wanted any piece of mind that he could give her. He reluctantly returned to his seat.

Archie leaned back and laced his fingers together over his abdomen. His hair had grown longer and now curled over his ears. He was trying hard not to look smug, but he knew he had Mick's undivided attention.

"Between his distraction and losing his son's financial expertise, Marius is almost broke," he explained, and smiled as the wheels spun in Mick's head.

"Yeah," Mateo chimed in. "There's no way he can hire any more mercenaries or pay that big-assed bounty he promised. Poor guy even lost his bodyguards when their last paychecks bounced. Boards and trustees have seized his companies, and he does not care."

Archie leaned forward to emphasize. "All he wants is Kit's head. The man has gone batshit insane."

"So tell me where he is and I can solve this right away."

Mateo shook his head. "DAG has been looking for

weeks. He's deep underground. He could survive a long time that way."

"Unless we draw him out," Archie finished.

"No!" This time, Mick's roar filled the deserted office space.

"We will *NOT* put her in danger again!"

"Of course we won't." Archie frowned and was silent until Mick calmed down. "We just need him to *think* she's vulnerable."

"Peter will never approve this." Mick sighed, even though the plan was appealing. "This would be an assassination."

"Which is why this will be on our own time," Mateo said.

What he was suggesting could get them all fired. Mick finally nodded for him to continue. He was torn. He wanted her to be totally safe, and in the end, that meant Marius's death. How could they accomplish both tasks?

It could work, if the Intel about Marius's state was true. They could not take on a team of professional assassins, but one man? Fuck yeah. Mick's finger itched to fire the bullet that would take the psycho down. For the first time in months, he felt hopeful. His head spun – he was almost giddy.

"Where do we set this up?" Mick leaned forward, eager to get started.

"At her house."

Mick's hands curled into fists, and he again flew out of his chair. He did not want to assault his friend, but he would if he did not stop speaking nonsense.

He turned when he was almost at the door and growled, "There will be *no* putting Kit in danger. We do not even know where she lives now."

"Malachai does," Mateo offered.

"How? He doesn't even work here anymore!"

Archie held up his hands to stop another tirade. "He somehow monitors her. She doesn't even know it. Just to make sure she is safe. He thinks this plan will work."

Mick sagged against the doorframe, furious and elated. Bless Malachai for making sure.

"We don't believe Marius will go for planted info," Mateo explained. "But if he can see that she has truly been in this location, the temptation will be irresistible."

Dammit to hell, they are right, Mick conceded. Archie sensed his buy-in and disclosed the details.

"She lives within a few hours of the compound Mateo stays at while in solitary. It's a safe house for CIA operatives and black ops mercenaries. In real life, it's an isolated sheep farm run by an old cohort of Daniel's."

"We switch her out with an agent, get Kit to another safe house," Mateo jumped in. "Have my guys waiting in hiding. These mercs are up for anything and would give us a good deal to carry this out. I'd love to be part of it, but with this injury, I'd be in the way."

"I have money. I'll gladly pay. As long as Archie and I are part of this," Mick insisted.

"I'll be lead." Archie nodded. "You'll need to guard Kit."

Mick laughed, and the sound was bitter. "She hates me. There is no way she would ever agree to that."

"Do you really trust anyone else to do it?" Archie

countered.

No, of course he didn't. No one else considered her precious, irreplaceable. No one else felt their heart jump whenever they thought of her. He snorted, realizing it would also give her the opportunity for payback. He hated to think himself a martyr, but he welcomed her fury. He deserved it.

Mick sighed. "Okay. I'll fetch some coffee and we can work out the details."

As soon as Mick was out of earshot, Mateo shook his head. "You know, after this, I'm going to start calling you Cupid."

Archie's smile was almost sad. "It's win-win. Take out the bad guy. Make our friend happy again."

"How are you so sure she won't send him packing?"

"She loves him," Archie said simply. "It may take time. Without Marius, Mick won't have an excuse to walk away."

He punched Mateo in his good arm. "True love may elude us, *cabrón*, but they deserve a happy ever after."

"THE DAY IS finally here, Mal," Kit announced to the big black mutt that lay by the fireplace.

The dog looked up at the mention of his name, but then returned his head to the rug when she didn't follow up with any commands or treats. The big mutt was a mix of many different breeds. When standing, his head reached Kit's hip. His thick black coat was medium length, like a shepherd, but his ears definitely came from husky genes. The local vet swore Mal also had some wolf blood. Not that Kit cared what breeds he had descended from. All that mattered was that he had become the perfect confidant, roommate, and guardian.

The shoebox was heavy in her hands as she sat it on the coffee table where she had previously laid out the bottle of whiskey and the shot glass. She wobbled a bit as she sat down. Excellent. Her journey to get drunk off her ass was going as planned.

"It's been a year. Time to give Katherine Hale Foster a proper wake." She sighed, feeling odd at uttering that name for the first time in six months.

The name should not have felt strange in her mouth since it had been her identity for almost thirty years. But she was such a different person now. A new name was fitting. Everyone now knew her as Edith, and she needed to begin to embrace that name.

And tonight was also about finally letting go of Mick. Or rather, the idea of Mick in her life. The Super Spy Exorcism, if you will.

There had always been a small hope that he would break and seek her out. It was a silly idea, dreaming that he would suddenly realize that he did love her. No, her instincts had been wrong again. Kit knew it was an implausible wish and made herself a promise that she would give it no more than half a year.

But the deadline had come. It wasn't as if she had truly believed he would come for her. She hadn't exactly put her life on hold. The city apartment that the agency had placed her in had been nice, and her job with a food pantry had been rewarding. It had just been too much, too different. Too many people.

Kit's skin had crawled every time another pedestrian

accidentally bumped into her. And why bother making new friends? Nothing lasted. She had superficial relationships at work. It was enough to satisfy her rare talkative moments. Even her therapist had not been able to get her to unburden herself. After four months of her new life, Kit was miserable.

Fate stepped forward in the form of Mrs. Winnie MacDougal. The pantry's largest benefactor had a soft spot for the new worker and was horrified to hear that she was considering leaving. So she made Kit an offer. Her massive cattle ranch in another state had an empty caretaker cabin. If Kit continued to do the pantry's bookkeeping long distance, she could live there.

Kit knew she had made the right decision when she clicked with her new therapist and when Mal showed up her second week. She wasn't hiding – she was recuperating. Not just from the trauma she'd suffered, but also from her relationship with Mick.

"How could I have been so wrong?" she asked aloud, and rolled her eyes when Mal yawned in response.

She had been so sure that Mick had held strong feelings for her. At first, she wished she had stayed and badgered the truth out of him. But she was too stubborn and had been too hurt and too prideful to consider it. She tried to rake a hand through her hair and was annoyed when it was stopped by a tangle. She was overdue for a haircut. Maybe tomorrow after the hangover wore off.

Collapsing on the ancient sofa, she gulped two more shots of the whiskey she'd bought specifically for tonight and then opened the lid of the shoebox. Months ago, she had pulled out everything that didn't relate to DC and had shoved the box in the back of her closet. Her plan tonight was to get drunk, burn the box and its contents, and begin her life tomorrow in earnest. Rehab time was over.

"I'll start dating," she informed Mal, her words beginning to slur. "Socialize. Join that trivia club that meets at the café. My therapist is giddy."

She ignored the fact that she had started down that road weeks ago. There were book clubs that met at the local library, and one focused exclusively on mysteries. She had attended two meetings so far and even managed to hold a conversation at the last one.

Of course the first thing she saw when she looked in the box was Mick's tank top. It took up most of the space. Kit pulled the wad of black fabric out and, before she could stop herself, brought it to her nose and inhaled. It smelled like cardboard. Of course, it would not have kept his scent after six months. Silly, she scolded herself.

But it felt the same. Kit's fingers smoothed over the wales in the cotton fabric. She doubted he had noticed it missing. He'd had dozens of them. The tears came before she was ready. Fuck, she had been so happy then. How could one bad decision have destroyed her whole life?

Keeping the singlet in one hand, she fished through the box with the other. Everything she pulled out, she studied before throwing it in the fire. Museum tickets, souvenir postcards, play programs. Oh, God. The night he'd asked her to live with him. When the tears obscured her vision, she used the shirt to roughly wipe her face.

Her crying was part of the purge, and she didn't try to temper her sobs.

She was about halfway through the box when Mal jumped up and ran to the bottom of the stairs. His growls started soft but then rose to menacing. Kit jumped to her feet to investigate and almost fell over. The room swam in front of her eyes, and she teetered on her feet.

Gritting her teeth in an effort to walk over to where Mal stood, she now wished she wasn't so intoxicated. Mal had probably scented another mouse, but what if...

"On guard, Mal," she quietly ordered.

Her vision wobbled as well as her legs. And Mal was growling as if someone was in her home. Someone uninvited. *Fuck.*

Kit peered up into the dark stairwell, wishing she had left the upstairs light on or had a flashlight. There was one in the kitchen, but that was suddenly miles away. She should give the attack command to Mal and let him tear the bastard up. But she hesitated.

She loved the giant black mutt with a vengeance. As deadly as he could be, she feared him being injured or worse. Not everyone loved animals.

"My dog is trained to go for your balls. I hope you can see what a strong jaw he has." Kit spoke carefully, praying that she did not sound drunk. "When he's ripped your junk off, he'll go for your fucking face."

"I prefer to remain in one piece, if you don't mind," the shadow at the top of the stairs said calmly, and then clicked the light switch.

Not only was she drunk, she was hallucinating. Her

mind was playing tricks on her. It was the only explanation.

A hysterical laugh slipped out of her. "Come to wish me a happy anniversary, Mick?"

Mick looked confused then turned his attention back to the growling dog. "Are you going to call off your animal?"

Kit's heart stopped. It was real? It was Mick, and he was here in her home. He was here and it was too late. Fucking rat bastard who did not love her! Fury burned through some of her inebriated state. Good. Anger was far better than grief.

"Down, Mal." She spoke and the dog stopped snarling but remained focused on Mick.

"I should warn you that he will still render you dickless if you try to get near me." She hooked her fingers in Mal's collar for moral support.

"Noted," Mick responded as he slowly descended the stairs.

Kit found that she did not want to look directly at Mick. She concentrated on his black boots before turning back towards the living room. Placing her feet carefully, she hoped he could not tell how much alcohol she had consumed. It would give him an advantage.

She chose the armchair and tucked her feet under her so Mal could sit in front. She shifted a bit in order to see around his furry head. Mick entered the room after her, quiet on his feet as always.

That ability had always amazed her. He was such a tall, lanky man. But he moved like a cat – graceful and discreet. He perched awkwardly on the edge of the sofa, still watching Mal uneasily out of the corner of his eye.

He noticed the fire and seemed to realize he was still wearing his thick jacket. Moments dragged by as he slowly removed it and folded it on the cushion next to him. His remaining clothes were jeans and a navy sweater. Thankfully, it was a loose sweater, and she was saved from being reminded of how amazing his muscles were. Thanks to the fire and the light from the stairway, the room was dim. Otherwise, she would see how blue the sweater made his eyes look.

Perhaps I am hallucinating, Kit thought. It was unlike Mick to appear so unsure. It was his super spy nature to always project confidence. His eyes – still a beautiful blue – roamed the room but skipped over her.

No doubt, she thought wryly. Dressed in leggings and an old flannel shirt, wearing ugly wool socks, she knew her hair was untidy and her face blotchy from crying. But then, she could not look worse than the last time he saw her. Not that she cared, anyway.

When his gaze finally rested on the coffee table, Kit's heart stopped before she noticed she had replaced the lid on the shoebox. She must have put the shirt inside, too, since she didn't see it. Thank God!

Mick nodded toward the half-empty bottle of whiskey. "Drink all that tonight?"

His deep voice, so familiar, wrapped around her like a warm blanket. There had been times when his voice had aroused her as much as his body. *Shit!* She did not need to go there. She needed to focus and remember how much she hated him. How badly he had hurt her.

"Fuck you," she scoffed. "What the hell are you

doing here? Too good to ring the doorbell like a normal person?"

Mick's brows rose in shock. Kit silently high-fived herself. Score one for the angry drunk chick. If she were sober, would she have flung herself in his arms? Possibly. So it was better if drunk chick took over.

Yeah, Mick was taken aback. She could tell as he blinked rapidly for a moment before centering himself.

Mick made a move to stand, but froze when Mal growled. He scowled and sat back down.

"He's named after Malachai?" he guessed.

"Hell no," she said. "It's short for Malnourished Fleabag, which was what he was when I found him. I saved his life. He'll die to protect mine."

This was a stretch. She had worked with a local trainer, teaching Mal one attack command and some other orders to make him look threatening. And he was protective of her. If someone tried to harm her, he would attack. But he was far from a trained guard dog.

"I saved your life, too," Mick reminded her, his voice a bit sharp. "Twice."

"And, if I recall, I died for you. Twice." She smiled, but it was patronizing, full of teeth. "Say what you want and leave."

"All right. There's new intel on Marius." Kit's gut clenched and she forced herself not to puke. "He is close to finding your location."

Mick's mouth twisted. "Which is impressive since it took a bit of work for me to track you down. What the bloody hell possessed you to move from Denver to the middle of nowhere in Wyoming?"

"I didn't like the city," Kit mumbled, her drunken brain trying to process the horrific news.

While she had all sorts of baggage from that experience, she honestly had not been afraid of being found. She had trusted DAG's skills, and she had genuinely believed that she would not be worth Marius' bother. While she had lived very carefully the past year, it wasn't as if she had bought a weapon or taken tae-kwon-do classes. Her lungs seized up. What was she going to do?

Mick seemed to read her mind, for he leaned forward, his face oh-so serious. "If we switch you out with an agent and have a force hidden here, we can capture him. This is our best hope in ending this."

"What about the others?" She hated that her voice quivered. "The other men who were with him?"

"Dead," Mick answered without hesitation.

Kit looked at him, the question in her eyes. Was he certain? When he nodded, she knew. *Oh.* He was positive because he had killed them.

The thought should have repulsed her, but she was too grateful. As much as she had hated the reality that he sometimes killed people, the fact that he had done this for her helped loosen the bands of fear around her chest. The others were dead and could no longer hurt her.

"The name you chose." Mick changed the subject. "It's quite...unusual."

"Fuck you. I was having a very bad day." Kit hoped her gaze looked fiery enough. "Edith was the name of my tenth grade English teacher. She was a cold bitch. I am hoping to emulate her."

"Don't cock your head at me!" Kit knew her voice

sounded shrill, but that habit of his brought back too many memories.

Mick's eyebrow rose in surprise and confusion. His face was bewildered. No doubt. Kit never shouted in anger. But Kit was gone. There was only Enraged Edith now.

"And stop doing that damn eyebrow thing!" She added.

Good. Mick looked pained. Fuck, when did she become such a bitch? Yet she was glad this hidden part of her personality decided to surface tonight. It was like armor, an extra layer between her and the man who could have destroyed her. There was no way in hell he was getting that close to her again.

Mick frowned again and shook his head in frustration. "You're drunk. We can finish making plans in the morning. You need to be out of here and on the way to the safe house by ten."

Kit formed both hands into a rude gesture. Mick merely raised his eyebrows.

"It means fuck you," she explained, and waved her hands around.

"I'm aware," he replied dryly.

Kit snarled at her inability to get a rise out of him. Why wouldn't h argue with her? She was sure she could win a fight tonight.

"I haven't agreed to anything," she reminded him.

He ignored her and shifted on the raggedy sofa until he was lying down. "We'll talk in the morning."

She watched in amazement as he stuck a pillow under his head and used his jacket as a blanket. Luckily, the sofa was huge, and he almost fit. She did not remember giving him permission to stay…had she? The booze, the late hour, and the stress of seeing Mick again was hitting her hard. Her mind was hazy, and she was so sleepy.

She shifted in order to get more comfortable in the chair. If he was staying, then she was going to remain alert and hide the shoebox after he fell asleep. She was confident she could stay awake that long. A few short minutes later, she was snoring.

MICK SETTLED BACK into the sofa, closing his eyes. It seemed to make the giant dog more relaxed. From under his lashes, he could see Kit fighting to stay awake. She would drift off, then jolt awake to glare in his direction. It was unfortunate that she was so intoxicated. Mick had no doubt that he would win this battle of wills, and that made him sad. He missed their stubborn matches.

What the fuck had happened to Kit? Edith, he corrected himself, even though he doubted he could ever call her that. Bubbly, open Kit was gone. In her place was a bitter, suspicious stranger. What had happened? She had not been like this in the hospital. Something had obviously happened to make her leave the city and hide out here with just a dog for protection.

Mick waited until he was sure that Kit was out before slowly sitting up and holding out his hand to the giant black beast. He had a hunch that the dog might kill to protect his master but was otherwise harmless. He was proven right when Mal trotted over, sniffed his palm, and then covered it in dog saliva.

Using both hands to reward Mal with a thorough

head scratch, Mick had to smile. The dog vibrated with delight then sat down on the floor at his feet. Now that he was certain he would not be attacked, he could give Kit his undivided attention.

She was slumped over in the large chair, snoring slightly. She had been crying. The bloodshot eyes and puffy face gave that away. Why? Whatever the reason, Mick wanted to fix it, to make her smile again. The reality was, he had thrown away that option when he had lied to her.

At least she looked healthy. Her hair was longer, the curls ending well below her jaw. The large flannel shirt she wore reminded him of the baggy t-shirt she had sported when they first met. Kit had a smoking body, but was not very comfortable in showing it off. Except she had for him. *Christ*, he could look at her for hours. Angry or sweet, messy or neat, she was still Kit.

He did not like that her home was so far away from the main ranch. How would anyone know if she were in trouble? She was a sitting duck here. Why hadn't she put more thought into her safety? He had so many questions. He sat back, looking around the small room. It was cozy, filled with mismatched furnishings and wood paneled walls. None of it spoke to her personality, so he assumed the home had come like this. Perhaps she did not intend on being here for long.

Then he noticed the shoebox on the coffee table. That he recognized. A bad feeling settled in his stomach, leaving him nauseous. He hesitated, then pulled it over to his lap and removed the cover. On top was a wad of black fabric. Shaking it out, he was shocked to see it was one of his old singlets. What the devil had she saved that for?

Below it were various bits of paper. Sifting through them, he found they were ticket stubs, tourist postcards, and parking passes from her time in DC. What on earth had she been doing with these? When he glanced at the hearth, he knew. Remains of what she had already tried to burn had drifted to lie among the wood ash.

She had to be intoxicated to burn the contents, he guessed, and blinked back tears. She was moving on. Destroying what little she had kept from their life together. He was too late.

His bitter laugh startled Mal, who raised his head in curiosity. Mick gave him another pat, and he settled back down. How fitting. Just one day late. He had known getting her back was one chance in a million. He had been right. Her hatred of him had not dimmed. Now the best he could do was save her life and wish her well. He owed her that much and more.

Christ, when she had flipped him off earlier, he had wanted to kiss her silly. She was such a fighter. Pressing the heels of his hands into his eyes did not relieve the knot in his chest. He wasn't sure if he wanted to cry from sadness or elation. What a night.

Mick waited a bit longer, watching the cozy fire before he rose to get Kit settled into bed. Mal woke and looked up at him with misgivings.

"Bedtime," Mick explained quietly.

It must have been a cue, for Mal trotted over to the kitchen door and waited for Mick to open it. He would let the dog in and lock up after he took care of Kit. He looped her arms around his shoulders and picked her up. Striding toward the stairs, he stumbled when she snuggled closer, rubbing her cheek against his sweater. He stopped to take a deep breath and center himself. *Get it together mate*, he cautioned himself. Tripping on the steps would be bad form. The only reason she was allowing his touch was that she was out cold. That did not stop his arms from tightening, pulling her even closer.

Mick carried her into the bedroom he had scoped out earlier. Thankfully, the light from the hallway was enough for him to be able to lay Kit down on the iron-framed bed without tripping on one of the many dog toys littering the floor. After settling her gently atop the covers, he turned on the bedside lamp so he could get her properly situated.

The first thing he noticed was the quilt that covered the bed. Recognition stabbed sharply at his heart. He remembered the day she had found it at a craft fair. His fingertip slid over one of the cotton squares as he recalled how excited she had been over a blanket that he had considered a flamboyant nightmare of colors. But the vibrant pattern suited who she was, or rather had been.

The rest of the bedroom was surprisingly bland, even for a rental. The heavy wood furniture had obviously come with the house. It was old and scuffed, probably traded out when new furnishings had been bought for the main house. The beige walls added no warmth to the small room, nor did the matching blinds covering the lone window. There were no pictures, no personal touches to see, even after months of her living here.

Besides the chest, the only other furniture was the bedside table and a giant dog bed in the corner.

Of course, she would make sure Mal's space was lavish. Even though the pillow took up an entire corner, Mick wondered if it was even big enough for the giant dog to stretch out on. It must be, for the plush royal blue cover looked well used.

The room solidified the change in Kit. This space matched the unhappy woman he had met downstairs. The bitter, drunk woman who had wanted to tear his eyes out. Perhaps he should have let her.

Mick maneuvered her body between the sheets and pulled the quilt up to her chest. Christ, she was still lovely. Before he could stop himself, he reached out, pulled on one of her curls, and smiled when it bounced back. The brown coils had a life of their own and still beckoned to him as if they were alive. The mutual fascination between her hair and his fingers had often led to his hand becoming so ensnared that it would take the two of them to untangle it.

The lamp light was dim, and he would not have seen the faint scars on her face if he hadn't known exactly where to look. He'd spent hours memorizing even the smallest of cuts and bruises while she had been in the hospital. He had to make sure he never forgot what she had suffered because of him.

As Mick reached to put out the light, her eyelids fluttered and she blinked sleepily at him. Oh, her eyes! They were still the color of French chocolate soufflé. Still had the power to stop him in his tracks.

He braced himself for another deserving tirade and

was stunned when a slow grin shaped her lips. The new frown line between her eyes faded as the grin changed into a welcoming smile. Her gaze, so icy and brittle before, was now so full of warm emotion that it made him gasp.

"I love this part," she whispered, her words slurred.

"What part, Angel?"

Mick's brow furred as he tried to remember what she was referring to. While he had escorted her to bed many times before, he could not recall her ever being tipsy.

"The part of the dream where you kiss me, silly," Kit said, her smile fading. "Why are you just staring at me? You're supposed to kiss me now."

Mick cleared his suddenly tight throat and thanked the universe for one last opportunity to kiss his brave girl. It was short, sweet, and devastating. She must have been dreaming of him before. Whatever the reason, alcohol or memory, he was grateful.

Chapter Thirteen

THE NEXT MORNING, Kit tried not to move when she awoke. Her headache throbbed throughout her entire body. The smell of booze seeping out of her pores was nauseating, and her stomach was in bad enough shape already.

Shifting slowly, she turned to her side to look for Mal. It was not like him to let her sleep in. Instead of an alarm clock, she used her dog's "I have to pee now" whine to make sure she was up on time. But his bed was empty. The bedroom door was also wide open. She always closed it.

That's when she saw the note on the nightstand. "Waiting downstairs. Mick."

Physical state be damned. She leaped up and rushed to the bathroom to puke up what remained in her poor stomach.

Shit! It hadn't been a hallucination! He'd obviously opened her door to leave the note and let Mal out. While she couldn't remember coming to bed, she had evidently crashed still wearing her clothes.

Shedding the smelly garments, she took a long, steaming shower. While that made her feel more human, she still looked ghastly. The reflection in the mirror had red eyes, a puffy face, and pale skin. Of course.

In all of her fantasies concerning running into Mick again, she had looked stunning. Kit scrubbed her teeth hard in frustration. Fuck him. He deserved to see her like this – hung-over and untidy. Why should she care? There had been dozens of times he had seen her looking put together, and he had still tossed her aside.

And if she remembered correctly, he wasn't here to try to win her back. He just wanted to save her life again. *Fuck.* Kit wasn't sure she was strong enough for this.

"Go do whatever it takes to make him go away," she told the sad woman in the mirror.

Mick's reappearance, combined with the booze, had given her such odd dreams. One moment they were discussing Mal, next, her nose filled with the scent of Mick and she felt his arms around her. *Oh, yes! This was the good dream!* She had floated for a bit before she seemed to land in bed. The strong arms had slipped away, and her mind had protested. This wasn't how the dream usually went.

However, there was no need to worry. Mick's face was right there. She smiled in relief. This dream had happened before. Several times in fact. His hesitation was a new wrinkle, but then the dream had returned to normal when he had leaned forward to capture her mouth.

Like most dream moments, a kiss can last for just that or go on for hours. How she wished this one had lasted longer. It was definitely her fantasy's handiwork because Mick had never kissed her like this. It was too sweet, too poignant. The kind of kiss only her imagination could create.

Ugh! She needed to erase that from her mind! Just a dream, and she needed all her wits to simply face reality today.

She rummaged through the closet for clothes after locking the bedroom door. She paused before getting dressed to look about the room. What had he thought of it? While the downstairs still bore some knickknacks from the previous tenant, the bedroom did not.

Only the corner of the sad room was plush. Mal slept on a giant cushion and kept it surrounded with many of his toys. While this place was just temporary for her, it was Mal's first home, and she wanted him to feel loved. Mick had probably thought Mal's corner was frivolous.

Who cares what he thinks? Mick's apartment looked similar, just with better furnishings. So what if she failed to spruce up a temporary living space? It meant she could travel light. Heaven knew she was used to not having a permanent home. Summoning up her angry persona from last night, she threw some clothes and minimal makeup on and marched downstairs, ready for battle. Well, as ready as one can be with a horrific hangover.

The living room was empty, and the scene that greeted her when she poked her head into the kitchen was shocking. Mick was sitting cross-legged on the linoleum floor with her vicious guard dog practically lying in his lap. Neither noticed her. Mal was too content with the head rub he was receiving, and Mick was grinning at the dog's enthusiastic reaction.

Kit quickly ducked out and leaned against the wall. That day back at the hospital, she was sure her heart had just winked out of existence. How wrong she had been! Right now, it was back and cramping hard enough to bring her to her knees.

Mick looked the same and yet better. Oh, God, his smile…the way his face had relaxed when he was at home and unguarded. How was she going to survive even an hour in his presence?

Remember the last time you saw him, her conscious whispered. *Yes!* The time when he had not asked for or even considered her opinion. The time he decided her future for her, as if she were too dumb to think for herself. The time he threw her away like a piece of garbage. His sunny smiles and magic hands meant nothing after that.

Kit straightened and took a bracing inhale. While she wasn't ready, she needed to get this over with so he could be gone.

"I assume you let him out to pee and found his breakfast." Her tone was snappish as she frowned at the man stroking her traitorous animal.

By the time his eyes met hers, Mick's face was once again a bland mask. "Yes. I wasn't sure what amount to give him. I chose two scoops."

The fact that he had guessed correctly pissed her off even more. Mal could sense something, for he bounded over to her side. Kit's anger at him lasted until he looked up at her with apologetic eyes. Rolling her eyes at how easily she let the dog play her, she leaned down for a hug and a wet lick on her cheek.

Only when Mal trotted into the other room did she look back at Mick. He had obviously made himself right at home, she thought as he handed her a cup of coffee. If she weren't so desperate, she would refuse. But right now, she needed the caffeine for her headache.

She turned sharply on her heel when he picked up his own cup. It made her dizzy for a moment, but it was better than watching him sip his coffee. She initially had thought that the way he held a cup was odd, but it turned out to be a British custom. Many men held cups by their rims rather than force their fingers through the small handles. It brought back too many memories of sharing a morning coffee with him.

"We don't have much time," he announced as she rooted through a cabinet looking for painkillers.

Ignoring him, she took the pill bottle to the sink and downed three with a glass of water. She then found a pack of crackers in a drawer and refilled her coffee before sitting at the small kitchen table.

"You have a lot of explaining to do before I agree to anything," she reminded him.

Mick sighed and sat down across from her. "Marius could be here as soon as tomorrow. You need to be far away when that happens."

"What about Mal and Mrs. MacDougal? There's no way I'm putting them in danger!"

Her heart rate increased. She could not bear it if anything happened to either one of them. None of this was their fault. It all came back to her and that stupid decision she had made to take that freelance offer. While the ranch was half a mile away, it could still be seen from this small house. Guilt wore down some of her obstinacy.

"The main house is far enough away that she would never notice what happens," Mick said. "We will have agents watching her just in case. As for Mal, there's someone who lives between here and the safe house who owes me a favor."

"I'm not putting him in a kennel!" She responded angrily.

"It's not a kennel," Mick rushed to explain. "It happens to be a farm. There will be other dogs there. I assure you Mal will be fawned over."

Kit blinked back tears. It hurt to think of being without the stupid mutt even for a few days. But if he stayed with her, there was a chance he could be harmed. Must be the hangover making her sappy, she reasoned.

Mick, sensing her capitulation, continued. "All we have to do is switch you out with an agent. After that, the others will sneak in one by one. Marius will never know anyone but a lone female is in the house."

A day or two in an anonymous location wouldn't be the end of the world, Kit admitted to herself. Sure, there would be a female agent there as a guard, but she could keep herself busy with a book. With Marius gone, she really could start her life over again. Damnit! Mick's idea fell perfectly into line with her own plans.

"Fine." She sighed. "I'll do it."

Mick nodded in approval. "Go pack a bag. The exchange can take place within the hour."

Kit packed a case for herself and one for Mal. Mick's plan involved her driving into town to the market while he snuck Mal and the bags out the back. He had a car hidden somewhere nearby. As much as it galled her to hand over Mal, she knew he was in good hands with Professional Mick. It was Personal Mick that she could never trust again.

As INSTRUCTED, SHE drove into the small town and bought some groceries. After that, she parked in front of a boutique that catered to the local wealthy ranchers.

DAG had overtaken the shop for a few hours. After Kit entered, an older woman locked the door and turned the sign to read Closed. The woman was Kit's height but older and thinner. She was either a new recruit, or an agent borrowed from the nearby FBI office. Kit did not recognize her, and the woman paid her little attention.

"Come with me," she instructed, and led the way into the stockroom where Mick was waiting.

The woman handed Kit a stack of garments and a pair of running shoes. "Put these on and give me what you are wearing."

Kit knew the drill. She had done this same routine with Amy when she had fled DC. Unsurprisingly, the clothes fit perfectly. But of course, DAG had her sizes noted somewhere.

The artfully faded jeans were comfortable, and the green turtleneck brought out the faint gold in her brown eyes. After tying the shoes, Kit emerged from the dressing room to see the woman tucking her short hair into a curly dark wig.

Kit scowled at the fact that the agent had to put on padding to fill out the outfit she'd been wearing. At least she had hips and tits, she snarked to herself and accepted the tan jacket Mick offered. After handing over her keys, she and Mick exited out the back door.

Seeing Mal in the backseat of the SUV brightened Kit's day considerably. Before Mick pulled out into the street, he pushed her head between her knees.

"Stay down until we get out of town," he explained.

That made sense, but all Kit could feel was his warm hand on her neck. She expected him to remove it in order to drive, but it remained there even as he maneuvered through the streets. A few moments later, his long fingers started stroking the curls at her nape. She bit her lip to keep from moaning at the familiar touch. *Fuck, no!*

"Don't touch me!" she hissed, knocking his hand away but keeping her head down.

Mick looked startled. Maybe the movement of his fingers had been involuntary. Kit didn't care. When Mick gave the all-clear, she tumbled over the seat so she could sit with her dog. She saw Mick's lips tighten, but he said nothing. Even with the darkened windows, the sunlight made the pain behind her eyes worse. Damn it, she had left her sunglasses in the shop! Oh well, she thought, now she had a decent excuse to lay her head back and close her eyes. Anything to block out the reality that she was once again alone with Mick.

THE EXITS ON the highway flew by, and Kit watched another chapter of her life disappear in the rearview mirror. It wasn't until her stomach grumbled that she realized how long they'd been on the road. What's worse was that Mick heard.

"I take it that means you'd like to make a pit stop?" Mick asked.

Damn him. If she wasn't starving and in desperate need of a sports drink to help her hangover, she'd have told him to keep driving. Talking about cutting off your nose to spite your face.

"Yeah, actually, if you wouldn't mind. I'm hungry and Mal could use a walk."

She was happy that Mick didn't say much. She kept her attention on Mal even though she was aware of every movement Mick made.

In the sunlight, she could see some threads of gray in his dark hair. His day-old beard stubble showed even more silver strands. There also seemed to be new lines on his face, but she refused to look closer. He was just as gorgeous as she remembered, and that was not a good development.

Another hour of driving through smaller towns and Mick turned down a road that was surrounded by pasture on both sides. They passed a few men in cowboy hats and jeans mending a section of fence. Mal woofed playfully at the groups of sheep he saw. Kit chuckled. Perhaps this would be a fun vacation for Mal.

Mick stopped the car in front of a small ranch house. Even though style was from the mid-fifties, she could see modern additions, like the floodlights under the eaves. Two dogs rushed out to greet them in a flurry of black and white fur.

At first, Kit held Mal's collar when they climbed out. While he was used to Mrs. MacDougal's small Corgi, he did not have much exposure to larger dogs. Luckily, the dogs knew how to act. The two shepherd mixes approached slowly and sniffed. Mal returned the butt-sniffing and wagged his tail.

When Mal continued to wag his tail, Kit let go to watch him frolic in the front yard with the other mutts. A man approached from inside the barn, and Mick greeted the rancher like an old friend, not just someone who owed him a debt. Mick was not wearing his super spy persona now. His smile was open and genuine as he gestured toward the knot of dogs playing nearby.

Kit's breath caught as he turned to look at her with that smile. It faltered in response to the frown on her face. She tore her eyes away and dredged up a polite smile for the sheep farmer as the men approached.

"I'm Kit." She extended her hand. "Thank you for agreeing to take care of Mal."

"Mateo." The man shook her hand with a firm, calloused grip. "Happy to help. All the men here love dogs. I promise he will be treated like a king."

Kit chuckled and relaxed a bit. Despite the coveralls and baseball cap, he looked nothing like a farmer. Especially with one arm in a cast. Was he an agent? She could believe that. His dark hair was long, pulled back with an elastic band, and his arms were full of tattoos. There were even tattoos on his neck, which made Kit cringe in the pain they must have entailed. If not for his warm brown eyes and easy smile, she might have felt intimidated by all that ink. He looked Latino but his accent screamed New England. Since Mick trusted few people, there must be some history between the two of them.

Mick turned down the offer of a meal and announced they needed to be going. Kit took the hint and pulled Mal's bag from the SUV. Blushing, she handed it over to Mateo.

"I over-packed," she tried to explain about the overflowing bag. "It has the food he likes, some of his toys, treats and a blanket. There's also a list of commands to stay away from. Uhm...unless you have something that needs attacking."

Feeling incredibly awkward, she turned to find Mal and say goodbye. Since she was still off-balance from the hangover and being around Mick again, she kept it short. There was no need to break down sobbing in front of a stranger and Mick. She needed to appear strong, so she swallowed her tears and put on a bland expression.

Thankfully, Mick rushed her back into the front seat and took off. Kit closed her eyes and took deep breaths. It was just a couple of days. She'd been through worse times. Mal was just a dog. As well as her best friend and only confidant. If anything happened to him, she would happily kill Mick and his friend.

"Is Mateo an agent, too?" Kit asked as she watched the pastures whiz by.

She was expecting an evasion, but Mick surprised her again. "Yes. He joined DAG shortly after I did. This is one of the safe houses we share with other government agencies. Mateo is currently working undercover, and his alternate identity is now in solitary confinement in a prison. He stays here for another month. He then gets 'released' and goes back to the gang he is infiltrating."

Wow. What a nugget of information. Was Mick part

of that op? Kit wanted details, but she was too stubborn to push for them. He was no longer her concern, anyway. She closed her eyes and tried to relax enough to doze.

MICK TURNED LEFT onto a twisting road that hugged the hill. Kit's eyes snapped open. A curvy route was not what her stomach needed right now. While her headache had faded, her gut had not fully recovered from last night's drunk-fest. Watching the scenery rush by wasn't helping, and she found her concentration moving to Mick's hands.

They were so graceful. And deadly, she reminded herself. But her mind skipped over the assassin in the woods and darted to all the reasons she'd deemed his hands magical. They moved carefully on the wheel, not gripping or tugging. They nudged the car around the curves with a light touch. Skillful was another adjective that sprang to her mind and caused blood to heat her face. This brought to mind all the ways those hands had touched her body and made it sing.

No! She ripped her gaze away with a small moan. *Best not to think about it.*

"Kit?" Mick slowed the vehicle, glancing at her in concern. "Are you car-sick? Should I slow down?"

"I'm fine," she insisted. "How much farther?"

"Just over an hour," he answered.

They traveled in silence for a bit until Mick finally spoke. "You didn't take much when you left."

Kit straightened in surprise. Of course, she assumed he would eventually bring up their past, but she had not expected this line of questioning. He had no right to know about anything that had happened after he'd left that hospital room.

"Starting over, you know," she snapped. "New life, all that jazz."

"I was surprised so much was still at the flat," he persisted, his mouth tight.

What on earth? He was angry! Ha! Was he irritated that he had to throw out the rest of her belongings? Other than the shirt, she had taken nothing of his. What had she left that he could possibly have an issue with?

Taking a wild guess, she choked out a disbelieving laugh. "You're pissed because I left the necklace behind? Are you serious?"

Dear God, he was. She could tell by the color that rose in his cheeks and the way his jaw tensed. *Good*, the evil part of her rejoiced. Her instinct to leave it had been a good one. It was a symbol of the lie that had once been his feelings for her. As much as she had treasured it, it was too painful to keep.

"Did you really expect me to keep it and cry over it every night?" Her voice climbed in time with her indignation.

"Of course not!" Mick bit out, and kept his eyes on the road.

"Anyway, it's not like I'm that angelic ball of light anymore," Kit sniffed, twisting the imaginary knife. "It wouldn't suit me now. Edith is not angelic."

Mick's jaw tightened to the point that she should have heard his teeth grind together. At least her final comments seemed to render him mute. Good. It was difficult to hear his low voice, even when it was cross. It could seduce her against her will. Back when they had been together, he could make her horny by simply reading the newspaper aloud.

THEY STOPPED FOR a bathroom break in a small town. After that, signs of civilization were few. Mick swerved to the left, turning down a dirt path that ran through a forest. Within minutes, they emerged onto a muddy field that contained a few tree stumps and one rusted aluminum house trailer. The late afternoon sun glinted off the exterior, making it look even seedier.

At Kit's astonished look, Mick smiled. "It is bullet-proof, runs off a generator and has running water and plumbing. There's also a perimeter alarm system and satellite phone service."

"Oh," Kit replied and looked around for another sign of life. "Where's the other agent?"

Mick stopped on his way out of the car and looked at her in confusion. "What other agent?"

"The one who's staying here with me." She spoke slowly, a bad feeling halting her words.

He had mentioned another agent, hadn't he? Other-wise, there was no way she would have agreed to this plan. No! This couldn't be happening. Panic swirled up from her gut to compress her lungs.

"I'm the one guarding you," he answered, and went to retrieve the bags.

Once Mick had tapped in a long password into the hidden keypad, he showed her to the small bedroom in the back. Kit shut the door for privacy to verbally kick herself while trying to steady her thundering heartbeat.

"This is what happens when you get drunk," Kit lectured herself. "You then get a hangover and cannot think correctly!"

This new development was bad, really, really bad. How long could she keep up the angry persona? It was exhausting. Yes, she was still mad at him, but the anger came from hurt. She had to find ways to keep from breaking down in front of him. That would be the worst thing that could happen. He could never know how wounded she was.

The tapping on the door caused her to yelp in surprise.

"I'm going to set the outlying alarms," Mick informed her. "There should be plenty of food in the kitchen. You can choose dinner."

KIT WAITED UNTIL she heard the front door shut and then emerged to explore the trailer. The main room contained a small kitchen and a living area. A table and two chairs were crammed into a corner. A large futon took up much of the space, and the only other seat was a rocking chair. One interior door belonged to a coat closet, and the other opened to reveal the bathroom. Kit had expected dark wood paneling, but found the walls covered with ivory textured wallpaper. Still, it looked thrown together, much like her rental house. She should feel right at home.

Something was off about the interior. The inside did not correspond to the outside, she realized. The great room should be bigger. Knowing DAG, there could be a hidden weapons room or something similar. Even after all the weeks she had been with Mick, this entire scenario was still unreal to Kit.

By the time Mick returned, she had a casserole nuking in the microwave and a salad ready. After dinner, she planned to hide in the bedroom. She was not ashamed of the cowardly plan. She needed to do whatever it took to mitigate her time with Mick. If not, she would do something horrifying like cry or kiss him.

Mick threw his light jacket on the futon and motioned her over. "If the alarm sounds, I need you to stay in this safe room."

He popped open another hidden panel and entered a shorter password. Part of the wall slid out to reveal a small room that contained an armchair and a few metal boxes of supplies.

"If you need this room, type in the password and add a seven. Once the door is shut, it can be opened only from the inside." Mick showed her the latch on the inside of the door. "I'll tap three times and then twice to let you know it's safe."

Kit nodded her agreement. Despite the fact that she wasn't claustrophobic, she didn't relish being in there for any length of time. It was a worst-case scenario anyway.

Mick was staring at her. Like he wanted to say something important. Something that Kit was sure she did not want to hear. Luckily, the pinging of the microwave saved her.

"Dinner is ready." She slipped past him to flee into the kitchen.

Chapter Fourteen

WHEN THEY SAT down to eat, Kit realized just how small the table actually was. She had to practically sit sideways to keep from brushing up against Mick. His legs took up most of the space underneath the tabletop.

Crap. How was she supposed to eat this close to him? Sitting in the car had been bad enough, but now there was no console between them. She could even smell his aftershave. Just her luck, it was the same brand he'd used before. She would just have to breathe through her mouth then.

At least now her pride was stronger than her libido. Yes, she wanted to run her fingers across the back of his hand and up the hairy expanse of forearm that his rolled-up sleeve exposed. Of course, the first man to have an effect on her body in a year would have to be Mick. Talk about unfair.

Kit moved her eyes to her plate and forced them to stay there. She was doing a good job eating on autopilot and trying not to smell when Mick's deep voice broke the silence.

"Malachai retired six months ago." He glanced at her and then back to his food.

She didn't want to have a conversation with him, but she was too curious. Malachai had been her friend.

"Was he pushed out or was it his choice?" Kit knew her tone was bitchy, but she had no fondness for Mick's employer after being forced into this new persona.

Mick's lips quirked. "His choice. Claimed he was burned out. I think he hated the fact that Marius somehow breached his system. He could not solve the puzzle of how it happened. He's well. Teaching hacking classes at the CIA for now. We had dinner just last week. There are bets that he will be back within a year."

Kit swallowed both a smart-ass comment and a lump of jealousy. She was the one who had dinner with Malachai every time Mick was out in the field. Yet another thing Mick had taken from her.

"How's Amy?" she asked.

She saw Mick frown out of the corner of her eye. "Not certain. She's been spending most of her time in Atlanta with family. I didn't realize you knew her well."

Kit hoped Amy was happy, that she had reconciled with her brother-in-law and niece. It was maddening that she had no way of knowing for sure. Of course, Mick had no idea about how she and Amy had bonded after he had ripped her heart out.

Her next response was petty, but she was hurt, envious, and off-balance. "My father died in January."

"Jesus Christ!" Mick dropped his fork. "I am so sorry!"

Kit looked away from the shock and dismay on his

face. He moved his hand to rest on her arm in a show of sympathy. She slowly pulled her arm away. The move was pointed and callous. The hurt that glinted in his eyes should have felt good to Kit. Instead, the hole in her chest widened.

Mick awkwardly moved his hand back to his lap. "Wait. How did you find out? Kit, you were not to contact your family. It was too dangerous!"

She scowled at him. "I did not break any damn rules! Before I left, Malachai gave me a safe way to access the security cameras at the home. I only hacked in once a week. He died peacefully, just watching TV in the common room."

"I am so sorry." Mick did look mournful. "I know you loved him very much. I know…it hurt you to not be there."

"Fuck you," she whispered.

Torn between wanting to punch Mick or crawl in his lap and cry, Kit pushed her chair back and tried her best to make a graceful exit. While it may not have been polished, at least she made it to the bedroom before breaking down.

SHE SPENT THE next two hours curled up on the bed pretending to read while listening to Mick move around in the other room. She should just go brush her teeth and turn in, but she kept hoping he would go outside so she could slip into the bathroom without seeing him.

As if he read her mind, Kit heard the bathroom door shut. What happened next had her certain that her hearing had gone bad. It sounded like the shower was running. That was impossible, right? Mick Harris *never* showered.

But as the sound continued, she realized that it had been half a year. There was no telling what other feats he had accomplished since she left. Or who had helped him.

This time jealousy had her bent over in pain. No! She'd had a plan. How she would slowly help him work up to being able to actually take a shower. It was the one way she had been able to contribute to his recovery. And now someone else had obviously stepped in and claimed that prize.

When Mick emerged from the bathroom, clad in a t-shirt and loose shorts, Kit was waiting in the bedroom doorway. He looked at her curiously while drying his hair with a towel.

"You showered." Two words were all she could get past the lump in her throat.

"Yes." Mick smiled in satisfaction. "I've been able to handle it for several weeks now."

The last thing she saw was his expression turn to confusion before she slammed the door and launched herself up on the bed. She prayed that he could not hear her sobs with the pillow over her face.

It was ridiculous that this one thing cut her the deepest. He'd not only moved on, but also had probably replaced her in his life. She needed to acknowledge that his affections for her were not what she had thought. No matter how much she hoped, he had not spent months thinking about her, regretting his decision. She had been the only one shattered.

When the tears finally stopped, Kit was exhausted.

More from thinking than actual exertion. She just had to survive the next thirty-six hours and then she could get her dog and find a way to get on with her life. *I can survive this*, she thought as she turned off the lamp and got into bed.

THE NIGHTMARE WAS always the same. While it had been weeks since she'd last experienced it, part of Kit could still recognize it as just a dream. The other part of her was terrified as usual. She was tied down on a dinner table in a room that looked like it belonged in a museum or period movie. Various men milled about until Marius walked in. The men snapped to attention as if the well-dressed executive was a general.

Once he took a seat near the window covered with ornate drapes, the brutality started. Kit pulled her mind away. Mal would be here soon. He always heard her cries and woke her up with sloppy doggie kisses and bad breath. Where was he?

The older man just sat and stared as Kit struggled, cursed, and spat at the man she would later find out was his son. His expression never changed as the son began to punch Kit in the face. Where was Mal? Kit started to panic along with her dream self. All she could hear was Mick's voice in her head. Why? Mick was not part of that memory.

Mal! She wanted to scream, but the nightmare always kept her mute. Mick's voice grew louder, and she latched onto that. The sound of his deep accent she had once likened to a blanket wrapping around her. It felt like the conscious part of her was crawling over jagged rocks, following the sound of his voice. But all she saw was Marius and his cruel son.

"Wake up, Kit!" Mick's voice was shaded with concern. "You're safe."

Kit plunged out of the nightmare with a cry. It was dark and all she saw was a shape looming over her prone figure. Panic made her shriek when she realized the person had captured her hands. She sat up quickly and tried to head butt the attacker.

"It's me, it's Mick!" The form insisted.

The voice was right and the size similar, but she had to know for sure. Jerking her hands free, she pulled up his shirt and moved her fingers over the warm skin of his torso. There on his right, her thumb slid into the indentation the bullet hole had left. It *was* Mick.

Kit sagged in relief and collapsed onto his chest. She clutched at his back in panic. He hissed when her nails sank in, despite the t-shirt. But Kit was unable to relax her hold. If she did, he might disappear. She burrowed in as close as she could manage. The strong arms she remembered returned the tight embrace, and he began to talk again.

"It was a nightmare. You're safe, Angel. I will not let anything harm you." He had dipped his head so he could speak into her ear.

Kit wasn't sure how long it took her to calm down. Could have been hours. Her body was lethargic, but her mind was slower to calm. Mick started to pull away and she clutched at him, her nails biting into the skin of his back again. An alarmed squeak escaped her mouth. Mal was not here and there was no way she could fall asleep alone now.

"Shhh. I'm not leaving. Slide over."

Kit gladly obeyed, and when he joined her on the bed, she draped herself along his side, desperate for his warmth. Mick didn't seem to mind being a stand-in for her dog. Mal always stayed on the bed until she fell back asleep. She pushed her hand up under his t-shirt again to find the bullet scar on his side. It was too dark to see, but this way she knew it was indeed Mick. Now she could sleep.

THE NEXT TIME she opened her eyes, the room had filled with dim sunlight that filtered through the window shade. She was so sleepy. Just five more minutes. She burrowed down into the blankets and dozed.

Her morning catnap ended when she was pinned to the mattress by something heavy. Her drowsy brain identified that it was warm, breathing, and had an erection. Before Kit could process the information, her body started fighting back.

She screamed, kicked, and elbowed with all her might. The covers tangling around her legs heightened her terror. Panic seized her lungs, but she kept struggling. Clawing her way across the mattress, she finally tumbled onto the wooden floor. Kit scrambled until her back thumped against the wall. Only then did she look to see who her assailant was.

Mick was sitting up in bed, peering at her with a mixture of concern and horror. His hands were raised, and it was obvious he had been asleep.

"It's just me. Mick." He looked confused as he slowly

moved to the edge of the bed closest to where she was huddled.

Kit was still panting, almost hyperventilating from fear. She remembered the nightmare and the fact she had begged him to stay. He must have rolled onto her in his sleep. But logic didn't keep her from shaking in reaction. She clenched her teeth to keep from moaning. She wanted to order him out, but her voice would not work. Why couldn't he just leave now and let her fall apart?

Mick slid off the bed and knelt a few feet away, his hands still raised. Every movement was slow, as if she were an injured animal. Which she was, in a sense.

Kit had landed with her back against the wall, shivering in her thin tank and shorts. Her mind was divided between fury and terror. She stared at Mick as she gasped for air.

His eyes were intense but his voice was oh-so gentle. "You're safe here. You don't have to be afraid. Just tell me who did this to you. Who raped you, Angel?"

Kit actually made a noise that sounded like a snarl. How dare he! Every morsel of loathing, despair, and anguish that she had borne the past year came shooting out of her eyes. Good thing she had no weapon, because she could kill him. Short nails dug into her palm as she made a fist. If he ventured closer, she could at least deck him.

Mick's eyes widened in shock. "No. That's not possible."

He shook his head. "No. The doctors said nothing about it. YOU said nothing about it!"

Kit calmed down enough to speak, though her voice

was scratchy. "And when was I supposed to have done that? When I was drugged out of my mind? While you were dumping me? Leave. I can't deal with you right now."

She glimpsed the self-revulsion on his face before she turned her head. She would examine this new information as soon as she was sure she wasn't going to throw up. When the door clicked shut, she curled up into a shuddering heap on the floor.

AFTER SHE PULLED herself together enough to walk, Kit took what might have been the longest shower of her life. She didn't want to face Mick, to see pity, or worse, disgust. How could he not have known? She had thought that DAG would have seen her records, medical secrecy acts be damned. A small part of her always wondered if that was why he had cast her aside. But the rest of her doubted that even he could be that callous.

"You're braver than this," she reminded herself aloud as she lingered by the door. "It's not like he can re-break your heart. It's dead, remember?"

Schooling her face into a bland expression, Kit walked into the kitchen as if nothing odd had happened. She refused to look at Mick head-on. He was leaning against the counter, sipping a cup of coffee. The smell wafted over her, making her stomach clench.

Tea would be a better choice this morning, she decided, and snagged a cup and tea bag. Caffeine would not help her unsettled stomach or frayed nerves. While the tea steeped, she found a granola bar and an apple. Only then did she force herself to turn and bring out angry girl.

"Stop staring," she snapped. "I find it very convenient that you claim to have not known."

Mick slowly sat his cup on the counter and held up his hands. His face was earnest and his eyes radiated pain. When he shook his head, a fringe of dark hair fell over an eyebrow.

"I swear, I had no idea —"

Kit's snort cut him off. "Even if I did believe you, it doesn't make a difference."

"No wonder you hate me," he murmured, hanging his head.

"Yes!" She cried, her old accent coming out. "You made the decision for me! Without a discussion, without any consideration for what I wanted!"

"I was trying to save your life!" Mick protested, his own voice rising. "I promised you from the moment we met that I would protect you! And I failed."

Kit could see him struggling for calm. He hated to be discomposed, unprepared. *Tough shit*, she thought and tried to hang on to the small victory.

"I just wanted you to be safe!" Mick threw his hand out in frustration.

"And yet here I am!" Kit gestured to their surroundings. "Back in danger from the same man who took me before! The same monster who watched his son and other men rape me like it was dinner theater!"

Mick froze, his voice cracking. "Men?"

Kit turned away. That was a low blow, she admitted. This wasn't the way the story should come out.

"Let me eat." Her voice was soft now. "Then we can

discuss it like adults. Okay?"

Mick didn't respond, but she heard him move away and then close himself in the bathroom. She managed to choke down the bar and tea despite the knot of emotion in her chest. Somehow, the fact that he hadn't known made it harder to talk about. She had never considered this scenario.

WHEN SHE HAD started therapy, she'd had a secret, malicious desire to make him listen to every horrid detail. She had wanted it to spew out for hours, for Mick to have to sit in the acidic pool of her memories. Just to punish him for rejecting her. Thankfully, that urge had faded.

It seemed that he had not cast off the "broken" her. Now she was clueless as to how to tell the story. Part of her still wanted to cause him pain so that he could have a taste of what she had gone through. That was childish, she knew. His own history was worse than anything she could conceive of. And the other part of her was just tired of the hurting and wondering.

The practical Kit knew that she needed to get this entire episode over with, move back to civilization, and finally get on with her life. This was the closure opportunity she needed. The longer she remained around him, the more likely she would convince herself that he had treasured her. She might even begin to hope that he still cared, and that would be the most dangerous fantasy ever.

"I'm ready," she announced as soon as Mick re-entered the room.

His brows rose, but he simply sat on the futon, his hands resting on his thighs, and waited for her to begin.

Kit started to pace as she spoke. "Just…please don't interrupt. I'll answer any questions you have after."

She glanced over to see him nod. His arms were loose at his sides, but his eyes never left her face. He had changed into another pair of jeans and an ocean blue Henley top that matched his eyes.

Fuck, but she wanted to throw up. It wasn't as if she hadn't told the story before. Her therapist knew every disgusting detail. Amy knew most of it. But this was different.

"The man who turned out to be his son was first. I woke up naked, tied to a dinner table in a fancy room. I guess it was one of Marius' houses. Marius was sitting nearby, just watching. Like a bored king waiting for the jesters to entertain him." She took a deep breath "When the son…started, I fought back as hard as I could. Turned out he liked that. Got to give daddy a big show by hitting me back."

Rubbing the back of her neck, she grasped it was easier now that she had started. Sneaking a glance at Mick, she saw that his fists had clenched. Otherwise, he hadn't moved. His face was a bland mask. There had been times during their doomed relationship that she had hated the poker face he had honed in prison. Right now, she was grateful for it.

"I kept fighting and I guess he'd had enough of that. I saw a syringe and the next thing I knew it was the daylight and we were almost at the warehouse."

"Doctors filled in the gaps." Kit could almost breathe

normally again. "The injection had been a muscle relaxer that was too strong. Lucky for me, Marius' son had worn a condom. The doctors found no DNA, just bruising and small tears, and couldn't tell me how many...I chose to think it was just him, but there were six men in that room."

She finally stopped to face Mick. His fists were now clenched so hard that the knuckles were white. The tension had spread from them to his entire body. His eyes were so blazingly blue they were hard to look at. His mouth was set, and his upper body was rigid with fury. She could see that he was slowly taking deep breaths in order to remain unaffected.

The mean side of her would have celebrated. But she hated to see him upset, even now. There was only one piece left. She walked over to him and raised her stretchy shirt a bit.

"While I was out, they left me a token." She then pulled down the waist of her yoga pants to expose her lower abdomen.

Right above her bikini underwear was a string of crudely etched letters. Obviously drawn in haste by a novice, the tattoo was comprised of jet black letters that were mismatched in size and thickness. It slanted up at the end. Amy had translated the German words for her.

Of course, multi-lingual Mick could easily read it. All he had to do was lean forward to trace the first letter with his finger. Kit didn't even flinch at the contact because his face had gone from anger to sorrow. The tattoo she knew he could empathize with.

"You are *not* their whore," he whispered, looking up

at her steadily, his tone emphatic.

"No," she agreed, "I'm not. That's why I haven't had it removed or covered up."

Mick nodded, probably remembering what she had said about his own ink. That they could help him remember his strength, that he hadn't been broken, that he was still alive after all that abuse.

Kit pulled her waistband back up now that the story had ended. She had expected to feel lighter, better. However, part of the knot was still in her chest. She widened her stance, hoping it would keep her upright. She was suddenly oh-so tired.

Mick seemed to age before her eyes. It wasn't as if all the fight left him. It looked like everything inside had leaked out. He sagged into the cushions, limp.

"I ruined you," he whispered, horror and despair written all over his face.

"Excuse me?" Kit's voice was sharp. "I am not 'ruined,' least of all by you!"

Mick raised his head, and the sorrow in his eyes made her lock her knees in order to remain standing. His smile was brief and sad.

"I knew I should have left you alone; let you leave after the interview at the office. Before me, you were so full of life, always laughing."

The corner of his mouth kicked up ruefully. "Now you are just like me – angry, suspicious, and bitter. I did ruin you."

Gritting her teeth, she forced herself not to cry. And not to run over to him. Shit, she could almost feel her arms curving around his body. Like her, he looked on the verge of tears.

"Just because I act like this around you, does not mean I am this way in my normal life," she bit out, hoping to not get caught lying. "I hate you and it has nothing to do with what happened with Marius. I hate you for what happened in the hospital."

Some of the life returned to Mick as he rose from the futon.

"I acted to save your life," he protested, indignant. "I watched you die – because of me!"

"No!" Her voice was quiet but vehement. "It was my fault. I ignored what you said. None of it would have happened if I had stayed in the flat. I knew the risks being with you carried. How could I not after the way we met? I'm the one who fucked up."

"But you did take all my choices away at the end!" She continued. "You decided!"

"So you would be safe!" Mick strode toward her, pointing his finger. "It was the only solution!"

"You should have asked!" Kit screamed.

"You would have declined to go." Mick bent his head to look her in the eye. "I know the choice you would have made. I had to decide for you."

"You son of a bitch." Kit was now so angry she was vibrating. "You didn't care about me at all, did you?"

With that, she shoved him with both arms, wanting him to be as far from her as possible. The move caused him to only rock back on his heels a bit. Grabbing her wrists, he pulled her even closer.

"No! I cared!" He hissed, his face inches from hers. "I

cared so much that I had to make you leave! To protect you!"

Kit was again blinking back tears, trying not to notice how warm and familiar his hands felt on her skin. Even more amazing was a tendril of want that seemed to move inside her. Just her luck that it would be Mick to bring that part of her back to life. That seemed to be the last straw. Before she could stop herself, she confronted him with the truth.

"No. You just didn't want me anymore." She hated the way her voice broke.

"Oh, no," Mick whispered, aghast. "That is so untrue."

He pulled her closer, leaving her hands to rest on his chest. She could feel his heart racing under her palm. His own hands reached up to tenderly cup her face. Kit knew he could easily see the pain in her eyes, but she was too spent to will it away.

"So very, very untrue."

Oh God, the way his low voice wrapped around her. The heat and emotion that she saw in his eyes. Mick shivered under her hands and then he dipped his head to kiss her. It was light, soft, but incredibly powerful. It was like the kiss from her dream. How did he know to kiss like Dream Mick? The perfection of it made her melt, and she leaned into him for support.

Mick held her loosely, giving her time and room to draw back. But there was no way she could do that. Not that Kit even wanted to. It was as if she had come in from the cold and entered a room with a roaring fire. She was desperate to thaw.

This time, desire was like syrup moving thickly within her, slowly saturating areas she thought had died. Such a relief to know that she wasn't faulty. Not traumatized for life.

On the next kiss, she parted her lips to lick into his mouth. Mick moaned, his fingers moving to tangle in her hair as his own tongue brushed hers.

Curving her arms around his waist, Kit twisted as close as she could without breaking the kiss. She had to whimper when she felt how hard he was. The answering throb between her legs made her want to cheer. She wasn't broken.

Mick came up for air, and she used the opportunity to nip at his neck. It used to drive him crazy. His muffled moan said he still liked it.

"Christ, I've missed your hair." His long fingers caressed her scalp. "The way it would capture my hands, winding around my fingers as if it were alive."

Kit shuddered, remembering how he would hold her head when she went down on him. Afterward, they would laugh at how long it took to untangle his fingers. Wedging her arms back between them, she slid both hands down to rub his erection through his jeans.

"Fuck!" Mick said, his head falling back in reaction, and gasped for air.

Yes, Kit thought as she pressed kisses along his collarbone. That was just what she needed. Just one fuck to usher her back into a normal life.

The moment she moved one hand to his belt, the

perimeter alarm began its jarring sound. Before she could even blink, Mick had his gun in hand and was moving toward the door.

"Lock yourself in the safe room. Don't come out until I come back!" he ordered, and was gone.

Chapter Fifteen

KIT SECURED HERSELF inside the panic room. She was dazed, elated, and distressed all at once. She collapsed into the sole chair and hugged her knees. Of course it was just her luck that Mick would be the only fucking man in an entire year that could make her want to get laid. Physically want, that is.

She had wanted so much to put it behind her, to get "over the hump." She'd tried dating, hook-ups…no one had given her more than a faint impression of warmth. Then one kiss from Mick made her go up in flames. Shit, this was not good.

Use him, the angry part of her whispered, have one for the road and walk away whole again. It would be just sex. She knew him – he would not hurt her, at least physically. She also knew just how skilled he was when it came to getting a response from her body.

"Stop it!" She hissed at herself.

It was no use getting so worked up thinking of him in that way. And it wasn't like she could come out unscathed. She had no illusions about that. Having sex with Mick again would damage her emotionally. But would it be worth the trade-off of knowing that she wasn't ruined? That she could be normal and enjoy sex again?

Feeling antsy, Kit jumped up and began pacing the small room. It was agonizing. As soon as she would make a decision, another question would come to mind. It made her head spin. What should she do?

MICK RUSHED OUT into the sunlight, pulling on his jacket as he went. Ducking behind the SUV, he pulled up the alarm system on his phone. Thank heaven for satellite internet! The breach was off to his right, about 300 yards behind the trailer. He moved steadily, hiding behind trees and treading lightly on the dried leaves that covered the ground. He tucked away what had just happened with Kit and focused on killing whoever had found them.

A loud noise caused him to freeze in his tracks. It was like an un-oiled door, but louder and sharper. Something you would hear inside a Halloween attraction. *What the fuck?*

Mick remained motionless, his gun out and ready. Just as he was about to move, something bulky shifted to his left. He swung around and watched as a large animal meandered through the trees, heading away from him.

It was huge, whatever it was. It looked like one of Santa's reindeer, but he doubted they lived this far south. He would have to ask Kit. If it lived in a forest, she would be able to identify it. The beast moved on, triggering the silent alarm on his phone as it left.

Mick relaxed, confident he had found the cause of the breach. He re-holstered his gun but hesitated before returning to the trailer. Once he was there, he would have to face Kit.

He knew he should not have put his hands on her. He knew his limits. They were woefully low when it came to Kit. When she accused him of not caring...he had acted on instinct. When she had started to cry, a different instinct had taken over and he had been helpless to stop. Nothing mattered except for healing her pain. Even if it meant exposing the lie he had told in the hospital. The second he had touched her, had felt her racing pulse under his fingers, it had been too late.

Groaning, he scrubbed his hands over his face. To say today had gone tits-up was an understatement. What was he to do?

He decided to walk the rest of the perimeter, just in case. It would give him time to think. Too much had happened so far to process. As much as he didn't want to explore her confessions, he needed to.

How many nightmares had she endured alone? Why hadn't he considered that? All the times she had been there for him, and he had just pushed her away when it was her turn to need him.

"You are such a bastard," he muttered to himself as he walked.

He had assumed that she had been locked in that van all night. Of course, she would have trauma from the abduction and the beating, but Kit was so resilient, he hadn't given thought to any other scenario. She had seemed so unfazed in the hospital. She had not provided details, and he had not asked.

This morning he had been awoken by her frantic scramble to escape from underneath him. He had been ready to apologize for involuntarily triggering a nightmare when he had seen her eyes. He'd known then. Beyond a shadow of a doubt.

Mick could have sworn that his heart had shattered multiple times over the last two days, but he now knew he'd been mistaken. As realization washed over him, he could almost hear the explosion in his chest. The feel of it, the pain, made him flounder for breath.

Sudden nausea caused his stomach to cramp, and he bent over, willing it to pass. He could not dwell on it. The thought of someone brutalizing her made a red haze cover his vision. It did not matter that she had been unconscious for most of it. Taking deep breaths, he reminded himself that he had personally taken out Marius' henchmen. Now he wished he had not been so quick about it. If he had known, he would have inflicted horrific torture before he'd put a bullet in their brains. His hands clenched, and he wished there was something around that he could safely hit.

The tattoo was the worst. He wondered if it had been Marius or his son who had crudely etched the words into her soft skin. In English, they roughly translated into "cheap whore." The irony wasn't lost on him, even though he doubted Marius knew of his own tats.

Her pain led back to him. He was responsible for all of it. The "ifs" crowded his brain again. If he had made her more afraid. If he had let her go sooner. If he had managed to keep her safe.

No matter what she said, it was his fault. He sighed when he realized his lap was complete and he was back at the trailer. He needed to let Kit know they were safe. Surely, she had reverted to Kit who hated him, now that she had been given time to think. Otherwise, he was unsure of how he would keep his hands off of her. He wanted to hold her and kiss her again. To love all those horrible memories away. But he was not worthy of that, and he knew the kiss before was an aberration. A mindless reaction to the emotion of the moment. She would be grateful if he pretended it had not happened.

He locked the door behind him, removed his jacket and gun, and braced himself for her wrath as he tapped out the code on the paneling.

IN THE CLOSET, Kit continued her pacing. Before long, she paused and realized Mick had been gone quite a while. Was he simply killing time, asking himself similar questions? Or was he hurt…or worse?

The idea that he could be dead galvanized Kit into action, and she lunged for the door. Fuck waiting. He might need her help. Just as her hand touched the latch, she heard tapping from the other side. Three raps, a pause, then two more.

She sagged with relief. It was Mick! He was alive, but was he injured? Panic had her fumbling at the lock then flinging open the heavy door.

Her eyes raked over him, looking for any blood, bruises, or trauma. No, he looked just like he had before the alarm sounded. He had returned in one piece.

"It was just an animal," he began to explain.

Emotion and memory overtook Kit and she jumped into his arms, just as she had done every time he had returned from a mission. Suddenly the decision was easy. She would risk her heart again for just one more night with this man. It would be worth it.

"Kit."

She heard the regret in his voice and knew the hands he moved to her upper arms were going to push her away. Probably "for her own good" to keep her from doing "something she would regret."

Screw that, she thought fiercely. Rising up on her toes, she grabbed a chunk of Mick's hair in order to pull his face down to meet hers. She kissed him with all the desire and desperation she had, praying it would be enough. She didn't want to be reduced to pleading.

"Kit." This time his voice was hoarse and his eyes dazed.

"Don't," she choked out. "I want this part of my life back. I hate that you are the first man to make me feel anything in a year, but that's life."

Keeping hold of his hair, she slid her other hand down to the front of his jeans. He jumped under her palm and began to harden. He could not deny his body's response.

"Then we should go slowly, ease into it," he protested, but was unable to stop his hips from rocking against her hand.

"No." Kit shook her head, her voice breaking. "Now. Or I will lose my nerve."

Mick was going to object, she knew it. She could use

guilt, claim he owed her. But she didn't want him to cave because of a perceived responsibility. Kit wanted all of him. Therefore, she used the one weapon she hoped still worked.

"Please."

It was almost as if she could see his every defense melt away before her eyes. His beautiful blue eyes turned sad as he saw the tears she blinked away. He raised one hand to slowly slide his fingers down her face. His eyes followed the movement, watching closely as his index finger traced her trembling lips.

"All right." He sighed and replaced his fingertip with his mouth.

The kiss was gentle, unlike the hand that reached down to cup her ass and pull her to him. That grip was firm, demanding, and carnal. It caused Kit to melt even more. Damn, it was so good. In their short time together, Mick had learned countless ways to make her breathless. He obviously remembered them.

KIT BROKE THE kiss, took a gasping inhale, and grabbed his hand. First, she pulled him into the bathroom. The cabinet was stocked with everything an unprepared guest might need, including a box of condoms. Then Mick took over, leading her into the bedroom that was lit only by the light coming in from the common room.

"Tell me what not to do," he instructed as he kissed his way across her forehead.

"Don't hold my arms down." She twisted to get closer. "Don't be sweet. I mean, don't treat me like I might break."

She felt him smile against her skin. "Not you, brave girl."

The sound of her old nickname caused her to be teary again. Desperate to keep that emotion out of this act, she pulled back in order to throw off her top and then began to attack Mick's belt.

As soon as she had it undone, she quickly rid herself of her socks, pants, and underwear. While fear of not being able to go through with it did spur her urgency, so did the idea of being with Mick again. Being together, skin-to-skin. Right now, she wanted that more than anything.

While she had been getting completely naked, Mick had merely managed to remove his shirt and undo his jeans. They hung open on his hips, exposing his black briefs and a mighty erection. Afraid that he might want to back out, she started to reassure him that she was serious, but lost her words when she looked at his face.

His slowness was due to the fact he was staring. He focused on her body, almost as if he was under a spell. Mesmerized. His lips had parted, and she could swear he was panting. Just from looking at her bare body. It was so…hot.

Kit shivered and felt her nipples peak. All from the heat his gaze generated as it slowly roamed her body. After he covered every inch with his scrutiny, his hands came up to trace her shoulders and collar bones. When his warm, magical hands covered her breasts, she moaned and sagged as her knees went weak.

Before she knew it, he had turned her around and had her lying on the edge of the bed. He leaned over her, his weight on his elbows as he closed his mouth on a nipple. His tongue traced the shape and then he used his teeth. Kit cried out in response, arching up to get more.

When he moved to the other breast, he shifted to lie beside her. His hand moved down her abdomen, but stopped before sliding between her legs. He waited until he could look into her eyes, and then slowly inched his fingers down. Kit returned his gaze, realizing he was watching her every reaction. He would stop the second she so much as frowned.

Even though she was terrified, Kit forced her thighs to open. She wanted this, but she was still apprehensive of how her body might react.

"That's right," Mick murmured. "Just look at me. It's my hand touching you."

His fingers lightly traced her folds. The next round, they delved in deeper. Kit kept her eyes on him, grateful that his touch was familiar. It allowed her to spread her legs farther apart.

She gasped when he grazed her clit and was glad when he took the sound as positive. She arched as his thumb drew circles around it the way he used to do. Suddenly, she remembered what she had forgotten to say, a fact he really needed to know. She would hate herself if he took her lack of response personally.

"I can't..." She stumbled over the words. "It has nothing to do with you but I haven't been able to..."

"Shhh," he cut her off, nuzzling her cheek with his nose. "I understand. Having an orgasm isn't a priority right now. Let's just focus on getting you as wet as possible, okay?"

"Yes," she gasped, and tried to relax.

Mick pressed a kiss to her cheek and then slid off the bed to kneel by the side. He looked up for her reaction before pulling her forward so that her bottom hit the edge of the mattress. He slowly placed her knees over his shoulders and lowered his head.

Kit moaned. He was so talented at this. Her fingers threaded through his silky hair as his tongue swiped her clit. Slowly and thoroughly it circled, the sensations sparking a fire in her. When her hips began to rock in reaction, his finger brushed at her entrance. She tensed up but then forced her body to relax. This was Mick.

"Go ahead," she encouraged, her voice husky.

The digit slid in slowly but easily. When she didn't freeze up, it moved in and out a few times, and his mouth continued to work its magic. Then there were two fingers. Kit was amazed. It wasn't too much. It was actually not enough. She wanted more. It was now or never.

She tugged on his hair until he raised his head to see what she wanted. When she mouthed the word "now," his eyes darkened with so much desire she grew even more soaked. He rose, finished removing his clothes, and rolled on a condom. He gestured for her to scoot back onto the bed so he could comfortably lean over her.

He braced a hand by her shoulder, watching her intently. The other one grasped his incredibly hard cock.

"Keep your eyes open." His voice was so deep with desire. "You know me. You know my body."

Kit forced herself to breathe, even though she wanted to hold her breath. She watched his face, set in stern lines as he fought for control. She used to love to shatter that same control, but this time she was grateful for it. She needed him to guide her through this.

When he breached her opening, her eyes flew down to where they were joining. A bead of sweat rolled down the tattoo on his abs to disappear into the dark hair at his groin. The burn from the stretch was more painful that it should have been. It was all in her memory, though.

Don't! Her mind reprimanded. Concentrate on Mick. That's the past. She watched in fascination as he was able to seat himself with just a couple of shallow thrusts. Was she truly that wet? The stinging sensation faded as he gave her time to get used to his girth. Kit relaxed a bit more. He was right – it did feel familiar, safe.

Mick held himself away from her, leaning over her with arms extended. When he looked at her, his eyes were blazing, intense.

"Okay?" He choked out the word with gritted teeth.

Kit saw him, so determined, all for her. Her channel pulsed, and she had no idea if it came from her, him, or a combination. All she knew was that nothing had ever been so right. He was correct – she knew his body. As long as she stayed focused on Mick, she could do this. Perhaps even like it.

"Better than okay." She smiled and managed to swivel her hips a bit.

As soon as he heard her, he let out an immense exhale and let his head sag. After a moment, he looked back at her, the side of his mouth kicked up in a rueful grin. This close, she could see how the ends of his lips curled up, like a secret smile just for her.

"Oh, angel," he groaned. "The way your body cradles mine…it has always floored me."

Kit blinked back tears. It was a thought she'd often had. That their bodies seemed made for each other. But right now, his obvious pleasure was helpful, making her see herself as stronger, more desirable, less defective.

As he carefully plunged in and out a few times, something within Kit started to shift. Having him inside her started to feel enjoyable. The slow drag of his thrusts was making her hips buck in frustration. For the first time in months, she felt like her old self. The daring woman who would leap first and then check for the net.

Knowing that he was still being careful, Kit smiled and whispered, "More."

Mick dazzled her with a grin of his own and started to move faster and harder. Ugly memories wanted to pull her attention away from his beautiful face, so Kit concentrated harder. Those bad times had no place here. She anchored her hands around his forearms, the only part of him she could easily reach.

"That's it," he crooned, as if he knew her demons wanted in. "Look at me, beautiful brave girl. Can you tell how inflamed you have made me?"

She could, the signs were obvious. Sweat dripped down on her from his face. His arms were starting to tremble from exertion. His entire body was taut and he was incredibly, deliciously hard inside her. She moaned and clenched around him, causing him to hiss in reaction. He was so ready to come, she could tell. But he was holding off for her. Kit opened her mouth to tell him there was no need to wait. She had gotten every-thing she had wanted and more. But Mick moved before she could begin.

He leaned down for one quick, frantic lick into her mouth. He groaned as he raised his head.

"There were times I would wake up with the taste of you on my tongue," he whispered, continuing his measured plunges.

Kit could not look away from the truth and the heat in his eyes.

"And I would be so hard," he continued, drawing out the last two words for emphasis.

While she managed to contain her whimper, she still shivered at his words and his dark voice. Her hips twisted as she pictured the scene in her mind. Mick, naked and ready, in their bed.

"I would use my hand." The deep tone of his voice ensnared her. "And fantasize it was your hand...your mouth."

There was no way Kit could hold back her moans now. She imagined him kicking away the covers, touching himself. The image was beyond hot, especially when he admitted he was thinking of her as he got off. She knew what he looked like when he came. How his lips would form to growl out her old name. In her head, she could see him unload all over the tattoo on his abdomen.

Her breath stuttered when he moved one hand down and stroked her clit. *Fuck, that felt good*, she admitted as her body quaked. The sounds coming from her mouth were incoherent, needy.

Because she knew he wasn't lying, not making up a story. She knew him well enough. Oh hell, that meant that he really had jacked off fantasizing about her. Perhaps more than once. So he had missed her, at least in a sexual way.

Between that realization and the emotion in his eyes, imaginary flames licked at her as if she were on fire. Heat rolled through her, centering on the spots between her legs where his cock and magic fingers were at work.

The sudden orgasm crashed into her, surprising and forceful. It was like an actual break; she could almost hear the snap. She had been so seduced by his tale, she had not been focused on her body's reactions, or lack thereof.

Her body seized up for what seemed like minutes before the warmth expanded and reduced her to a pile of quivering goo. She heard herself chanting Mick's name in between sobs. Her short nails were probably leaving bloody crescents on his arm, she was squeezing so tightly.

As amazing and unexpected as the orgasm was, she almost came again as she looked up at Mick. She watched in awe as he threw his head back and gasped her name. Her real name. Christ, he was utterly beautiful when he released. Muscles bulging and sweaty, gasping and shuddering, spent and blissful. Seeing Mick let go was a gift. Kit just wished her view were less teary.

Mick's arms gave out and he collapsed on top of Kit. Instead of feeling restricted or trapped, she welcomed his weight. She was a sobbing, shuddering mess right now and needed to be close to him. She could feel it as Mick gulped in air, and she loosened her hold on his back to make it easier for him to breathe.

When he rose up on his elbows and started to pull away, Kit grasped desperately at him. She was crying too hard to speak but wanted to scream for him not to leave her.

"Shhh," he murmured, kissing her forehead. "Need to take care of the condom. I'll be right back. Slide under the covers."

Kit tried. Boneless from the orgasm and blind from tears, all she accomplished was rolling onto her side. In seconds, Mick was back to gently maneuver her into place. He slid in beside her and gathered her back into his arms.

Kit had cried a good bit in her life, but not like this. Every hurt inside her seemed to be in a race to make it past her throat. Eventually, the sobs ended and left heavy tears. Mick wedged part of the sheet under her cheek to catch the wetness. He stroked her back, her hair and whispered comfort and encouragement. His skin was so warm and familiar against hers.

"That's good, angel. Let it all out. I'm here. They took nothing from you that you cannot get back," he assured her.

Except you, she thought. But if he didn't love her enough to stand by her, then the relationship had been doomed anyway. Marius had just hastened the end.

Lord, she had cried so much the past few days. Her father had always told her that only cowards don't cry. He insisted that strong people stayed that way by experiencing emotion and not blocking their feelings. After all, he had endured and overcome. She believed in what he said and had always tried to emulate her hero.

AS HER WEEPING tapered off, she was surprised that she wasn't sleepy. Maybe it was due to being physically tangled with Mick. The coarse hairs of his thigh abraded the skin of her leg that draped over his. Her free hand was currently anchored around his side, and she could feel the muscles shift as he inhaled and exhaled. This – Mick holding her in the quiet – was what she had needed since that awful day she had been taken. She wanted to catalogue every minute detail since this time, as she knew it was soon to end.

Even though the crying had subsided, Mick continued to stroke her back. Perhaps he didn't want to break the spell, either. Kit doubted he wanted angry girl to come back. He probably didn't know what to say. She certainly didn't. Luckily, Kit's body saved the day when her stomach rumbled with hunger. The sound was deafening in the quiet room. And it was perfect when they both snorted with humor.

With the blackout drapes on the windows, it was impossible to tell what time of day it was. Mick glanced at his watch and gave her a quick squeeze.

"I'll make some sandwiches," he grunted.

Kit didn't argue since she wasn't sure she could sit up, let alone walk. The dim light didn't keep her from ogling Mick's bare back as he stood beside the bed and redressed. Getting to see his naked ass once more was the cherry on top of the day's sex sundae. It was thrilling and heartbreaking at the same time. The lines of ink on his back shifted as he pulled his clothing back on. Perhaps she should get a similar tattoo – *I suffered, I learned, I changed.*

After Mick left the room, Kit tried to pull herself together. For her pride's sake, it was vitally important that she seem unaffected by what had happened. Or at least blasé about him being something other than an ingredient in her healing. He must never know she still had feelings for him.

When she finally managed to get out of bed, she realized the thought of tight clothing or underwear was offensive. Her skin felt electrified, tender. So she pulled on the tank and cotton shorts that she used as pajamas. While lacking in the armor department, they were loose and baggy. Absolutely not seductive.

MICK WAS OPENING a bottle of wine when she exited the bedroom. Giant sandwiches sat on plates next to a bag of pretzels on the table. Kit wanted to smile in affection. Obviously, Mick still went overboard when it came to food after sex.

"Thought you might need this," he explained when he handed her a large glass of wine.

His glass held water since he was officially on duty while they were here. Kit accepted the wine with a grateful look. They sat and ate in a silence that wasn't uncomfortable.

Mick stopped eating, set down his sandwich, and pointed to her left hand.

"Is that Amy's ring?"

When Kit nodded, his eyebrows shot up. "Ah. I think I understand why she was so cool to me after you left. Of course. Only a despicable bastard leaves a battered woman."

"Mick." Kit wanted to defend both he and Amy.

"Don't fret," he bid with a frown. "She thought I knew. I'm grateful she was there for you."

"I have some work to do on the laptop," Mick changed the subject and nodded toward the computer at the end of the table. "You can sit on the sofa and read if you like."

If Kit hadn't cried every tear she had, his offer would have called some up. He had a sense, an accurate one, that she desperately did not want to be alone right now. While he cleared the table and started to work, she got her book from the bedroom and poured another glass of wine. Kit spent the next hour alternating between trying to read and stealing glances at Mick. He was deep into whatever super spy puzzle he was trying to solve online. He would type furiously, and then scowl and sometimes rub his jaw in frustration. Was it one of DAG's math puzzles? While he loved fieldwork, Mick had also relished the opportunity to dig through financial records of groups they investigated. If DAG could pinpoint how the organization funded themselves through the sale of drugs or guns, they could shut them down and move onto the suppliers.

She was glad he was so preoccupied. It made the air more relaxed, and it gave her the chance to watch him like the stupid lovesick idiot she was. She had loved to watch him work before. Sometimes, she could swear steam came out of his ears as his brain worked furiously with numbers. The math nerd part of Mick had excited her as much as the super spy part.

She couldn't beat herself up too much. She made the decision to sleep with him knowing it would end with another broken heart. If she just dwelt on the present, her feelings could remain positive. It wasn't like she regretted her choice, no matter how this turned out. So she forcefully turned off her brain. Plenty of time later to fuss.

Chapter Sixteen

MICK PULLED UP the file that Del had emailed. It contained financial records of a government arms contractor illegally obtained by DAG. Mick wanted to have a go at solving the mystery of how they were being paid by a group of radical terrorists. Proof of the arms sale had been found, but no one had a clue where the money was.

He was grateful for the distraction. While he wasn't one of DAG's forensic accountants, he loved these puzzles. It was similar to the work he'd excelled at in Iraq. Heaven knew he needed a diversion right now.

Peeking through his lashes, he saw that Kit was still engrossed in her book. His mouth quirked. Of course, she would have brought a book. He'd bet his retirement that there was also a backup stashed somewhere in her travel bag. The sight of her curled into the corner, immersed into the pages, was so familiar it made his heart ache. How many evenings had they spent like this? The only difference was that then, he had been sitting beside her, not across the room.

Christ! Had he really given in and made love to her? Of course, he had. Mick swiped a hand across his suddenly dry mouth and wanted to groan. He was half-hard from just the memory. Yet he hadn't given in because of the lust or even her use of the word *please*. It had been the way she had launched herself into his arms. That had not been cautious, angry Kit. That had been his Kit, demanding that he ravish her, to hell with propriety or consequences. Leaping before knowing if the net would catch her.

The fear in her eyes had almost changed his mind. It had been fear of herself, of how she might react. Fear that she might break down or disappoint him. He had never been so determined to not fail. He was still in awe that he had been able to make her come. That had been well worth the blue balls. It had been glorious.

He gritted his teeth and pulled on the denim around his suddenly snug crotch. He needed to concentrate on his math puzzle, not on Kit. This was not the time for another erection.

The woman in question shifted on the futon, and he was unable to look away. She was now facing the bathroom, her profile to him. The loose sleep shorts had ridden up to expose all of her thigh and a slight bit of purple knickers. His fingers tingled from the memory of how soft her skin was. Christ, she was so lovely. He had missed her every moment they had been apart.

A movement on the screen snagged his attention, and he saw it was an IM from Archie. He quickly opened the encrypted message, hoping for good news.

Archie: *Done. Op was a success.*

Mick: Identity confirmed?

Archie: Fuck yea. This one was my pleasure.

Mick: Collateral damage?

Archie: None. Target was solo. Mrs. M at charity dinner.

Mick: Owe you. Send pic to my cell. She will need proof.

Archie: Will do. Give us time to clean up then bring your lady home.

Archie: Do what it takes to get her back you idiot. Home is DC, not this isolated hellhole.

Mick smiled sadly and signed off. If only he could. She hated him and had good reason, too. Despite their remaining sexual compatibility, he doubted she could ever love him again. He had royally killed that, even more than he had planned to. Just because the threat was gone did not mean she wanted to go back to her life with him. He was too damaged and had destroyed the enchantment.

But she is now safe, he reminded himself and felt that weight slip from his shoulders like a leaded cape. He had accomplished that, at least. He picked up his phone and moved to sit beside her.

"Marius made his play," he announced, resting his free hand on her arm. "And before you ask, Mrs. MacDougal was away at a charity function, so she is safe and unharmed."

The hardback book dropped into her lap, and Kit sagged with relief. "Thank God! What about the agents?"

"Everyone is well," Mick explained. "Marius came

alone. Despite all his money, he's had trouble hiring goons the last few months due to his obvious mental instability."

"What happens to him now?" Kit asked, envisioning having to face him again in court.

"He's dead." Mick showed her the picture on his cell phone.

It was grainy, shot outside at night. Nevertheless, it was clearly the face of the monster she remembered. Although the bullet hole in the center of his forehead was new.

The bands around his chest loosened even more as Kit's entire body relaxed. Archie was a crack shot, and the damage in front was minimal. Mick was thankful she could not see the back of the bastard's head. There would be little left of it.

"Thank you," she choked out, still looking at the photo.

Mick turned the phone away and said, "I know you miss Mal but I'm pretty knackered. Can we leave first thing tomorrow?"

Kit nodded, still dazed. She looked exhausted. He wanted to reach out and hold her, yet hesitated. Before he could act, she rose to her feet.

"I'm going to bed. Goodnight."

With that, she disappeared into the bathroom. Mick could not blame her. This trip had been surreal and now it was ending. He could imagine she was just as exhausted as he was. Too many emotions, thoughts, and questions were swirling. He should check all the alarms and turn in soon himself.

When bedtime arrived, Mick bypassed the futon with barely a thought. He needed to hold Kit again. His hands ached from barely touching her all evening. The day had pulled him apart in so many ways, and the only way to feel peace was to be near her. He also wanted to be there in case she had another nightmare.

He made the right choice, he thought as he slid into the bed and Kit scooted closer in her sleep. She must need him too. At least for another night. He placed his hand on her hip and felt peaceful for the first time in months.

SOMETHING WOKE KIT later that evening. She could tell by how stiff her body was that she had been asleep for hours. Her senses weren't alert so it hadn't been a nightmare. She could hardly see anything. At night, the only lighting in the trailer was a small bulb glowing in the bathroom.

She stayed quiet and listened. The noise came again, a low hum she recognized. She turned her head to see a dark mound to her right. The mound was Mick's back, and the noise was him snoring.

Kit wanted to giggle and cry at the same time. She had assumed he would sleep on the futon again. There was no telling why he had picked the bed. Could be it was just more comfortable. She was sure he hadn't fit on the small sofa very well.

Careful not to wake him, she kept still while her mind ran a marathon. On one hand, she was overcome with shame. She had spent the last year hating him. While she still despised the way he had gone about it, he had put her safety first. He had cared that much.

And he hadn't thrown her over because of what Marius had done. His not knowing about the rape still confused her. Would it have made a difference? Doubtful, except to make his remorse even heavier.

Kit sighed. As for what had happened earlier…damn, his balls must have been bright blue. He had held out so long, just to make her come. Despite her insistence that it wasn't necessary and likely impossible. She could just mark it down to male ego, but she thought guilt was the more apt reason. Perhaps mixed with the emotions he'd once had for her.

Now could they both go on without the past haunting them? The thought ripped her guts out, but she needed to be fair and realistic. She wanted him to be happy, despite everything. To not feel self-reproach when he thought of her.

After all, that could be the only positive outcome. It wasn't as if one instance of great sex would make him fall in love with her. If it had not been true before, a few days with angry, fucked-up Kit wasn't going to change that. This short time together was the only consolation prize she would get.

Giving in to the urge to touch him, she turned on her side and snuggled up against his back. She only had mere hours left, and she didn't want to waste them. Her hands delved under his shirt to rest against his skin.

Mick murmured and reached back a hand that landed on her thigh. She could feel it as he slowly awoke. He rolled over and pulled her closer, tangling their legs together. Was he coherent or operating on instinct? Kit didn't care.

With her free hand, she stroked as much of his warm skin as she could reach. She tucked her head under his chin and breathed him in. Here in the dark, it was as if they were the last people on earth. There was no DAG, no bounty, and no pain.

Kit's hand swept up the center of his back but snagged on a long, jagged scar. It was new. She had not noticed it before, but admitted that his ass had taken all of her attention. She gently traced the outline. It was about three inches long; the tissue was still raised and puffy. She could not stop the strangled sound of distress that came from deep inside her.

"Now, now," he whispered. "It wasn't that bad."

She knew he wasn't lying. Mick had a massive tolerance for pain, thanks to his time in captivity. She doubted that neither the wound nor the stitches to close it caused him much discomfort. But it still caused *her* pain.

His hand tangled in her curls and pulled her face away from his chest. His other hand slowly tipped her head back for a thorough kiss. His tongue leisurely remapped every inch of her mouth. By this time of day, he had enough beard stubble to lightly scrape along her chin when he changed angles. The contrast between that and his soft lips was striking.

The fingers that were not caught in her hair moved across the skin of her back. Kit melted under his touch. Those damned magic hands. Mick pulled back slightly and when he spoke, she felt his breath tickle her lips.

"Let me have you," he uttered. "Just once more."

Kit trembled from the plea she heard in the soft words. Without speaking, she turned to fumble for the box of condoms on the nightstand. Pulling one out, she laid it on her pillow so she could quickly shed her clothes. Almost blind in the dark, she sensed Mick doing the same.

Thank God, she thought. This time would be all for him. She planned to touch every inch of him. To somehow show him all the forgiveness she felt in her soul. The love that filled her heart.

As soon as she pressed the condom into his hand, she shoved him onto his back and began to nibble her way down his torso. He relaxed with a shuddering exhale and again slid his fingers into her hair.

She squeezed him in her hand the same moment she took him into her mouth. Humming in approval, she felt him swell under her tongue. Damn, she missed this. It was the quickest, easiest way to drive Mick insane with lust.

"Kit." Her name came out deep and guttural from his throat.

She remembered everything he liked. Things she had loved doing to him. Kit worked her tongue over him, meticulously covering every inch. Soon, his hips were pressing into the mattress, and his breathing was labored.

"I won't last," he gasped, lightly tugging on her hair.

She moved out of the way so that he could put on the condom. The second it was on, she threw her leg over his hip and reached for him. His large hands palmed her ass as she worked his cock inside her.

It was so much like their first time. It was fitting, she

decided, since this was now their last. She only wished it were lighter so she could see him. Mick was gorgeous all the time, but even more so during sex. But being in the dark made it secretive, special.

This time, neither of them lasted very long even though the act was slow and tender. Kit brushed away her tears, grateful that Mick couldn't see. The way he moved his hands over her was almost reverent, but she was sure he was just following her lead. Mimicking the way she was touching him.

She worshipped his body the best she could. She only hoped that he had sensed her regret, her apology. The last thing she wanted now was for Mick to feel guilty or to be unhappy.

THE NEXT MORNING, Kit was surprised when she woke first. Surprised yet grateful that she could sneak out of bed before Mick stirred. She needed some time to compose herself, to put the pieces back together and re-erect her barriers.

Of course, he grumbled in protest when she tried to slide out from under his arm. *Don't look at him*, she cautioned herself, *just move*.

"Need bathroom," she whispered, and was relieved when he moved his arm and rolled over.

As soon as the bathroom door latched, she collapsed in a heap on the ugly green rug. Christ! Had she been insane? Had she honestly thought that a tumble with Mick would not scar her soul?

She had planned on everything except the tenderness and how the second round had made her feel...

cherished. Oh, and waking up with him twice in one night. Boy did that bring back poignant memories. What a mind-fuck.

It's just because of the rape, she reasoned. *You know how he is about guilt. That's where the emotion came from. He still thinks he was at fault.*

Grabbing the edge of the sink, she hoisted herself up and brushed her teeth. The flaw in her sneak-out-of-bed plan was that she was naked, and all of her clothes were in the same room as Mick. Snarling in frustration, she decided to take a shower. Hopefully, the sound would rouse Mick and he would be up and dressed by the time she was done.

Thankfully, the towels were large, and she felt less exposed when she later peeked out from behind the door. As soon as she spied Mick in the kitchen, she ran for the bedroom, again locking herself in.

"Really smooth!" she congratulated herself sarcastically as she tidied her hair.

SHE EMERGED DRESSED in a red flannel tunic over jeans tucked into hiking boots. Mick, on the other hand, had thrown on yesterday's clothes and looked deliciously rumpled. He also looked uneasy, barely looking at her as he sipped his coffee. Kit carefully fixed her own cup, praying she appeared calm and serene.

"Kit," he began, but then seemed to lose his train of thought.

"Don't," she cut him off, her voice gentle but firm. "I think we did much better with our goodbyes this time. Don't spoil it."

He glanced at her, his jaw tight. He shook his head and practically slammed his cup on the counter.

"I'll wash up while you get your things together," he stated, the words sharp and tense.

"Thanks." She tried to smile. "I'm really anxious to get Mal back."

He nodded and grabbed his duffel before exiting the room. Kit frowned. There was no need for him to be so angry. Just because she denied him a farewell speech. She was sure it was full of guilt, self-sacrifice, and regret. She knew all that. He didn't have to remind her.

THEY WERE ON the road within twenty minutes. Kit had wrapped up some muffins and protein bars and had stocked the car with water and juice. She wasn't sure if Mick had eaten or not. Her stomach was in knots, but she forced down a muffin with the last of her coffee.

Mick glowered the entire way to the sheep farm. They didn't speak. Kit stole glances at him from behind her new sunglasses. He'd shaved, which meant he'd needed aftershave so he smelled delicious. He'd thrown a black fleece on over a white tee and some jeans. She had loved it when he wore black because it reminded her of their original meeting.

Stop! Quit dragging out old memories! And stop staring at his hands and his thighs. She sighed and closed her eyes. It would be easier once they picked up Mal. She could get into the backseat with her dog and ignore Mick the rest of the way home.

When the SUV rolled up the unpaved drive to the farm, Kit became anxious because she didn't see Mal. He would normally run out to meet her if he were outside. But just as her heart began to seize, the large wooden door to the house opened. Out spilled three dogs, one of them Mal.

Mick had barely stopped the car when she bounded out the door. She bent down for a hug and was immediately covered in happy dog slobber. Mal licked her face so forcefully that she toppled over. Kit had to laugh when the silly mutt lay across her chest so that she couldn't sit up.

"Missed me, huh?" She giggled and rubbed his ears.

She was faintly aware of Mateo and Mick chatting near the car. The other two dogs sat nearby, probably hoping for their share of hugs and head scratches. But Mal wouldn't budge.

"Goofy dog," Kit laughed. "I'm not going to leave you. I'm here to take you home."

By the time she got Mal to move, Mateo had disappeared, and Mick was walking toward her with Mal's bag in his hand. He bent to greet the other dogs as well as Mal.

"I wanted to thank your friend. It looks like Mal was happy. And someone bathed him." Kit found it was easier to talk if she didn't look at Mick.

Mick straightened. "I thanked him. He understands you're anxious to get back home."

Great. Kit sighed. Even after seeing his friend, Mick was still Mr. Grumpy. His words were terse and he looked...sulky. Whatever could be his issue? Did he really want her to behave like last time and make him bleed? Or, God forbid, cry? She couldn't imagine that.

Whatever the reason, it was out of character for him to be so unsettled.

When she jumped into the backseat after Mal, Mick frowned at her before speeding back down the lane. They drove for a bit, Mal providing the only sound with his panting.

THE AIR WAS so thick with tension that Kit wanted to demand that Mick pull over and explain himself. But he seemed to have the same thought and suddenly veered off into a small meadow.

Mal was happy to exit the car and ran off to a nearby tree to mark his new territory. Kit knew he wouldn't go far, so she made herself face Mick, who was rubbing a hand along the lower half of his face as he paced. He was several feet away when he finally looked at her.

Kit's breath caught. His eyes, so blue in the sunlight, were troubled. She steeled herself for whatever was coming. Had she not given him enough reassurance that she did not hold him responsible for the rape? Surely, he knew her well enough to see that she meant it.

She hoped he didn't want to rehash the hospital scene. Her behavior had been embarrassing. And she now realized that he had been trying to do an honorable thing with making the choice for her. It still pissed her off, but he hadn't dumped her just to get her out of his life. It was no one's fault that he just hadn't loved her enough. That was the final truth, as much as it hurt. They just were not meant to be.

"During the times when I would ache from missing you." Mick's voice came out anguished. "I would remind myself that at least you were alive…and happy. I always imagined you happy. I couldn't envision anything else."

Kit tightened her lips so a cry of grief didn't escape. Shit. His eyes, his voice, were ripping her apart. She could never bear to see him distressed, and now he appeared tortured. And the part about missing her…she would have to file that away until she was emotionally capable of thinking of it.

The corner of his mouth kicked up without humor. "But my being selfless wasn't the only motivation. I could not comprehend that someone like you – so steady, so joyful – could really care for someone so fucked up, repressed and unworthy."

Kit started to protest his depiction of himself, but he held up a hand to stop her.

"But you've been just as miserable as I. You don't smile, you barely speak. And last night." He paused to catch his breath.

"Last night you showed me your love. It was so clear, even after all the ways I buggered up what we had." Mick shook his head.

Without releasing her gaze, he came to stand closer to her. Kit was confused, her mind a messy whirl. What was he saying? That he didn't know she loved him? Of course she had, it had been so obvious. She still did, even though she didn't want to. What did it matter now?

"I don't think you'd trust the words, so I need to show you in a way that is equally clear." The despair on his face was gone, replaced by conviction and something that looked like adoration. What on earth?

Kit watched in disbelief as Mick slowly lowered himself to his knees. Numb with reaction, she must have looked ridiculous because Mick could not stop a tiny smile.

"When I said that there was nothing that was worth begging for, it was before you left my life. You, brave girl, my angel, are worth begging for. Please forgive me."

One part of her wanted to scream at him to get up, to not associate her with anything to do with his time in prison. But the way he was looking at her kept her frozen. Was he saying what she thought? Or was he just wanting her forgiveness again? She focused on his beautiful face since the rest of the world was spinning.

"Of course I forgive you," Kit answered through bloodless lips, still shocked and confused.

"But will you give me another chance?" He asked, looking up at her.

"Wait." Kit's mind finally latched on to what was happening. "You want us to be together again? Are you trying to tell me that you lo—"

She couldn't say it. Not after what had happened in the hospital. She couldn't make herself utter that sentence again. His response last time had shattered her. She wasn't that brave. The air would not even leave her lungs.

Mick grabbed her hands in his. She saw in his face emotions that she had dreamed of seeing – admiration, hope, and love. Oh God, it looked like love.

"Go on," he encouraged gently, his eyes shining.

"You...love me," she finished, her voice soft with amazement.

"Totally. Completely." He spoke without hesitation.

"I love you Kit, Edith, whatever name you choose to go by. The woman you were then and who you are now. I love you."

Was this real? Kit thought so. Her hands were enclosed in his warm grasp. Tears blurred her vision. She could feel the sun beating down on them and hear Mal romping through the tall grass nearby.

"And you still love me?" The silly man actually looked nervous now.

"Of course I do." Kit's heart raced so fast that she was dizzy.

"Even the filthy, broken bits?" Mick pressed, his eyes suspiciously damp.

Kit laughed through her tears. "All of it, Michael Andrew Harris. Everything that makes you who you are. I love you with all my heart. I always have."

Mick smiled, a full smile, something that Kit had seen only a few times. It was broad and showed off his straight, white teeth and the uneven ones on the bottom that she loved. Then he laughed. He laughed in utter delight, throwing his head back, the sound coming from deep inside him.

Kit knew her heart was back. Unlike before, this time Mick caused her heart to explode in millions of brightly lit sparks that moved through her body, leaving her warm and tingling. And alive. Christ, she felt alive!

"Will you come home with me?" He asked. "Or should I leave DAG and live with you?"

"No!" Kit was aghast. "You love your job! I wouldn't complain if you were in the field less, but you cannot quit!"

Alarm washed over her and she said, "But I don't know if I can live in the city again. And what about Mal?"

Mick laughed. "Of course Mal comes too. He's family. We'll look for a house with some land for him to explore. Whatever it takes to make you feel comfortable."

Hearing his name, the black beast ran over to the couple. Since Mick was on his level, Mal began to lick his face, causing both of them to snicker.

"I think he approves." Kit smiled. "And I think you need to stand up and kiss me."

"Gladly." Mick grinned back and complied.

It was almost like the kiss from her dream. While it was harder, more urgent, it was just as full of emotion. Kit's skin tingled. She was alive. This time, she was Snow White and Mick's kiss was breaking the spell she'd been under. It was silly, but she was too happy to care. Her very own Prince Charming was in her arms and back in her life to stay. She could have happily kissed him all day.

Too soon, though, he pulled back. "One more thing."

Kit watched as he dug in the front pocket of his jeans and then held out his hand to her. In his trembling palm was her necklace. Dear God, he had not only kept it, but also brought it with him! She took it and managed to secure it around her neck. She looked at him in confusion.

He made a rueful face. "I asked Archie to keep an eye on Marius. When he found that Marius was close to finding you, I forced myself onto the case. I wanted to make sure you were happy. It was vitally important that you keep the necklace. As proof of what you meant to me. No matter the outcome, I wanted you to have that."

Kit beamed and hugged him. "Take me home, super spy. I need to start packing."

This time, Kit sat in the front seat, her hand on his thigh as he drove. They opened a window so Mal could enjoy hanging his head out in the breeze. Mick didn't say much, and Kit had a sudden idea of what might be troubling him.

"Let me tell you about the day I met Mal," she started.

And so she began to talk. At first, it was like putting on clothing that was two sizes too small. It felt restrictive, uncomfortable. Even though she had spent most of her life being chatty, she was out of practice. However, the more she went on, the more Mick smiled. And the more Mick smiled, the more she talked.

Epilogue

A FEW WEEKS later, Mick, Kit, and Mal had settled in a farmhouse across the river from DC. Mal loved chasing squirrels and romping in the creek. Kit had several job interviews lined up. Mick was settling back into work. He had been right – Malachai returned to DAG. In addition, they were headed to Atlanta this weekend to surprise Amy. Kit was overjoyed to spend time with her friends again.

On their way to dinner one night, Mick had inquired if she had selected the name she wanted to go by. Stay Edith, go back to Kit, or pick a new name?

She answered that she had decided and her choice was Mrs. Harris. Mick agreed that it was a brilliant choice and they should see to making it official right away.

Acknowledgements

There is no way this book would have happened if not for the support and understanding of my husband and children. They are my inspiration, the reason I keep trying and the best parts of my life.

My amazing critique partner Abby helped every step of the way and made me feel talented on days I felt like a hack. My Beta Readers Bobbette, Erica, Abby and Audra helped me to focus the story through many revisions. Cady saved my life with her proofreading. Alexandra read my mind and created a beautiful cover. I want to give my editor Lauren Plude credit for inspiring me to expand the story and dozens of other suggestions that took my draft to another level. Many thanks to all the established authors who offered encouragement, advice and friendship.

More than anything, I am grateful for my husband – who has always encouraged me to go further than I think I can and gives me a safe place to fall when I fail. He is the reason I believe in love.

About the Author

Kel O'Connor lives with her husband and teenagers in the mountains of North Carolina. In addition to reading and writing, she loves coffee, loud rock music and subversive humor. She collects graphic t-shirts and hates to vacuum. You can find her online on Twitter, Facebook and at keloconnor.com.

66769109R00167

Made in the USA
Lexington, KY
24 August 2017